DEFIED
MARIA LUIS

DEFIED

BLOOD DUET, BOOK 2

MARIA LUIS

ALKMINI BOOKS, LLC

I am both a sinner and a saint, but I bleed vengeance.

For years, I've lived in the grey... until her.

Avery Washington didn't belong in the shadows, but I dragged her into the darkness anyway.

One kiss, and I would stop at nothing to possess her.

One caress, and my need to destroy wavered.

Our attraction was poison and pleasure.

They say the devil recognizes his own, but I never saw Avery coming.

She's determined to light the matchsticks, and I can't resist going down in flames...

Defied (Blood Duet, Book 2)
Maria Luis

Cover Photographer: James Critchley

Cover Model: Charlie Garforth

Cover Designer: Najla Qamber, Najla Qamber Designs

Editing: Kathy Bosman, Indie Editing Chick

Proofreading: Tandy Proofreads

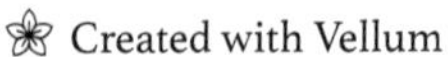

For my girls in Book Boyfriends Anonymous - thank you for encouraging me to write Lincoln & Avery's story when I shared a snippet of the prologue months and months ago. Without your interest, without your encouragement for me to take a leap of faith, the Blood Duet would still be gathering dust on my laptop. Thank you for always having my back, and I love you guys, tons.

*

*

*

*

Good job, honey.

1

AVERY

The chill of the metal gun to my temple was like ice skittering down my spine.

Every inch of me was frozen—fear working its way through my limbs, immobilizing me until all I could do was struggle to breathe.

In.

Out.

In.

Out—

The muzzle of the pistol slid from its place against my temple to that sensitive spot behind my earlobe. Chills erupted over my skin, and there was nothing I wanted more in that moment than to cup my hands over my mouth and quiet the humiliating whimpers escaping me on every exhale.

Be brave.

Be bold.

The stranger's words finally registered, pushing through the blood pounding furiously in my head, and suddenly the ice turned to heat, and I worried I might vomit all over the front seat of the SUV.

My gaze latched onto Lincoln, the man who'd just brought me to orgasm not even an hour ago. *Multiple orgasms*, my brain offered up, *not just one*.

"Ahhh, I see," the man in the back of the SUV drawled pleasantly, like we'd all sat down for tea instead of a feast of guns and terror, "you didn't know."

How could I have known? My stepfather had never spoken of having kids when he'd been married to Momma. There'd only been me. His stepdaughter. His only child. *Apparently he'd lied about that too.*

The urge to throw up returned, tugging on my gag reflex, but not because of who Lincoln Asher was—we had no ties to one another. Nothing to bind us. His father had my mother murdered in cold blood, and the way I saw it, that one fact destroyed any familial bonds society could have ever deemed existed between us.

No, I wanted to vomit because that was yet another lie Jay had fed us.

Another lie, another way to keep us in the dark and create an illusion of gentlemanly behavior that held no truth to it.

And Momma and I had believed every word, sucking them up like they were a paragon of all that was right in the world. *He'd never lie to us,* he'd always whispered—but he had.

Every. Single. Day.

"Take the gun off her," Asher clipped out, his voice pitched so low I could barely hear him over my thundering heart. "If you're going to kill someone, it's going to be me. Not her. Do you understand?"

The gun on the underside of his jaw shoved up, pushing hard enough to cant his head into an awkward angle.

"The one with the gun at your head is the one who gets to call the shots here, Sergeant. And that ain't you."

In the light of the vehicle, Asher's scars flexed as his cheeks hollowed with a dark laugh. "*Ain't*, huh? You suddenly forget every bit of schooling you learned back in the day, Joshua? Or is it that when you're slumming, you feel the need to speak like us regular folk and forget all about your fancy Pershing presidency?"

My eyes went wide. The Pershing presidency?

The man holding me at gunpoint was *Joshua Hampton*?

It was so absurd that I almost laughed out loud. Maybe I would have, if it weren't for the pistol getting so closely acquainted with the back of my skull. As it was, my voice tremored when I spoke, like the very devil himself was the one seated behind me. "What do you want from us?"

"So, she speaks." The backseat cushion squeaked as he shifted his weight. "There are *many* things that I want, Laurel, but first . . ." He cocked the hammer on the revolver at Asher's jaw, the sound swallowed by the hum of cars honking their horns as they passed us. "We need to take a little trip. In case you're concerned, Sergeant, you've got enough gas. I checked when I had Templeton break in for me and hide me under all your uniforms back here. I'd suggest bringing them to a laundromat soon."

"*Motherfucker.*"

In the driver's seat, Asher jolted, twisting at the waist and hands lifting into motion, and then—

Click.

This time, it was the hammer to the revolver at the back of my head, and I wasn't the only one who stiffened in fear.

Asher's limbs locked in mid-air, his jaw working as he went still, his familiar blue eyes fixed on me.

Dread. Terror. Grief.

I read it all in his gaze just before he blinked and his customary mask slipped back into place.

Would he tell Hampton to pull the trigger? When it came down to it now—him or me—had he changed his mind? He looked at me like he cared. But there was no denying the fact that we barely knew each other, and at the risk of saving his own neck . . . would he sacrifice mine?

I wouldn't cry out. I wouldn't *cry*. But there was no stopping my lids from falling shut as the realization set in that I was at Hampton's mercy for reasons that were completely unbeknownst to me. I would die, probably, not knowing. Without having peace. Without vindicating my mother. Without *living*.

"Put your hands on the wheel, Asher." Hampton lifted the revolver from the base of my head to my temple. "Unless you want this SUV looking like a crime scene, you're going to do exactly as I say. You understand?"

With reluctant slowness, Asher's hands went to the steering wheel, gripping at ten and two.

The pressure holding the gun to my head didn't slacken.

"Good," came the Pershing president's soft murmur. "And if you think, for even a second, that I won't put this bullet through her head, all you have to do is take a glance in the rearview mirror or at the cars on either side of us and check out the drivers. She'll die before you even have a chance to make a move." There was a small pause, and then, "Now drive straight until I tell you otherwise."

2

AVERY

We drove for close to an hour.

Joshua Hampton's revolver never wavered.

Between fits of panic that I was one trigger away from having my brains blown out remained the nagging fear that I was missing something crucial here. Besides Asher's relationship to my stepfather, besides the fact that I'd never even heard Asher's name before two weeks ago, was one lingering thought: "Big" Hampton knew my name.

My *real* name.

Which meant that he somehow knew my stepfather was full of shit, pretending after all these years that Laurel Peyton had committed suicide.

It was both a relief to know that I was "alive," so to speak, and also terrifying.

If Hampton knew, who else did?

Who else could use my identity against me?

With the revolver kissing the base of my skull, I watched the street lights speed past my window as Asher drove down Airline Highway, somewhere just east of Baton Rouge. The fact that Hampton had no worries about us knowing our final destination meant that he either planned to kill us before the night was over *or* the location was a setup for tonight only, never to be used again.

I desperately hoped for the latter.

"Up here," Hampton murmured, "take a right up at the next traffic light."

He spoke like we were being directed to a restaurant or somewhere equally unassuming, but when Asher made the turn and the street went from gravel to dirt, there was no mistaking the fact that we were in the middle of nowhere.

My fingers dug into my thighs.

For all his pompous air, Hampton wasn't an idiot. Within minutes of us driving out of New Orleans, he'd forced us to hand over both guns. There was no telling him to screw off when we were sitting ducks—every which way I looked there were black, unmarked SUVs, and I wasn't enough of an idiot to think that they were simply accessories to a man who liked to make a grand entrance.

No, each one was packed to the brim with men who carried firearms. If I squinted hard enough, I could make out their outlines through the tinted windows.

Our own SUV bumped along the uneven road, the seatbelt locking me in place.

I'd rather go through the windshield than be stuck in here.

The thought came just as quickly as it went.

It wasn't true, not really. I hadn't managed to escape my stepfather's notice for over a decade just to roll over and give up now. Momma would never forgive me for giving in. I wouldn't forgive myself.

"Are you going to kill us?" I demanded, my voice scratchy from pent-up nerves. "Is that your plan?"

Pershing's president chuckled. "Want to answer this one, Sergeant?"

With my heart in my throat, I stared at Asher. Even after an hour of sitting on the new information, I couldn't believe . . . I couldn't even fathom that we . . . that Jay—

I dropped my gaze to my thighs, breathing through the jitters, only to hear his deep timbre to my left: "We're not dead yet, which, if memory serves correctly, means we're likely to keep our heads on our necks for the time being."

"You remember so well," Hampton murmured with an air of snobbery. "I figured our last run-in made enough of an impression on you, and I suppose I was right."

"Our last run-in had nothing to do with me. If your side-piece wanted some better cock—some *younger* cock—than what she was currently getting, that's not on me, you piece of—"

Pft! Pft!

Glass shattered before me as my ears rang from the shot of a pistol, my hair swinging forward as the SUV slammed to an unexpected stop.

Lincoln.

I tried to turn to him, but the seatbelt jerked me back—and the revolver at my head never eased. Asher's arm shot right, across my chest, keeping me in place as though he worried I'd go flying from my seat and through the splintered window.

My lungs inflated with much-needed air, and it was only in the far recesses of my mind that I realized I was clawing at his bulky arm, trying to draw him closer.

He was okay. *He was okay.* He wasn't dead.

"Put the gun down," Asher bellowed, his voice harsh in the dimly lit car, "if you fucking shoot one more time, I will—"

Behind me, Hampton's breathing came loud and heavy. "Finish that sentence, Sergeant, and I'll put the next round through you. Better yet, I'll aim for Laurel here. How does that sound? You mess with me and she ends up as collateral."

It sounded like Joshua Hampton had spent too many years watching blockbuster thrillers at the theaters, but I wasn't about to risk my neck by giving voice to the sarcastic retort.

One second passed, and then another, and then Asher stiffly pulled away from me and set his hand on the steering wheel again. A single glance at his profile was all I needed to know that he was a man balancing on a very thin tightrope.

Like me, he was no good at obeying.

In pure silence, Asher hit the gas again and we rolled on, farther into the darkness, farther into unknown territory. I watched the digital clock on the dashboard like my life depended on knowing the precise moment everything went straight down the gutter, and by the time Hampton instructed Asher to park the car, another thirty minutes had trickled past.

"Don't move," Pershing's president grunted as he popped the back door open and slid out from the SUV.

A half-second later, the passenger's side door swung open and an unfamiliar man stood there. "Put your hands out," he ordered. I wasn't given the opportunity to do a damn thing—he clasped my hands in his, drawing them out, and then efficiently circled them with a set of metal handcuffs. The lock clicked into place, and then he was hauling me out of the SUV.

Was Asher being subjected to the same treatment? Was he getting manhandled just like me?

My bare feet tripped over the dusty soil as I stumbled forward, my weight off balance from the man's hand directing me forward. Although "directed" was too gentlemanly sounding. No, the man at my back shoved relentlessly.

Temper snapping, I twisted back to glare at him. "Ease the hell up before I eat dirt, asshole."

Dark brows lifted, and to my satisfaction, the pressure at my back slackened.

It didn't make me feel any better.

Off somewhere to my left, I heard Asher protesting, volatile curses falling from his mouth, and then . . . nothing at all. *Oh, God.* I craned my neck to stare at where he'd stood before, searching for him, needing to catch sight of his powerful frame, only for the jerk behind me to push me roughly all over again.

"Keep walking," he growled.

Within the binds of the cuffs, my hands curled into fists. Rage claimed my every step, the soles of my feet beyond the point of protest as I stomped over gravel, dirt, pebbles. My dress rode high on my thighs, every step inching the hem up to expose more skin. I was far beyond embarrassment, though, and I didn't touch it. Didn't try to yank it back into place, even though I was still panty-less.

I wanted someone to make a comment.

I wanted someone to leer.

And when I finally got my hands on a damn firearm, I'd wipe that stupid look right off their faces with a single bullet to their most precious jewels.

Boom.

Head up, chin lifted, I stormed forward. Crying did nothing for me. Worrying only wasted my time. If Asher was wrong, and we were going to be killed tonight, I'd go out in a blaze of glory. The particulars hadn't formed into a solid plan yet, but I refused to roll over and call it quits.

Be brave.

Be bold.

I always had been, and I wasn't about to change now.

The scent of swamp infiltrated my senses, pungent and smelling of rotten eggs. Cypress trees dotted the horizon, swarming my periphery, concealing the moonless night sky above, and up ahead was a small wooden shack that looked like it belonged to Huckleberry Finn and not the twenty-first century. Seated on tall pilings, the house hovered some ten feet above the water with wooden steps leading from the ground level to the front door.

"Up we go," Jerk muttered, giving me another push when we reached the base of the steps. "Don't even think about getting frisky."

The wood grated the soles of my bruised feet, and I bit back a curse when a jagged splinter cut just below my big toe. Hissing, I sucked in a quick breath and shoved past the pain. If I couldn't hear Asher, then that had to mean he was dealing with more than just a wounded foot—at that thought, the rage in my system burned hotter.

It wasn't until my eyes registered the figure sitting at the table in the brightly lit, one-room shack that I blinked and then blinked again, just for good measure. Maybe Big Hampton had accidentally knocked me over the head without me realizing it because there was *no* way I could be seeing who I thought I was.

Nat sat at the table.

My Nat.

My friend Nat.

Betrayal struck me straight in the heart, savage like an unexpected blade to the chest when you were expecting a hug. If she was here . . . if Joshua Hampton knew who I really was, then that could only mean . . . I swallowed the hurt—the lies that Nat had fed me all these years as she sat at my table in Jackson Square.

Somehow, she'd found me out. Deduced the truth. Kept my secret until it suited her to spill the tea and throw me to the wolves.

"How long have you known?" I didn't bother getting more specific. From the way her gaze flicked over my body to my shoeless feet, she knew exactly what I'd gone through tonight . . . and I had the sneaking suspicion that she'd been part of its orchestration.

"Long enough," she answered in that maybe-French-maybe-not lilt of hers. Her lips pursed. "Your feet look horrible."

That was what she had to say? Seriously?

Back stiff, I snapped, "I didn't have the luxury of keeping my shoes on when someone was trying to kill me."

"Not you, *cherie*. You were never meant to be in any harm."

I blatantly looked down at my cuffed wrists, lifting them up as though to say, "Stop with the bullshit."

Nat tilted her head, one shoulder lifting in a delicate shrug. She was still dressed in her gown from earlier in the evening. Still looked just as elegant, as though she weren't sitting in a shack in the middle-of-no-where-Louisiana. "Inconvenient, of course. I do hope you'll understand why we'll need you to leave them on."

A startling *thud* echoed in the room. The tiny hairs on the back of my neck prickled, and I spun around—or as far as I could go with the jerk still holding me in place.

My heart dropped clear to my feet, my stomach roiling at the sight of Asher.

His fists were cuffed like mine, although his were locked behind his back. But his face . . . Bile rose in my throat, threatening to put on a performance for everyone to see, as I absorbed the horrid sight of him. The half-closed right eye, already purpling from what had to have been a fist. The blood trickling from his nose, a single droplet glistening on his bottom lip. His scars, already tinged a faint pink, were a brilliant red as though he'd been roughly shoved up against something—and held there with force.

I wasn't even aware of darting forward, of my voice splitting the quiet of the room, until arms banded around my chest and yanked me backward, toppling me into a chair. Hands pressed down on my shoulders, limiting my movement, as a thick cord of rope wrapped around my ankles, tying them together.

"Shut her up," Hampton said, entering the room in my periphery and moving to stand at Nat's side. "I don't want to hear a single word from her."

When a palm closed over my mouth, I bit down on the calloused flesh without regret.

"Fuck!" my jailer shouted, just as Asher surged forward, my name on his lips: "*Avery*."

He didn't get far.

I watched in horror as a fist from one of the men collided with his stomach, and he folded at the hips, dropping to his knees as he coughed harshly, hands still linked together behind his back.

My gaze went to Nat, tied feet twisting on the floor as I squirmed in my chair. "What the hell is *wrong* with you?"

She didn't look away, simply returned my stare. Calmly. Easily. Like this was the norm for her. "I wish you hadn't come to Whiskey Bay tonight," she said. "You weren't supposed to be involved in any of this." She tipped back her head when Hampton shockingly slid a hand over her hair.

Holy crap.

Were the two of them *together*?

I stared at Hampton's hand, at the way he smoothed her hair, tucking the strands behind one ear in a typically sweet gesture. She reached up to grasp his wrist and tug his hand down to rest over her collarbone, where she played with his fingers.

Pershing's president met my gaze, startling me with the lack of warmth in his expression. "You'll have to excuse my behavior, Laurel. It wasn't my intention to frighten you."

There he went *Laurel*-ing me again, without even dropping a hint as to how he knew my identity. Everything in me tightened, especially when Nat gave a short nod, like she was pleased with Hampton's half-assed apology.

I wasn't pleased by it, and one glance at Asher told me that he wouldn't be pleased by it even two centuries from now.

"You're worried about him," Hampton murmured, returning to stroking Nat's hair like she was some sort of precious pet. He jerked his chin in Asher's direction. "It's sweet of you, of course, Laurel, but I wouldn't stress. Your sergeant has been through so much worse."

Worse than being pummeled while handcuffed?

A beat later, Hampton tacked on, "Isn't that right, Sergeant?"

Asher swayed on his knees, his bruised eye swelling rapidly as he blinked his good one in the president's direction. His full mouth twisted in a sneer. "Fuck you."

Hampton's ridiculous hair-stroking paused, his hand suspended mid-air. "He's as crude as you warned me."

Nat's eyes turned to slits. "Some things never change."

Through a rough laugh, Asher drawled, "Screwing your husband's competition is definitely a new change.

Ambideaux have any idea that you're taking it up the ass from enemy number one?"

"*Ex*-husband," Nat snapped, practically vibrating in her seat with fury. The part of me which considered her a friend wanted to shout at Asher to watch his language; the part of me which felt betrayed by her deception silently urged him to keep going. "Don't be mistaken—Jason and I haven't been on speaking terms for *years* now."

Hampton cleared his throat. "In actuality, that's the reason you're here, Sergeant."

"To listen to y'all's bullshit?" Asher straightened his shoulders as much as he could with the cuffs, and my heart squeezed at seeing him—a strong, independent man—struggle to keep his balance. "Fuck no," he growled, "I'm gonna take a hard pass."

"Will you, really?" Stepping away from Nat's side, Hampton closed the space between him and Asher. The president didn't kneel to Asher's level, nor did he crouch down, but he did stand less than a foot way. The close proximity forced Asher's head up in order to maintain eye contact.

He's in so much pain.

To the outside observer, they'd never notice . . . but I could. I could see it all: his shoulders flexing from his restrained position, the uneven way his chest lifted and fell, the slight pinch to his brow. The way it took all of his strength to climb to one foot, with no use of his hands, and then to the other, his chest muscles flexing under his shirt as he rose to his full height and moved toward Hampton.

He towered over Pershing's president, imposing and brutally beautiful.

Hampton visibly stiffened.

In a low voice, Asher spoke. "This shit ends now. I'm done playing games."

The entire room descended into silence, and it struck me then that when Hampton had quipped that Asher had dealt with worse in his past . . . perhaps he'd meant that Asher had personally dealt *out* worse. *It would explain all of the guns trained on him, like they expected some savage to pop up in his place at any moment.* And it would explain why no one said a word when he slowly limped to a man standing by the door.

Not a soul moved. Not a soul breathed.

"Take out your gun."

3

AVERY

Even I startled at the deathly quiet way Asher uttered the words, my bare heels digging into the floor, my back shooting straight.

The man's eyes volleyed from Asher to Hampton and back again, a look of frenzy in his expression. "I-I—"

"I said"—Asher stepped closer, invading the man's personal space until his back collided with the wall behind him—"take out your gun." I couldn't see Asher's face from my position, but there was no mistaking the way his head ducked down as if he'd run his gaze over the man and found him lacking.

"Mr. Hampton," the man edged out weakly, "I—"

My gaze fixed on Hampton, who clenched his hands into fists at his sides. "Do what he says, Charles. The sergeant clearly wants to make a point."

With awkwardness and a visible tremor, Charles fumbled with the gun at his hip. The distinct scent of urine saturated the air, and it sure as hell didn't belong to me.

The man had pissed himself.

His legs shifted from a squared-off stance to squeeze

together, and the misery on his face said it all. Embarrassment cloaked him like a second skin as he clutched the gun in his hand, his gaze bouncing everywhere but never landing on the man directly before him.

Asher would not be ignored.

He knocked the man's wrists with his bound right arm, and the guy was so on edge that he nearly let the gun drop to the floor. Scrambling, he reassumed his position, gulping audibly.

Turning around to face the room, Asher rasped, "Put the gun to my head."

Wait. *What?*

Was he absolutely *insane?*

My ass came off the seat in an instant, and I managed one step before remembering that my ankles were tied together. My elbows broke my fall.

As did my chin.

Teeth crashing together painfully, vision swirling, I lifted my face to see Asher staring at me, his expression tight. His one good eye narrowed with concern, his lips pulling thin, and then he seemed to come to a decision in his head.

He wrenched his gaze from me just as masculine hands went to the back of my dress and hauled me off the floor. It was a miracle the damn material didn't rip in half, and God knew how many people had just seen my naked crotch.

If I came out of this alive, I really needed to stop for new underwear.

Walmart would do.

Walgreens would do.

Anywhere would do.

"I'm not getting any younger," Asher barked like a drill sergeant, and the gun he was so desperate to have aimed at his head lifted up, up, up until the mouth was in place, and every single person in the room took a collective inhale, all at once.

Except for Pershing's president.

Haint-blue eyes homed in on Hampton. "I'm giving you one chance for this. You pissed I decked your precious kid? You ticked off that I'm a crude motherfucker?" He stepped back into that gun like a man without fear, and that icy feeling returned to my skin, raising the hair on my arms. "I've giving you one chance. You skip it? The next time you even try to come after me, I will snap your neck before your next breath."

He paused, the silence lengthening, and then added, "But maybe you're trying to prove that you can play with the big boys—and we both know that you don't have the balls to kill someone, Hampton. You'll rough them up, hold them at gunpoint, but at the end of the day, you're still that rich asshole sitting in your perfect mansion behind twenty-foot walls with twenty-four-seven security ensuring no one disturbs a blade of grass on your damn lawn. But, hey, maybe for the first time in my life, I'm wrong. Maybe you'll follow through." Asher's bloodied lips lifted in a smile that would send children scurrying for their mothers. Hell, it made *me* want to scurry away. "Tell him to shoot."

My mouth fell open.

He. Was. Insane.

There was only one reason why he'd do something so asinine as to tell someone to *shoot him*. And where the hell did that leave me?

Dead. That's what.

If we lived, there was a good chance I'd bust his other eye—just for giving me a heart attack. The bastard deserved it. One-hundred percent.

Hampton's expression tightened, hands balling into fists at his sides as he glanced over his shoulder at Nat.

Nat, who'd tricked me into this mess.

Nat, who'd lied to me for *years* when she'd known all along that I was Laurel Peyton.

If given the chance, I'd bust her eye, too.

The metal handcuffs chafed my wrists, and I settled down, temporarily resigned to my restraints.

"Make up your mind," Asher clipped out.

Hampton slammed his eyes shut. Then, "Take the cuffs off him."

"Surprise, surprise." Not even relief or smugness registered on Asher's face. Like he was completely composed of marble, he nodded stonily in my direction. "Avery first. Now."

The jerk who'd cuffed me earlier moved before me, unlocking the handcuffs, untying my feet. My limbs, already accustomed to the constraints, felt heavy, my toes numb. I wriggled them, but I might as well have been watching someone else's appendages move because I couldn't feel a thing.

Hampton spoke up. "I brought you here because I have a proposition for you, Sergeant."

"Then you should have called me like a normal fucking human, instead of playing the Hollywood villain and staging an abduction." Asher sneered, rubbing his wrists after they were freed. "Give me my guns and my damn car keys."

Pershing's president dipped his chin, and someone off to his right scurried forward with the goods.

"We have a common enemy between us, Sergeant," Hampton said, trying to get Asher's attention when he stepped forward, into Lincoln's line of sight. "Your father . . . he has something that I want."

Asher's father.

My ears perked up, and I shifted forward, biting back a howl of pain when my poor feet scraped along the floor. Asher's eyes flicked to me again, went to my feet, and then he immediately crossed the distance between us.

His arm went around my waist, and he hoisted me close to his side.

His familiar scent felt like safety, but I couldn't . . . God, it was weird. So weird. We shared no blood, and I waited for disgust to sit low in my belly. I waited, and yet it never arrived. My fingers clutched the back of his shirt, holding onto the fabric for stability.

When Asher spoke, I felt his chest reverberate against my cheek. "I don't give a fuck what you want. You don't own me. You don't get a say in what jobs I take on. You are *nothing*."

A hard light entered Hampton's dark eyes. "Perhaps I'm nothing, but is she?" He indicated to me with a casual tilt of his chin. "It seems imperative to note that our lovely mayor fully believes *Laurel* is dead. Clearly, he went so far as to bury the poor girl before the masses when she's standing before me now, breathing, alive." Mouth curving in a sinister grin, he added, "But a single word from me will change all that. I, for one, would love to see his reaction to her *miraculous* return from the dead. So, let me repeat my question to you, Sergeant. I might be nothing to you . . . but is she?"

Asher's arm tightened around my waist, which may as well have been a hand around my lungs, squeezing, squeezing, squeezing until they burst with a climactic *pop!* My vision blurred at Hampton's words.

I was the pawn.

Since that day twelve years ago, I had run my life as the queen of the chessboard. I directed the ship. I operated everything from behind-the-scenes.

In the span of a breath, Hampton's words had demoted me so swiftly I feared suffering whiplash.

I opened my mouth, fully prepared to take control of my fate.

There was no opportunity to do so.

"Take your threat and shove it up your ass, Hampton," came Asher's gruff reply.

His arms swept me forward, directing me toward the front door of the shack. I jerked to look back at Nat, at Hampton, at my fate dangling on the precipice. Pity lined Nat's pretty features. There was nothing but resolute hatred in Hampton's.

"No," I whispered, "no, I—"

Asher's heat left me, and I whipped around just in time to see him grip the man who'd pissed himself by the throat and shove his face into the wall. There was a crunching sound—the wall or the man's bones splintering upon impact, I didn't know—and then Asher was leaning in, his hold so tight that Charles's face began to purple from lack of oxygen.

My hands went to my mouth, holding in my gasp.

"You *ever* throw another fist at me like you did earlier tonight," Asher said, voice deathly low, "and I will end you." His knuckles whitened as his grip tightened. "Understand me?"

"*Lincoln.*"

That was me. My horrified whisper. My rapidly beating heart. My unrelenting fear.

His lips thinned at my tone, and then he brutally tossed

the man to the floor, where he curled in a fetal position, his hands at his throat as he gasped for air.

"Let's go," Asher muttered, hands reaching for me.

I stepped back.

I didn't want his hands on me.

I didn't want him *touching* me.

He was—he was . . . I looked at Charles with the imprint of Asher's hand around his neck, and this time when the bile rose, it had nothing to do with my stepfather or his lies and everything to do with the monster masquerading as a man before me.

In the end, my feet stole the fight from me.

They wobbled under my full weight, burned with an intensity from the scratches and cuts that scored the soles.

Asher's arms swooped below my butt, hauling me into his arms, bridal-style, as he strode from the shack.

Cop.

Devil.

It didn't matter what you called him—in the end, Lincoln Asher carried me all the way back to the SUV, his rugged face bruised and bleeding, his limp shortening his usual long-gaited stride.

He thought he was doing me a favor.

He thought he was helping me.

In reality, by turning down Joshua Hampton's offer, he'd just sealed my fate.

And I was as good as dead.

4

LINCOLN

She wouldn't talk to me.

Hell, she wouldn't even *look* at me.

If I'd been alone in this SUV, I would have bellowed out my rage. Buried my fist in the dashboard. Hit the gas, burning rubber so fast that I could forget everything that had happened tonight as the outside world sped past me.

None of those were options with Avery sitting in the passenger's seat.

No, not Avery.

Laurel Peyton.

Christ. I shoved a hand through my hair, tugging on the strands relentlessly.

It made sense that I'd have no idea who she was—I was nine years older. Had spent my entire youth bouncing from foster care to foster care after being dropped off with the Ursuline nuns as a toddler. Until Jason Ambideaux had stepped into my life, I'd had little understanding of my parents or why I'd been unwanted. Even then, there'd been no mention of Jay Foley. Not until much, much later.

I'd gone to the Ursulines with nothing—not even a surname, or so they said.

One of the nuns had named me "Asher," after a man she'd once fancied herself in love with, long before joining the cloister.

I wasn't a Foley, like my father.

I wasn't a Meriden, like my mother.

And I'd never been treated as such, always the forgotten bastard son left to his own devices.

Squeezing the steering wheel, I fought to see the road out of my good eye. Did my best not to let my frustration seep through like an infectious poison when I muttered, "We're stopping for the night."

That got her attention.

Her shoulders twitched though she didn't turn to look at me. Only sat there, face forward, shoulders squared off. "It's only an hour or so drive back to N'Orleans."

My muscles tightened at the distrust I heard in her voice. "You know how to drive?"

At that, she turned to glare at me, her chin lifted stubbornly. "No."

"Thought so." She'd told me nothing, but I'd survived thus far in life because I paid attention to the details. And the details were obvious: when I cut a hard turn, when I took a second too long to start easing off the brakes, Avery remained at ease. She never reached for the oh-shit handle or pressed down on a nonexistent foot pedal on the passenger's side. Another driver would be terrified; Avery was completely unaware.

And it all made sense.

Laurel Peyton had died from suicide in her early teens, that much I remembered from reading the newspapers. Long before she would have studied for her learner's permit.

Long before she'd have had the chance to steal her parents' car and go for joyrides.

Long before she would have learned to trust anyone enough to give up her virginity.

A visual of her backside as I thrust into her body hit me, and—*fuck*. I couldn't go down that road, not right now.

Grip tightening on the steering wheel, I focused on evening out my breath and not squeezing my eyes too hard. The swollen one hurt like a bitch, and regret swarmed me for not ending that asshole's life when I'd had the chance.

One word from Avery, however, and I'd dropped his ass to the floor.

I'd heard the terror in her voice.

Had seen the fear in her hazel eyes.

Good. That was . . . good. No matter the fact we were barely related, Avery—*Laurel*—didn't deserve to deal with my bullshit. I'd never win an award for upstanding citizen of the year, even on my best day.

Rough. Brutal. Deadly.

Those were the words which best described me.

Poisonous, too.

Ill-timed laughter filled my chest because wasn't that the damn truth? Nothing good in my life ever lasted for very long. Like an infectious disease, the sinner in me had a way of converting everything I touched.

Avery didn't deserve that.

Especially not after the life she'd lived.

Trying to soften my voice, I took the next exit and veered left at the merge. "There's not a chance in hell that I'll be able to make it back to the city." Spotting the first bright neon motel sign on the quiet interstate, I pulled into the parking lot and found the first available spot. "I can't see worth a damn. We're lucky I haven't already driven us into a ditch."

There was a small pause and then, "Your eye does look like shit."

"Yeah, well, it feels even worse." Turning off the ignition, I sat back in the driver's seat, head resting on the cushion behind me. My good eye fluttered shut and I drew in a deep breath. "I can barely see," I muttered, "and I'm in no mood to teach you how to drive. Staying the night is the only option."

Six hours ago, we'd been fucking in the Basement, not a care in the world.

Now, she couldn't even relax beside me, like she was worried that I might launch myself at her and tear her limb from limb.

I was a monster. I was cruel. But only to those who deserved it.

Letting my head fall to the right, scarred cheek pressed to the headrest, I stared at the woman who'd made me believe, even for a moment, that more existed in this world than what I'd always believed possible. *And she's your stepsister*. Sort of. Barely.

I palmed the car keys in one hand, squeezing so tight that the serrated edge tested even my roughly calloused palm. The pain, unlike the one in my heart, felt good. A reminder that, at the end of the day, you could always count on reality to dump you on your ass and level out the playing field.

Happiness wasn't in the cards for me.

If I didn't understand that now, at the age of thirty-four, then there was seriously no hope for me.

Opening my mouth, I hesitated on the words I so desperately wanted to say:

You can trust me.

I wouldn't hurt you.

Please don't be scared.

In the end, I didn't say a damn thing. Cranking open my door, a grimace on my face, I stepped out and slammed it shut behind me. Crossed around the hood of the SUV to Avery's side, just as her bare feet connected with the dirty, glass-ridden concrete.

She could hate me again in ten minutes when we had a set of rooms and there was nothing but carpet everywhere.

Without any warning, I scooped her up in my arms, tugging her in close to my chest, hating that the instant her body collided with mine, my cock twitched in my pants.

"Put me down!"

Her voice was throaty, audibly exhausted.

I ignored her protests. Ignored the pain in my right knee, thanks to one of those bastards coming at me with a crow bar when I'd least expected it outside that damn shack.

Avery's hands scrabbled for purchase as I limped my way to the front door of the shitty motel. Dead potted plants sat on either side of the door, and a junkie reclined on the circular front drive, a matchstick in one hand and a spoon in the other.

Nothing said romance like staying the night in a shithole like this.

Not that romance should be anywhere on your mind after tonight.

"Asher," Avery snapped, sharply tugging on my shirt, "put me down. I can walk on my own. I don't *need* you."

Propping the front door open with my elbow, I angled us in. "Your feet are worse off than my eye."

She snorted derisively. "You're only saying that because you haven't seen your eye yet. It looks—"

"Oh!"

"—like shit."

The receptionist behind the front desk blinked up at Avery in my arms. Except that her eyes weren't on Avery. They were trained on me—on my swollen eye.

Guess it is that bad.

Readjusting Avery in my arms, I returned the receptionist's stare. Short and with skin weathered like worn leather, the woman had to be over eighty. On a good day.

I forced a grim smile. "We need some rooms."

"Oh." The woman's smile dipped, losing some of its luster. "I . . . Listen, sir, but I'm sorry to tell you that we"—her cloudy blue eyes refocused on Avery—"are booked solid for the evening."

Booked solid, my ass.

"Is that why you got a junkie on your front doorstep? Because you're *booked?*"

"Lincoln."

"No, Avery." I didn't believe for a single second that there wasn't even one room available for the night. We were in Bumfuck, Louisiana, not New Orleans, and if the druggie outside was any signifier, then this motel was hurting. "Two rooms," I ground out, feeling Avery's eyes on me. "If you'll sell to a junkie, then you'll sell to us. I need two rooms, second or third floor, with windows facing the parking lot."

The receptionist stiffened. "I don't like demanding guests."

"Yeah, well, I don't like—"

A hand clapped over my mouth, silencing the rest of my sentence.

Avery threw me a harsh look, eyes narrowed into slits, before turning back to the woman. "You'll be doing us such a huge favor," she murmured softly, "and we'd be so appreciative. Unfortunately, we were camping when Lincoln here came in contact with a black bear . . . let's just say that the bear won. He's a little embarrassed about it." She cupped a hand around her mouth and dropped her voice to a barely audible murmur. "Actually, he's a little emotional. We've been driving for hours and we simply can't go on any longer tonight."

Black bears?

If the state had any black bears at all, they weren't south of Baton Rouge, that was for sure.

The woman's straight brows eased, unpuckering until the crease at the center of her forehead finally smoothed. "That's *horrible,* dear," the receptionist whispered.

"It was. It *really* was." Avery nodded, her cheek brushing up against the planes of my chest. "You know what's worse? The fact that . . . well, the fact that the bear somehow managed to steal *all* of our clothes. Including my shoes . . . and my underwear."

Christ.

The receptionist gaped at Avery's fabricated tale, and I didn't know whether to applaud or jeer, demanding that she tell the truth about her missing panties. The panties *I'd* torn right off her before dominating her body.

With a shaky smile and a quick glance around me to the front door, the woman behind the desk turned to grab an old-school key fob off a hook. "Two-twenty-one," she edged out, "second floor, facing the parking lot." Her blue eyes went to Avery again. "I live here on site. I don't know if . . . I don't know if you'd be interested, but I do have an extra pair of underwear. They might be a bit big—"

"She's fine," I bit out, letting Avery slide down my body so that I could pull out my wallet. It was almost a miracle it'd survived tonight's activities. "We'll just take the rooms."

Avery's hands latched onto the lip of the chest-high front desk, holding herself steady as she settled her weight on her heels. "That is such a kind offer . . ." Leaning forward, her hazel eyes drifted over the elderly receptionist, pausing at the woman's pinned name tag. "*Sue*. I'd love a pair."

"They're clean," *Sue* said, all brilliant smiles and crooked yellowed teeth.

Avery returned the smile with one of her own. "Even better."

God save me from—

I slapped my credit card down on the counter, startling both the receptionist and the woman hell-bent on driving me insane. "We'll take the two rooms." Beside me, Avery bristled, and I gave in with a grunt. "And the underwear."

Sue shifted her weight, taking my card. "Just the one room, Mr. . . ." She peered down at my name embossed on the credit card. "Asher. Two-twenty-one, as I said. It's all I got."

One room.

Something told me that I'd have a pillow smothering my face before the night was over—Avery did *not* look pleased. Even so . . .

I nodded curtly. "We'll take it."

"We won't."

I ignored Avery's protest, grimly picking up the key and tucking my credit card back into my wallet. "Knock when you have the panties, ma'am. It's much appreciated."

Bending at the knees, I let out a tight breath at the twinge in my right leg, and then—

"I can walk, Lincoln," Avery snapped. "No, seriously, I'm fine—"

She bounced high on my chest as I stepped away from

the front counter and headed for the hallway off to the right. I needed a shower and a bed, the sooner the better.

Catching the flowery scent of Avery's shampoo, I swallowed.

Maybe it was a good thing we were sharing a room. We had a wide array of shit to discuss, starting with the fact that she was Laurel-fucking-Peyton. *You knew she'd been bullshitting you when she gave up her name.*

Yeah, I'd suspected that she'd fed me lies.

But there was no way I could have suspected *this.*

My good eye narrowed at the computer paper taped to the elevator with chicken scratch scrawled across it. Broken —of course.

"This has got to be the shittiest motel in the history of motels," I growled, turning my head in search of the stairwell.

In my arms, Avery snorted. "You chose a place called Bedding Down. Beneath the logo was the tagline, 'No more than twelve people per room.' What else did you expect?"

"That's not a tagline. That's a calling card for orgies." I hooked my thumb through the door handle to the stairs and drew it open with a low groan. "If I'd actually been able to see that, I would have kept driving until we hit a Motel 6."

"You should have kept driving until we hit N'Orleans."

"Then we wouldn't have made contact with the only pack of black bears in this part of Louisiana. Who knew they liked women's lingerie so much?"

"You should feel lucky they don't fancy dicks even more." With *that* comment, Avery squirmed in my grasp when my foot hit the first stair rung, muttering, "I can walk. Stop treating me like I'm an invalid."

She wanted to walk? Fine.

I checked back my grimace when her mouth twisted in

pain as her feet made contact with the cool tile of the stairs. I wanted to swing her back into my arms, but she was right.

She was capable.

She was independent.

And I was smothering her like a man obsessed.

Resigned to letting her crawl up the steps if that's what she really wanted to do, I turned back to the stairwell and stifled a groan at the pain in my knee. She wasn't the only one feeling the course of the night, and with each step I took, my mood soured several more degrees.

By the time we reached the second floor, Avery's face was three shades paler than normal and I was minutes away from coming unhinged. I'd spent twelve years separating my life from the corruption of our city's finest leaders—unless it directly involved work for the NOPD.

Twelve years of keeping my head down and trying to do the right thing.

Twelve years of staying in my lane and off the radar of men like Jason Ambideaux.

Twelve years of trying to build a life that wasn't blood and terror day-in and day-out.

I didn't miss the way Avery skirted out of reach when I let her slide past me into our shared room for the night. And I sure as hell didn't miss the way she slid a distrustful glance in my direction when I drew the blinds shut over the windows, as though she questioned my need for privacy.

Frustration welled up, suffocating in the way it clawed at my chest, until I finally let loose the words that had been on my mind since she'd watched me shove that man into the wall at the shack.

"If I wanted you dead, *Laurel*," I growled, "you'd already be lifeless."

5

AVERY

Funny how more than one person had called me Laurel tonight, and not a single time did I feel like they were talking to me.

I'd always thought that hearing my real name would come with a sense of freedom, like I'd broken free from my jail cell after so many years of being locked away in the darkness.

That wasn't the case.

In reality, it felt foreign. Strange.

I wasn't Laurel, not anymore. Laurel Peyton was a thirteen-year-old girl with starry-eyed fantasies of becoming a well-known vet and saving any animal that entered her practice. Avery, on the other hand, was simply content to foster strays and give them enough love so they never felt unwanted while they waited to be placed with a permanent family.

Laurel knew nothing but family picnics, an obsession with Brad Pitt in *Mr. and Mrs. Smith*, and that her momma, despite her affinity for drinking a little too heavily, never put up a fuss about random karaoke jam sessions with her only daughter.

None of that even related to me as Avery.

"Nothing to say to that?"

Asher's deep timbre yanked me from my reverie, drawing me back into the shadows of my reality. "Don't call me Laurel."

With the blinds drawn shut, I could barely make out his features and his scars were completely obscured. His dark chuckle, however, was perfectly crisp in the otherwise quiet room. "You've got to be kidding me—the secret's out and you're still trying to keep up the act. Listen, *Laurel*, there's no reason to pretend anymore."

I bristled at his sneering tone. "Do you really want to play that game?" Biting back a howl of pain, I took a step closer to him. "At least my biggest sin is pretending to be someone who I'm not. How many people have you murdered, *Sergeant?* How much blood truly stains your hands?"

His chest heaved, mouth twisting harshly. "You have no idea what you're talking about."

"No?" The memory of him squeezing that man's throat was not one I'd ever forget. It made me sick to think of it. Sicker to think, even for a moment, that I'd enjoyed Asher's hand around *my* neck as he'd fucked me. What did that say about me? What did that say about the kind of person *I* was? My stomach churned at the disturbing thought, threatening to upend the dinner I'd eaten hours earlier.

I turned away, unable to meet him in the eye.

"Just say it, Avery. I can practically taste your desperation to be the saint here."

I wouldn't face him, no matter the fact that he was right. My brain was on fire, thoughts rioting through me, demanding to be voiced. Struggling to maintain my cool, I let my head hang low and kept my gaze rooted on my still bare feet.

I must have taken too long to speak or maybe it was that his patience was threadbare. Whatever it was, I didn't expect to feel his hand on my elbow. He whipped me around, and my toes burned from twirling so fast on the scratchy carpet. Our chests brushed, and if that wasn't enough to make me feel unbalanced, being the sole focus of the hard glint in his one un-swollen eye was like experiencing vertigo.

The room swirled, my lungs heaved, and I bit down hard on my bottom lip to keep from gasping out loud.

"Say it," he growled, his hand still locked like a vice around my arm. "*Say it.*"

He pushed and he pushed and he pushed, and it wasn't my fault that I snapped.

Teeth clenching, I stared up at him, refusing to back down. "If I hadn't said anything, you would have *murdered* that man without thinking twice. I could see it in your eyes, the resolution there. And, for what? Because he punched you?" Shaking my head, I gave a dismissive laugh. "That doesn't make you a hero—it makes you a cold-blooded killer."

Silence.

It reigned in the scarce space between us, suffocating in the power it held.

And then, in a tone that sounded like it'd been pulled from the depth of his soul, Asher growled, "You're right, sweetheart. You want to know the number of people I've taken out?" He leaned in close, his hot breath wafting across my face. "I don't know. How's that for a confession? *I don't know.*"

Eyes widening, I tried to pull back, away from the anger

in his expression, away from the shock of heat that hit me square in the belly. "Lincoln—"

He didn't let me go. Didn't let me flee.

Instead, he invaded my space. Step for step until my back bumped into the wall and his arms came down like iron bars, locking me into the space between his chest and the plaster behind me.

"Should I confess some more?" he whispered like the devil himself. "I want to fuck you, Avery." His mouth dropped to my left ear, nudging at the soft skin there with the crooked bridge of his nose. When I gasped, he answered with a rough laugh. "Does that shock you? That even now that I know my asshole father married your mom, it doesn't make me want you any less?" He nipped at my skin, keeping me caged within his muscular embrace. "I want to bend you over and fuck you. Me, a *cold-blooded killer*. I want to mark your skin and wrap my hand around your neck just the way you like it and thrust into your tight pussy until you confess."

With every word that left his mouth, my breathing grew more erratic. I needed to breathe; I needed to remember that Lincoln Asher was not the man for me, for more reasons than just the recently made obvious. And yet, my response wasn't a set down and it wasn't a rebuttal.

To my utter humiliation, my response could be summed up with only three words:

"Confess to what?"

One masculine hand landed on my hip. "That you want me as I am. A murderer." His palm skimmed up my body, past my ribcage. "A cop." Over the curve of my small breast. "A sinner." Gently circled the base of my throat as his lips made contact with my hairline and a shiver worked its way down the pearls of my spine. "A man who is, beneath it all, just a man like any other."

But Lincoln Asher wasn't like any other man.

He stepped into a room and people cowered in fear.

He took a breath, and grown men pissed themselves.

Tonight, one of the most powerful men in the city had sicced his lackeys on Asher, just so that they could have the slim chance at an upper hand.

And *still* they'd failed in grandiose fashion.

My tongue darted out to wet my dry lips, and Asher's blue eyes tracked the movement hungrily. He said he was a man like any other, but I'd spent too many years watching and observing to take the words at face value. If I gave an inch, he'd steal a mile.

And if I submitted, he'd continue to believe that I was his for the taking.

Whenever he wanted me. *However* he wanted me.

How long until he turned those fists on me? How long until I ended up just like Momma, dead on my dining room floor, at the hands of a man who spun pretty words and yarns of lies?

At the hands of my stepfather's own blood—his *son*?

Chin kicking up, I fixed my gaze on his battered face and made a confession of my own: "I'm not Laurel Peyton anymore. I'm not naïve or trusting or looking for a savior. I'm not in the market for one. And the next time you make a decision for me, taking my voice away because you think you know what's best, just remember that I am *not* like other any other woman who will heel just because you tell her to."

Haint-blue eyes burning furiously, he rasped, "Is that so?"

I would not cower, not like the rest of the population who saw him and ran. "Yes, it is."

His lips pulled downward, jaw clenching tightly, and then he wrenched around with a violently uttered curse. "Any other confessions tonight?"

Fighting the urge to sag against the wall, I stood tall, shoulders back. My heart thundered in my chest. "I saw it the very first night you sat at my table in the square," I said, struggling to keep my voice steady as I watched his back flex with his labored breathing. "You're a man who's haunted by your past, Lincoln. I won't go down in that fire with you. I've got my own flames to put out."

With a bitter laugh, he glanced at me over his shoulder. "And what flames are those?" His tone baited me, daring me to rise to the challenge swirling in his gaze like a chaotic sandstorm. "Hiding in the shadows for another decade? Pretending to be someone you're not? Sitting at your little table with your deck of fortune-telling cards and *collecting* information? You can judge me all you want, but don't be mistaken. The only flame you're fighting is your own cowardice."

He might as well have stabbed me in the heart, slicing at the beating organ until every self-doubt of mine was splayed open for all to see.

I couldn't catch my breath. Couldn't see beyond the rage clouding the periphery of my vision.

"That's what I thought, *Laurel*," Asher murmured, his bruised lips turning up smugly. "Keep sitting on that high horse of yours. I'm sure the smell of bullshit is *real* sweet where you're at."

My feet were frozen, my limbs unmoving, as he turned for the door.

"Where are you going?" I heard myself ask, my voice faint in comparison to the blood pounding in my head.

He didn't look back. "To sleep in the SUV where the air is a little less judgmental. I'll get you in the morning."

Fisting the doorknob, he drew it open and then froze, broad shoulders stiffening. "Ms. Sue," he murmured, "thanks for bringing this by."

She said something I couldn't quite catch, and then Asher was turning around, a slip of white fabric in his big hand. He held it out, a silent challenge for me to step up and take it from him.

With wooden feet, I closed the distance between us.

Just before I would have clutched the material, he jerked it back and waited until I looked up, past his wide chest, his thick throat, to his hard blue eyes.

"White," he said, voice low, his gaze crudely skimming my body, "how fitting for someone determined to be such a saint. You of all people should know that the world isn't black or white, sweetheart." I watched, eyes wide, as he purposely let the receptionist's underwear fall to the floor at our feet. The tips of my ears burned with embarrassment as he tacked on, darkly, "I can't wait for the day when you're forced to make the decisions I've made in my life. What's that saying again?" He snapped his fingers dramatically. "Oh yeah, I remember. *How the mighty have fallen.*"

Heat swept over me, and it was hard to distinguish between the anger and the humiliation at knowing what he wanted—for me to get on my knees in front of him if I wanted to pick up the underwear he'd dropped.

"Fuck you," I whispered, my voice vibrating with fury, my hands balled into tight fists.

"I wouldn't want to stain your pristine innocence all over again, sweetheart, no matter how much you liked it." He lifted one brow and then idly dropped his gaze to the scrap of white fabric on the floor. "But, maybe," he drawled, "if you begged for it, I'd be down to tear off your panties again. We can blame black bears for their disappearance, if it makes you feel any better for sleeping with a murderer."

With a wink, he disappeared out the door and closed it shut behind him.

I don't know how long I stood there.

I don't know how long the rage lasted, burning in my veins, threatening to drown me.

I *do* know that I went to bed panty-less, refusing to even touch Ms. Sue's kind offering.

And as I stared up at the dark ceiling, I had only one thought: Lincoln Asher wasn't just dangerous. He was the devil.

I punched my flat-as-hell pillow, turning onto my side, slamming my eyes shut.

Sleep eluded me, and by the time the sun began to peek through the blinds less than two hours later, I couldn't shake off our heated conversation and the horrid realization that, like the devil himself, Asher had sussed out my inner truth.

I was a coward hiding in the shadows.

Had *always* been a coward hiding in the shadows.

It was time I did something to change that.

6

AVERY

For the second time in less than twenty-four hours, I was back at Whiskey Bay.

Unlike yesterday's visit, it was broad daylight now and unseasonably warm. The mid-afternoon sun beat down relentlessly, warming the crown of my head, turning my back so sticky that my T-shirt clung to my damp skin.

After driving back to New Orleans this morning with Asher—in pure, unforgiving silence—I'd only stayed at the Sultan's Palace long enough to shower and pull myself together before grabbing a cab to the Bywater.

You're an idiot for coming back.

Or maybe I was finally just making a move. Albeit, hopefully not an idiotic one.

The bouncer from last night was missing as I tugged open the door to the strip club. The dim lighting inside was an instant relief, especially compared to the hotter-than-hot weather outside.

Whiskey Bay might as well have been a different bar at this time of the day. The tables were scarce of gamblers, the dancers missing from their stages. Hardly anyone mingled at the bar, and I spotted only three Birkenstock-wearing fellows over by an old-school jukebox.

Movement behind the bar caught my eye.

Time to bite the bullet—not literally, of course.

With fake confidence, I ambled over, picking my way around tables and chairs. Slid onto a stool, elbows on the bar top. Like I'd seen in the movies, I lifted one hand casually, hailing down a bald bartender from where he was taking pint glasses out of a steaming dishwasher on the other side of the register.

Be brave.

Be bold.

"Hey there!" I exclaimed when he was an earshot. Pinching the fabric of my black T-shirt at my neck, I pulled it away from my clammy skin and made a show of fanning my face with my free hand. "Jeez, it is *so* hot outside."

Dark eyes, glazed over with a lack of enthusiasm, didn't so much as blink. "It's N'Orleans in spring. That's what happens."

Huh. Guess bartenders weren't generally happy at this time of day. I could have sworn I'd seen him here last night, mixing up cocktails and laughing with patrons. Then again . . . I squinted at his face, taking note of his bloodshot eyes. Maybe he was hungover.

It seemed silly to wish that *my* problem could be as simple as a hangover, but no, I got the shit end of the stick.

A stepfather who wanted me dead.

A sort-of stepbrother who I both wanted to bash over the head with a heavy object *and* climb onto his lap for non-bashing activities that involved both of us being naked from the waist down.

I never said it was great to be me.

In fact, I wouldn't recommend it.

"I'd love a cocktail," I said when the bartender seemed uninclined to ask me what I wanted.

"It's two p.m." Somehow, he managed to sound both disinterested and disapproving all at once. "And I'll need your ID."

"Yeah, sure!"

I pulled my wallet from my purse and handed over my fake. Like last night at the door, this guy gave the laminated plastic a cursory glance and handed it back over. "You look young for twenty-five," he said after I ordered a screwdriver.

I lied about many things—my age wasn't one of them.

"The perks of high-end skincare products." With a casual shrug, I added, "And good genes. My mother had *perfect* skin."

"Great."

This guy wasn't much of a talker.

Time to scrap the casual conversation and go straight for Plan B.

I edged my elbow a little farther on the bar, then scooted my ass to the very edge of the barstool. "Listen . . ."

He slid the screwdriver over to me. "Wanna open a tab?"

"Uh, sure."

"Great."

Any more of that Great-ing and he'd be giving Tony the Tiger a run for his money. "Right, thank you." *Because you're any less awkward?* This was so much harder to do now that I was here. And if I really wanted to dig deep and be honest with myself, I was suffering from a bad case of cold feet. Taking an irreparable step was a lot more terrifying when I had only myself to blame if shit went south.

Deep breaths.

Wrapping my hand tightly around the cocktail glass, I

swallowed my nerves and mentally whipped my ass into gear. It was now or never.

"I'm looking for Nat."

The bartender's dark eyes flitted over me, assessing. "Yeah?"

I gave a curt nod. Forced steel into my stone. "I read cards for her weekly. Unfortunately, she couldn't make it down to Jackson Square for our usual appointment and asked for me to meet her here instead. Do you mind letting her know that I'm here for whenever she's ready?"

Half terrified to breathe too sharply and give myself away, I waited and waited and waited for the bartender to make his call. White rag in hand, he wiped down the bar near the register, then swapped towels for another set, the latter which he used to buff the wine glasses dry.

"Nat's been in a meeting all day," he finally said, hooking the rag over one shoulder as he put those glasses up and grabbed another four by the stems from the dishwasher. "But I can see if she'd like for me to put you in one of the rooms while you wait."

One of the rooms.

Immediately, I thought of Asher and myself at Stage One, him on his knees with his face buried between my legs. It was wrong, *so* wrong, and there was a good chance I'd be more likely to shoot him than hug him the next time we saw each other, but I still wanted . . . Well, I guess it should be noted that I'd been on edge all day.

Sitting next to a man for over an hour while wearing no panties—not my finest moment.

Also not my finest moment? Spending the entire hour of that drive wondering if hate sex was as magical as everyone always boasted that it was.

Sipping my screwdriver for fortitude, I waited in my

corner of the empty bar until the bartender returned some twenty minutes later, tossing the rag from hand to hand. "She's ready for you."

Four little words, and yet I grinned like he'd spouted out the entire dictionary from start to finish.

"Great!" Now I sounded like Tony the Tiger, too. Pushing the cocktail away, I belatedly tacked on, "I'll close up my tab after I speak with her. Any chance you can point me in the right direction?"

He closed a fist around my discarded glass. "The Basement. She said you know where to go."

An uncomfortable laugh bubbled up in my chest. Yeah, I knew where that was. Both the stairwell that led up to it and the fire escape that led *out* of it. Twenty-four hours was definitely not long enough to scrub the memories from my retina. Twenty-four *years* seemed only slightly more likely.

"I'll help myself there, then." Clapping my hand on the bar, I hopped off the stool and offered a short wave. "Thanks for the drink."

It was time to put on my *I-can-do-this* attitude. Remember that—

"Want a suggestion, Miss Washington?"

No. I was actually rather convinced that I'd already hit my suggestion quota for this quarter. But because I wasn't an unthinking asshole like Lincoln Asher, I kept my opinion to myself. Plastering a smile on my face, I peered over my shoulder with what I hoped was a friendly expression. "Sure," I said, grinning way too brightly. There was a good possibility that my smile read *screw you* instead of *you're so nice to help me out.*

That was the problem with reaching the end of your rope—you were incrementally closer to giving less and less fucks about playing nice with the world.

The bartender stacked one dry pint glass on top of another. Then, finally, he spoke: "We all know you were here last night, Miss Washington. Nothing stays secret in this place for long." He added another pint glass to his tower, eyes on his masterpiece and not on me. "Nat's not your most subtle creature, and she's never been particularly fun to be around when she's pissed."

"Is anyone?"

Dropping the rag to the counter, he fixed his attention on me. "She came in this morning and fired one of my guys for serving an Irish coffee without whipped cream. Kid's been with us for six years. Guess what I'm trying to say is, Nat's in a special mood today, and if you've got any sense of self-preservation, you'll turn around and head right back out that front door."

Slowly, a smile worked its way across my face. "How fortunate, then, that I'm in a mood, as well."

I didn't give the bartender the chance to convince me otherwise.

Turning on my heel, I erased the distance to the hallway. Men's bathroom. Women's bathroom. Ah, here it was—the elusive General Storage Room. Sending a quick glance down the hall, I pried open the door, surprised to find it unlocked, and entered the so-called closet of Whiskey Bay. Then immediately took the stairs two at a time.

Like the main room downstairs, the Basement lacked a lot of its mystery during the day. Light glistened from the large windows, the curtains flung open wide to reveal a view of the winding Mississippi River and the grassy West Bank just across the width of the water. The stages were idle, empty, the chairs and settees and couches that circled each platform all arranged neatly in preparation for tonight's activities.

"I see you've decided to show your face, *cherie*. How utterly daring of you."

At the delicate sound of her voice, I breathed hard through my nose, expelling my nerves, and then turned to face her. Her evening gown had been swapped out for a skirt with larger-than-life patterns and a deep, V-neck top that plunged down to expose the inner swells of her breasts.

Straining for a nonchalance that I did not feel, I smiled. "It's surprisingly less difficult than I thought it'd be." My smile stretched a little wider. "Tell me, was it incredibly hard for you to lie to me for all these years? Or are you surprised that it wasn't that hard after all?"

If I hadn't been watching her face so closely, I would have missed it—the gentle arch of her brows and the twitch of her upper lip. Casually, cruelly, she murmured, "To be surprised entails that I was emotionally invested in the outcome of your life. I can't say that I've given much thought to it until recently."

Ouch.

Her words were like little pinpricks needling my arms. As though they were an actual physical threat, I ran my hands over my arms, swiping the little bastards away. If I could flick Nat into nonexistence, as well, I would have without second thought.

At the very least, I couldn't let her see how she'd wounded me, however minimal the puncture.

Slipping my hands into the back pockets of my jeans, I swept my gaze over the Basement, touching on everything and nothing all at once. Rocked back onto my heels when I said, "I won't lie, Natalie—from your cards, this isn't so far off from what I thought you did for a living." I paused, drawing in her curiosity before slipping in the verbal knife: "Only, I always assumed that you were the one putting out.

Although perhaps that's a more *recent* venture with the city's favorite university president?"

It didn't take long for my implication to click with her, and Nat's elegant hand lifted, hovering like she wanted nothing more than to strangle me, before snapping back to her side. "Acting a cunt doesn't become you, Laurel."

I turned to Whiskey Bay's queen, refusing to shrink before her. "How fortunate," I drawled, "that me and Laurel had a falling out some years back. Turns out I was too much of a *cunt* for her liking."

Her brows arched.

I stood my ground.

Seconds passed, and I watched her—a woman I'd considered a friend until yesterday—work through the scenarios in her head. Pristine white teeth sank into her red-painted lower lip. "You're here for a reason."

It wasn't a question. Wasn't even a statement, really—more like a thought voiced out loud.

"Yes," I said. Striving to appear casual, I kept my hands in my pockets, thumbs hooked over the denim fabric. With no one around to overhear, I opted to skip beating around the bush and go in straight for the kill. "Whatever deal Hampton planned to offer Asher, I'd like to take it on."

Take it on?

Because *that* sounded convincing or even halfway lethal.

And it seemed that Nat agreed with me.

Unblinking, she stared at me. "You couldn't handle it."

If I argued or protested, I'd sound like a petulant child throwing a temper tantrum—and I couldn't afford to lose this opportunity.

Big Hampton's threat still rang loudly in my ears, and I'd yet to shake off the worry that I was hours away from meeting my fate: death. Whatever Joshua Hampton wanted, whatever he needed of Asher, I was willing to make happen.

For that to even be a possibility, I needed to play it cool.

Stay unfrazzled.

If only my heart would get with the program.

I shoved aside the concern that Nat could hear its incessant thumping in my chest and zeroed my gaze on her face with a silent prayer that she couldn't read my inner feelings. "What's he want?" Pulling my hands from my pockets, I dropped my arms to my sides. *Look confident. Act confident.* "For Mayor Foley to die?"

Nat's mouth quirked. "You'd like that, wouldn't you? To be the one who finally ends your stepfather's life?"

Yes. I wanted nothing more. Had *never* wanted anything more than to see the blood pool around his body, his eyes unblinking, just like he'd had done to Momma.

Still, I said nothing.

Waited, hoping, for Nat to give up because of my silence and divulge more information.

She didn't . . . at least, not in the way that I'd hoped.

"I've always found this city so fascinating," she began, moving toward the closest stage and leaving me to follow. With an elegant fluff to her skirt, she settled into a velvet-padded chair. Her hands curled over the lip of the armrests, and she glanced at me as though she were actually peering down at me from a throne. Without waiting for me to take a seat, she continued. "You never know who you can trust. It was such an odd adjustment when I moved here."

"From Hungary?" I asked, thinking of her accent and her mention of her immigrant parents.

"No." She gave a thin-lipped smile. "Baltimore, actually."

Right.

I took the seat opposite hers, careful to remain facing the

stairwell up to the Basement. Just in case. After last night, I'd never look at Nat with a sympathetic eye again—and I'd come armed with my gun in my purse since my taser was probably in the Gulf of Mexico by now.

"It took me no time at all to understand that I would *never* understand the way New Orleans works. My first year here, a few of our finest men in blue murdered a man just over there"—she pointed toward the window, and I had the feeling that she meant across the river—"but, of course, they couldn't just let that slide. Couldn't risk having a target on their back if anyone found out that a drug stop had gone so wrong." She propped an elbow up on the armrest, positioning her chin in the palm of her hand to watch me with glittering eyes. "So, they torched him. Shoved his burnt body back in his car. Drove him up onto the levee and fled."

Bile climbed my throat, and I swallowed hard.

Nat smiled, slowly. "But, of course, that wasn't enough. They set the car ablaze before they left, too, just to be sure."

"Why are you telling me this?"

"Because I can understand why you wouldn't have gone to the police when your mother died." Forehead creasing, Nat's expression turned sympathetic. "You must have been *terrified, cherie,* not knowing who you could trust. Not knowing where to go. A man like your stepfather is supposed to be one of the most trustworthy—a family man, an overseer of our precious jewel of a city, a protector for those who can't protect themselves."

My soul cried out at the truth in her words, and just like that, she'd shoved me back into my thirteen-year-old body. Listening to my stepfather argue over my disappearance, my nose buried in my bent knees, my arms clasped around my shins. The fear that clung to me as I scrambled to my feet and slipped out a cracked-open window on the first floor.

Physically, I'd escaped that night unscathed.

Mentally, emotionally, it felt as though the chains of those long-ago fears would never break.

"Jay Foley is a bastard," I whispered, the curse sounding so underwhelming in contrast with the pure hatred I felt for the man. A word like I needed just didn't exist—not in English, at least, and I didn't know any other languages. I'd dropped out of school the year we were finally offered a language elective.

Nat nodded, her hand dipping with the force of the movement with her chin still in her palm. "Yes, *cherie*, he is. But I must say . . . of all the cocks I've sucked in my life, his is perhaps the best."

"I—"

The words died on my tongue.

Everything went rigid: my limbs, my heart, my blood, if that was even possible. It *felt* possible. In this room, in this old factory seated along the Mississippi River, in this *city* which had stolen so much from me, every iota of heat dissipated from my body.

"What did you say?" My tone was hard, unforgiving, and Nat smiled like she'd been waiting for this moment. Possibly even for years.

"You were right," she said after a moment, crossing one leg over the other, her skirts moving like silk, "I did put out. I *do* put out, as you so politely put it. And Jay is by far one of the best customers I've ever had. Your mother was a very lucky woman."

Hatred seethed like poison in my veins, twisting and turning and nearly strangling me with the force of it. "My mother was *murdered*."

"Oh, I'm aware. He let that slip, once, when he was deep in the liquor bottle." Nat straightened in her seat, hands clasping together in her lap—the very image of demure respectability. "He has a photo of her by his bed, his precious *Catherine.* Anytime he fucked me, it was with me on my knees, your mother's picture inches from my nose. I could have kissed it, especially when he got carried away in the fantasy and thrust too hard."

Stop. Stop, no more. Please.

The urge to dry-heave overwhelmed me, and it was only a testament to my strength that I didn't turn and vomit all over the floor. I despised the images she planted in my head. Didn't want to think of Foley—

"*Catherine,* he'd whisper into the crook of my neck as he fucked me," Nat went on, a nasty smile curving her red lips. "And next to her picture was one of *you.*"

I couldn't stop it.

My body twisting, my hands landing on the chair's armrest, nails biting down into the fabric, my chest dropping as my stomach unloaded itself.

"With the number of times I *put out* for him, I had the opportunity to learn your face very well, *cherie.* The crook in your nose with the scar right over the bridge. The birthmark near your hairline. The smattering of freckles over your cheeks, and the green ring around your hazel eyes. You may have swapped out your blond hair for black, Laurel, but one glance at you in the square was like a time portal to every fucking I ever received in your stepfather's bed."

Eyelids screwing shut, I exhaled through my nose. "Please," I edged out, my palm scraping across my lips. "I don't want . . . I can't—"

I heard the creak of Nat's chair, and then her hand gently landed on the back of my head, stroking my hair in much the same way Hampton had done to her last night. Her touch reminded me of Momma's, soft and soothing—and that alone had me wrenching away, jumping up from the chair before the sensations of wanting love, my *mother's* love, could sink me back under.

"No wonder you came to see me so often," I worked out, my stomach still queasy as I stood out of reach, arms locked around my middle. "How much did you report back to Jay once you found me, huh? Everything?"

Nat's nose scrunched as she glanced down at my vomit, then hooked a foot around my rejected chair, her hands on the back, and dragged the chair over the spot where I'd literally lost my lunch.

Satisfied, she returned to her seat, turning her head slightly so I remained in her line of sight. "Nothing. I told him nothing."

Highly doubtful. Suspicion laced my tone as I spoke, "And why should I believe you? You clearly told Hampton about me."

"I like to have people in my debt, *cherie*. It doesn't work in my benefit for your stepfather to know anything."

"And it works out for you if Hampton knows?"

Her shoulders lifted in a delicate shrug. "It earned me his trust. Joshua is a powerful man, and he and Jay claw at each other's throats at every chance. So, yes, him knowing about you put me in place for what *I* wanted."

There was something in her tone that I didn't like.

I stepped back, gaze dropping to my purse—which had fallen from my lap when I'd made the leap of faith from the chair. Dammit. *Amateur move.*

Nat's voice cut through my thoughts: "I wouldn't do anything drastic just yet, *mon amour.* I'm about to offer you the deal of a lifetime, and it'd be a shame if you were to grow too hasty before you could enjoy it."

The deal of a lifetime, huh?

Casting a quick glance over my shoulder, I was once again treated to pure emptiness. The sense of isolation was both a blessing and a curse, and I chose to focus on the blessing part of it all as I asked, "Is this the same deal Hampton planned to offer Asher last night?"

Head cocking to the side, Nat brought her hand up, index finger and thumb millimeters apart. "With a change or two, but yes."

"And if I take on the job, will you continue to keep my secret from Jay?"

The room seem to still, the energy itself grinding to a halt, and then: "*Cherie*, there won't be a secret to keep once you kill him."

7

AVERY

"Why?"

Like a queen, Nat leaned back in her seat. "Don't play the idiot, Laurel. You know exactly why."

Yes, but—

I shook my head, trying to right my thoughts when everything seemed so terribly confusing. "I know why Hampton does, but why would *you* want him dead? Because he, what? Called you by my mother's name and hurt your feelings? That's enough to kill someone?"

Visibly stiffening, Nat kicked up her chin. "Those reasons lay with Hampton, and he was *incredibly* disappointed with Sergeant Asher's decision to walk out last night."

"He shouldn't have kidnapped us."

"He prefers to do things on large scales." Nat sniffed. "He's just that sort of man."

"A limo pickup service would have been better appreciated by all parties. Maybe pass the information along."

Dark eyes narrowed in my direction, and I had the

distinct feeling that my most frequent tarot client was running through all the reasons she'd like to kill me off—in her head.

Out loud, however, she only slipped back into the role she played so well: the owner of Whiskey Bay, elegant and all too proper. "You want Foley dead, *cherie*. Hampton wants him dead. So, dead he shall be."

My mouth gaped. "I'm sorry, but are you hearing yourself right now? *Dead he shall be?* First, who talks like that—you're from Baltimore, Nat, not the Gilded Age. Second, you're expecting *me* to kill him? Me. Kill the mayor of N'Orleans. I didn't spend the last twelve years hiding out just so I could end up in prison and someone's lady friend."

"So, you what? Hid for twelve years to . . . keep hiding?"

Well, no. Obviously not.

It'd always been my aim to kill my stepfather, but the *how's*, the *where's*, and the *when's* had always eluded me. They *still* eluded me.

After all, I wasn't Lincoln Asher—murderer extraordinaire.

I didn't even know how to use a gun, let alone stage an elaborate plot to kill the city's most elite politician.

Opening my mouth to tell Nat that she had the wrong girl, I was soundly cut off.

"I'll set up everything, *cherie*. It's what I'm good at, after all, and I do have a few people who I can ask to help with the logistics."

Throat dry, I croaked, "If you're handling all of the logistics, then why don't you or one of your minions take him out?"

"I was under the impression that you wished to avenge your mother. Here I am offering you everything you've ever wanted and you're balking. Am I to assume that you *want* your stepfather to learn about you?"

"*No*, of course not." Why couldn't I breathe? Why was it suddenly so hard to draw air into my lungs? I fisted my right hand and set it against my heart. Through my black T-shirt, I could feel the heavy thud of my heart against the fleshy outer part of my fist. "I-I want this."

"Then why the fuss?"

Because I was a coward, as Asher had so politely told me, and that was something that needed to stop. Now. "I want to bring justice to my mother," I said, voice shaky. "I can do it."

Nat's answering smile was wide and serene. "You've waited a long time for this."

I had, she was right.

I'd lived in fear and worry, slept on the streets and on the hardest beds the city had to offer in the homeless shelters. I'd been pawed at by greedy, masculine hands and had been told countless times over that all my troubles would disappear if I just opened my legs and gave up my self-worth for a quick buck.

"Is this like a calendar-coordinating thing?" I asked. "Planned far in advance with maps and backup plans so I don't end up incarcerated after?"

Tipping her head back, Nat released a healthy laugh. "All of the above."

Maybe it wasn't so difficult to be Lincoln Asher, after all. Maybe he looked at each kill with a series of pros or cons. The way *I* looked at it, the pros far outweighed the cons in my book for murdering my stepfather.

Hell, the only con, really—besides the possibility of getting caught—was the matter of my own moral conscience.

I wanted to save the world. I wanted to save every stray animal. I wanted everyone to feel safe and loved and happy.

At the end of the day, however, I could handle my guilt over ending a life.

I had to do it for Momma.

I had to do it for myself.

If I wanted to make myself feel even more justified, then I was also doing it for Nat, who'd been forced to screw Jay Foley while he called her by another woman's name. *My mother's name.*

"Great," I said with a short nod. "I'm glad we got all this settled and squared away. I'm just going to grab my purse"—I crouched low and snapped it off the floor—"and be on my way. I'll wait for your call or something. Give you some time to figure it out. It's all been a great talk."

My feet beat it to the stairwell, and I had *almost* managed to get the hell out of dodge before her voice stopped me in my tracks:

"*Mon amour*, a deal is two-sided."

"Yes . . ." I glanced over at her, where she'd yet to move. "I want the same thing Hampton does. What you would have offered Asher last night."

"But it isn't what *I* want, and as I'm the one who could personally ruin you, it seems imperative that I get what I want, as well. Perhaps even more so . . . unless you don't mind having your *heartbreaking* tale told to everyone tomorrow."

She rose, crossing the space between us, until she was less than two feet away.

That spidey sense was back. Her tone had turned sly, which matched the devilry that I saw in her dark eyes.

I clutched the stairwell railing. "And what is it that you want?"

She leaned forward, eyes glittering.

"I want Lincoln Asher dead, *cherie*, and you will be the one who kills him."

8

LINCOLN

It was probably an omen that no one stopped me as I busted in Ambideaux's front door to his fancy St. Charles Avenue townhouse. Not a single house alarm went off as I stormed through the powder-blue parlor or the blood-red dining room.

In a different life, this townhouse had been the hub of all activity.

Politicians smoking cigars with the city's richest real estate mogul.

Elegant women reclining on the settees in the parlor.

New Orleans was a city that clung to its traditions—and no matter how many years passed, its snobbery remained intact without a single crack.

Money and pedigree guaranteed entry to the upper class. Without it, you'd be lucky if your ass was even allowed to stand on the front step.

I should know.

In Ambideaux's eyes, I'd always been the perfect fit when it came down to his Basin runs. Entering his house, on the other hand, had always been off-limits. Like the dogs, I'd been kept outside to watch the perimeter of the property.

Always on the outside looking in.

Always experiencing life through the windows I'd crack open just to catch the scent of a cigar or hear the titillating sound of feminine laughter.

Don't go down that road, man.

Molars grinding, I checked back my impulse. Snapped my hand back to my side from where it'd been flirting with a priceless antique vase Ambideaux had once sent me to "collect" from a man named James Mayer.

The vase sat on the gold-leaf table at the base of the circular stairwell.

James Mayer sat at the bottom of the Atchafalaya—or he had when I'd dropped his body in when I'd been nineteen.

My lips twisted in a sneer, which I caught in the table top's reflective mirror. Swollen eye from last night's activities out in the swamp. Cut lip. To say nothing of the right half of my face, where the flesh remained raised and red.

I was tired, *so* tired of dealing with all the bullshit.

And you're in a shit mood because of Avery . . .

Fingers twitching, I stared down at my reflection. Reached out to wrap my hand around the base of the vase. It wasn't massive, and my thumb and middle finger easily touched as I took its weight in my hand.

One million dollars sat on my palm.

In the next breath, one million dollars had been hurled at the wall.

It shattered upon impact, bursting apart like fireworks composed of centuries-old Chinese porcelain. Fell to the marble flooring like shards of ice.

A single piece skipped along the flooring, aiming

straight for me—I crushed it with my right boot, finding a sick sense of satisfaction when I felt the delicate pottery crumble beneath my weight.

"That was from the Yuan Dynasty. Almost a thousand years old."

Following the direction of the familiar voice, I looked up to see Ambideaux meandering down the stairwell.

I flicked my gaze down to the mess I'd created. "It had a good run."

My former boss stopped at the base of the stairwell, one hand on the balustrade. "You never understood the significance of antiquities."

No, I didn't.

Antiques were for people who could appreciate them—those who had the luxury of raking in millions of dollars each year, or more, and who never had to wonder when they'd eat next.

Antiquities were for men like Jason Ambideaux, who practically shit wads of cash on command.

They weren't for me.

"I didn't come here to talk about your vase."

"My *broken* vase."

Ignoring him, I pulled out the notebook full of names he'd thrown at my feet a week ago. Then waited until he'd locked eyes on it before continuing, "Why do you want them dead? Josef, Zak, these are people you know . . ." I dropped the notebook on the table, and its coiled-spirals pinged as it landed on the mirrored top. "You've always been a cold-hearted bastard, but why them? And don't bullshit me on this."

Growing up, I'd never trusted Ambideaux to give me the full truth. When I'd been real young, he'd kept some things secret to "watch out for me," he'd always said. By the time

I'd hit my teens, I'd learned that he liked to manipulate the truth, stretching it and forming it until *his* version of reality was so skewed from real life that I was convinced he believed every lie he told.

Probably explained the state of his marriage—which was to say, his *non*-existent marriage.

Not even Nat, the Queen of Bitches, could handle his shit.

I flipped open the notebook, flipping through the lined pages, and then stopped when I reached the handwriting that looked exactly like mine. "You played me pretty good, Jason," I said, referring to our little *meeting* in my kitchen from the week before. "You always have. It's what happens when you grow up with no family but one asshole prick—you latch on. Grow soft. Hope, maybe, that they won't stab you in the back when you look in the other direction."

Without giving him the opportunity to speak, I went on in a low voice. "You've stabbed me a whole hell of a lot, some instances worse than others." His gaze lifted to my scars, and I didn't look away. *Refused* to look away. "So, we can do this one of two ways. You can either give me a good enough reason to go after Zak Benson and Tabitha Thibadeaux *or* I can solve a lifelong problem I've had and permanently shut you up."

Ambideaux's blue eyes opened wide. "You wouldn't."

"You don't know that." Pushing away from the table, I strolled near him, hands loose at my sides, until only a foot separated us. He was decently sized, but I was bigger—taller, stronger, broader. "Fact is, Jason, you don't know *me* any longer. So, let's operate on the assumption that I wouldn't give a damn if you stopped breathing." I paused, cranked my grimace into something resembling a smile. "Now why do you want them dead? What the hell made you so desperate that you went so far as to blackmail me out of my job and go out of your way to hit Big Hampton where it hurts?"

Silence reigned, stretching and growing, until finally he bent at the knees to survey the broken porcelain. "He's leaving Pershing to run for mayor when Foley's term is up."

Every response that had been ready to leap from my tongue died in an instant.

And then I tipped back my head and laughed. Hard.

So hard that Ambideaux grumbled something beneath his breath and snapped, "Why the fuck are you laughing? I've been in the political world for years now. The people want—"

"The people don't know what they want." When he reached for a shard of pottery, I kicked it out of his way. He was a sneaky asshole, and I wouldn't put it past him to plan out an entire plot to kill me off with nothing but some Yuan Dynasty cast-off. "You think they want another eight years of dealing with bullshit politicians who have a tendency to run their opponents—*any* opponent—into the ground?"

With narrowed eyes, Ambideaux straightened to his full height. "That's politics for you, son. Everyone is determined to win."

"Sure they are, but I can guarantee that the public isn't expecting death as a result." Fingering the coiled notebook, I tacked on, "And we all know that death is something you dole out exceptionally well. I'm guessing that Josef and Micah were your handiwork—too lazy to make the drive all the way out to the Basin?"

His mouth flat-lined, and I had my answer.

Got you.

"Did your recruits bail?" I asked, resting my ass on the table. It was sturdy enough that I gave it my full weight, folding my hands over the edge as I studied him. "Let me guess. You went over to Central City . . . Galvez and Fourth —nah, Galvez and Third would be more your speed." I drummed my fingers on the underside of the table, straining my ears to listen for approaching footsteps. I'd be dead before being caught off guard again. "What'd you offer them? Crack?"

Face flushing, Ambideaux's jaw clenched. "I offered them enough that they took it."

"They played you, Jason." I grinned, slowly, methodically. "You want to run this city and you can't even figure out the difference between a group of junkies and their dealers. Let me clue you in on how that works: dealers don't work for *you* but I'm sure they appreciated the free cocaine."

"They're idiots if they think they can get away with—"

"They already did, and that's why you got desperate and ditched Josef and Micah in the river yourself." Pushing away from the table, I ambled toward him. "You've lasted this long without getting caught because you're smart. Dumping bodies in the Mississippi? That's sloppy work." The shattered porcelain cracked under my boots when I stopped, a foot separating us. "What made you fuck up after all this time? We both know there's a reason—and don't give me a bullshit excuse about you and Big Hampton competing for office."

Ambideaux's blue eyes shot to the side, avoiding staring at me straight-on.

I waited, already knowing the answer that he'd give.

And because I was a ruthless bastard, I twisted the knife a little deeper, backing him into a proverbial corner that he couldn't escape. "You blackmailed me into taking out people who worked for *you*. I remember Josef and Micah from back in the day, and if there's an idiot here it's not me. Every single one of them has your damn tattoo branded on their skin. You marked them. Promised them protection. Now you're taking them out one by one. *Why?*"

He cracked.

Shoulders hunching, eyes hard, Adam's apple dancing down the column of his throat as he swallowed. "Because they chose *her*. All of them."

Bitter laughter nearly suffocated me. "You're too old for that shit, man."

"Nat is—"

"A crazy bitch who won't stop until you're dead and she's watching you bleed out."

Ambideaux shot a hand out at me, clearly aiming for my throat. Speed and age were on my side, though, and it took me only a half-second to register his intent and reciprocate. Weaving to the left, I caught his elbow in my fist and spun him around like a middle-aged ballerina. His back slammed up against my chest and I locked his wrists at the base of his spine, my hands holding him in place.

He'd taught me the move when I'd been ten and desperate for some sort of guidance.

Now, his dyed dark hair was all I saw, and his heavy breathing was all I heard.

"Sloppy," I muttered, shaking my head. "Without Godzilla here to protect you, you're fucked." Squeezing his wrists in warning, I let him go—but not without a move of my knees at the back of his legs that had him toppling over.

He crash-landed with a *thud*, the broken pottery going every which way as his arms flailed to catch his weight.

Before he'd fed me to the gators, I probably would have felt a measure of guilt in seeing the only man who'd ever been like a father figure to me splayed on the ground.

But it wasn't guilt I felt now—more like regret that I'd lived.

That I was stuck in a damn cycle that I couldn't break free of, no matter how desperately I wanted to. I was chained to this city, both emotionally and physically, and I was beyond ready for the shackles to shatter just like the Yuan Dynasty vase I'd broken.

"You killed her brother," I said, voice low, my temper tightly leashed, "because he counted cards at a friendly game of poker with his *brother*-in-law."

Ambideaux hoisted himself up on his hands and knees, and I watched as his palm sank into a splinter from the vase. He reeled back with a curse, lifting his palm to examine the wound. With it cradled to his chest, he glared at me. "*You're* the one who did him off."

It would be so easy to angle my boot and push him back to the ground, to let off the steam boiling from the last twenty-four hours.

The goddamn "abduction."

Learning that Avery's mother had married my father.

Watching Avery as she stormed out of my SUV this morning and slammed the front door behind her as she disappeared into her building.

My foot shifted back, and I set my weight on the sole. Repeated the action again and again until there was a safe enough distance separating me from the city's richest bastard. I needed some patience—at the very least, I needed to not act when provoked.

"I'm not gonna take responsibility for your divorce. Like any good soldier, I did what I was told. You ordered. I made it happen."

Blue eyes hardened in my direction. "You're not making it happen right now."

"You don't own me anymore."

"You still marked?"

At the invasive question, my hand shifted to the base of my skull. Egotistical prick that Ambideaux was, he enjoyed knowing those who worked for him were always aware of who held the upper hand. The placement of the quarter-sized tattoo always changed—mine had required me to shave my head so that the tattoo artist could ink the back of my head. Women, generally, were marked in more prominent areas—their collarbones, their arms or their faces, like Tabitha Thibadeaux.

The men worked under Ambideaux's employment.

The women for Nat at the Basement—either as dancers in Whiskey Bay or on the stages or rooms upstairs.

Sexist. Masochist.

Jason Ambideaux reigned as king of it all, threatening to tear down any pawn that didn't fall into line.

And he thought he'd be a successful mayor? I'd rather have my asshole father for another eight years.

"Don't want to answer that?" Ambideaux taunted. "You're marked, Lincoln. You took a vow. You—"

"Yeah, well, you took a vow that you'd let my mother out of her goddamn cell."

His nostrils flared. "It's not a cell—"

"She hates it," I growled, hands curling into fists at my sides before I did something ridiculous—like strangle the man before me. "You don't get to choose what's best for her just because the two of you were childhood friends. She's suffered."

Jaw working, Ambideaux got up close in my face. "If there *is* anyone who knows what she went through, it's *me*." His knuckles connected with my chest—but even with the weight behind his shove, I didn't budge. Not even an inch.

It was like the last twenty years hadn't even passed. I was the troublemaker kid pushing all the right buttons, knowing what to do and what to say to send the people around me into a downward spiral.

And maybe he was right about my mom.

Hell, it wasn't like she'd wanted me. When I was two, she'd given me to the Ursuline nuns. I had no memories of her from that age, no splices of a vision of her cradling me against her chest. Nothing. It hadn't been until Ambideaux entered my life when I'd been seven that I was even made aware that my mom was still alive.

Ambideaux had fashioned himself as my mom's best friend. A neighbor from when they'd been kids. Promised me that if I did everything he said—if I behaved—he'd take me to her.

So I'd behaved.

Everything he'd wanted of me, I did without question.

I was desperate, and it didn't occur to me until years later that in those intermittent five years between when I'd met Jason Ambideaux and when I'd first seen my mother, he'd stripped every bit of my conscience.

I stole. I cheated. I threw my entire body, soul, and mind into being good enough to run with the older guys who worked for Ambideaux. At eighteen, the tattoo on the back of my head had felt like a rite of passage.

A reason to live. A reason to fight.

Particularly when only Ambideaux had ever cared if I lived or died.

Nat hadn't cared.

Neither had my mother.

And yet I still gave a fuck, even when she didn't give a damn about me.

When I opened my mouth, my voice emerged like I'd

smoked a pack of cigarettes all in one go. "I'm taking myself out of this equation. You pissed that your crew ditched you in favor of Nat? Find someone else to do your dirty work. And when it comes to Big Hampton, maybe try doing shit legally for once. You never know—you might find that it's not so repulsive."

I turned to leave.

Had made it two steps when Ambideaux's hand at my elbow pulled me to a stop.

"What about your mother?" His voice echoed in the room, hammering on my dead heart as I stared at the broken shards of priceless pottery on the floor.

The doctors had always said that a concussion like the kind my mom had experienced after her car accident could change a person. I wasn't a doctor, had never studied medicine, and had technically only "met" my mother, Victoria, after she'd survived the traumatic four-car pileup on the Greater New Orleans Bridge. She'd lost the use of her legs, the metals of the car twisting and turning and crushing the lower half of her body. I'd only been allowed to see her at the age of twelve; I'd never known her any other way.

When I'd first met her, she'd been hooked to a ventilator and had spent her days binging on *Jerry Springer* and every court show TV had to offer. Although the ventilator was long gone now, her bills continued to be expensive—more so than I could ever afford to pay—and Ambideaux used my limited funds to his own benefit. He ensured my mother's welfare, kept her healthy, and I paid the price for loving a woman who'd never love me back.

I'd heard her laugh, once.

When I'd been down the hall, a bouquet of flowers clutched in my seventeen-year-old fists, ready to surprise her for her birthday.

Her laughter had died the moment I rapped on the hospital room door and entered the space. Disgust had lined her features, and the hatred that narrowed her eyes was one I'd always been familiar with.

As were the words she greeted me with: *I don't want you here. You aren't my son.*

"The concussion," everyone always assured me. "She doesn't realize what she's talking about."

I wasn't stupid.

I'd been two when the car accident stole the use of her legs, and it seemed unlikely to me that fifteen years could pass with the same old excuse of her concussion working like a charm. No, for a reason I'd never understood, Victoria Meriden hated me. Despised me.

I wasn't her son just as I wasn't Jay Foley's son.

By blood, maybe, but nothing more.

I shook off Ambideaux's hand like he was nothing but an obnoxious fly, then sent a quick glance up, my gaze following the curve of the oak stairwell. Somewhere in this townhouse, my mother was set up in her room like the princess she never was, which had to be an improvement for her from her routine hospital visits.

"Lincoln," Ambideaux demanded with an unwavering stare, "I warned you what happens if you screw off on this. I want Benson and Tabby taken care of. If you don't, your mother will regret it. *You'll* regret it."

I met his gaze unflinchingly. "She's not mine to regret. She never was."

The only thing I heard on my way out was the pottery cracking one last time under my weight, and then the non-existent sound of Jason Ambideaux's plans withering like wood set ablaze.

The smile that slipped onto my face as I stepped back

into the world was perhaps the first genuine one I'd ever experienced in thirty-four years.

And while I wasn't free from the bullshit of New Orleans politics, I would be. Soon.

I refused to have it any other way.

9

AVERY

I was experiencing déjà vu.

Me at my table in Jackson Square, shuffling my Thoth deck mindlessly as I waited for someone to look my way and ask to have their cards read.

Him storming toward me, emerging from the shadowy Pirate's Alley alongside St. Louis Cathedral.

Except this time, I knew the taste of his lips and the hard brush of his athletic body alongside mine. I knew what it felt like to be wrapped up in his embrace as he thrust into me, the pressure so acute with each shift of his hips, the pleasure in his blue eyes only that much more erotic when he groaned my name.

And I knew now, though I wish I didn't, what it meant to look a man in the eye and realize that it came down to him or me.

I hadn't agreed to Nat's proposal, but I hadn't turned her down either.

The guilt was eating me alive.

Guilt which only surged forth like a thunderous wave as Lincoln Asher took the seat opposite mine. Forty-eight hours since I'd seen him last, and I soaked up his presence like I'd been starved of sustenance.

You can't. Don't even go down that road.

I couldn't stop.

My shuffling slowed, the backs of my hands resting in my lap, each half of the deck clasped in my palms. He said nothing, and I didn't either. We'd parted ways in anger, our words dripping like poison in that motel room, and the awkwardness of this moment stole my words and kept my mouth sewn shut.

Should I apologize for speaking my mind? For trying to push him away and avoid the future hurt?

Or maybe you should whip out the I'm sorry's for sort-of agreeing to kill him?

Fingers tightening around the deck, I dropped my gaze to his plain clothes. Dark jeans paired with a plain black T-shirt. Unwanted approval hummed in my veins because there was no denying that he looked good tonight. "You're not wearing your uniform."

For a conversation starter, it could have been better. I'd maybe rate it a C-minus on the scale of A-F—nothing higher because, really, *that* was the first thing to come out of my mouth considering everything that had gone down between us? Utterly pathetic.

But it seemed to break the slab of ice, even just a little, because Asher let out a low chuckle that sent shivers of awareness twirling down my spine. I sat up a little straighter when he said, "Guess I never broke the news to you. I've been suspended."

"*Suspended?*"

The bottom of his chair scraped against the concrete as he positioned it directly before mine, the toes of our shoes touching when he sat down. "Suspended," he confirmed with a small dip of his chin, his right forearm landing on the table. "Want to take a guess as to why?"

Knowing him, it could have been a number of things.

He was stone and fire, all at once. Unreadable and yet in possession of a temper that ran on a short leash—if there was a leash at all.

"Did you talk smack?" I asked, all too aware of our shoes getting closely acquainted with one another's.

His mouth hitched, the side with his scars, and as I watched them crinkle and stretch, I felt a wave of protectiveness sweep over me. Could I do it? Could I be the one to take away the vitality in his Haint-blue eyes?

Lincoln Asher wasn't a good man, and I wasn't entirely sure he was even likable when he went on one of his ridiculous alpha bents, but that didn't mean I had the right to take his life.

Now you're just being a hypocrite—do you have the right to take Jay Foley's either with that logic?

No, I didn't.

And yet I'd thought of nothing else since leaving Whiskey Bay yesterday.

What would it be like to walk free in this city without watching my back? Would each breath I brought into my lungs taste a little sweeter?

My cards slipped from my grasp, and it took my brain a moment to register the fact that Asher had stripped them away from me and was setting them out on the velvet-lined table.

"You're not doing it right," I muttered, reaching forward to take them back.

His shoe eased against mine, a silent warning for me to give him space. He followed it up with a husky, "Let me try."

After our argument—after being called a coward,

however right he was about that—I should have raised my foot and plowed it straight into the apex of his thighs. He was a cocky bastard, and there was not a single reason why I had to put up with his bullshit. Not. A. One.

But I was a junkie and Lincoln Asher was my chosen vice, and so I caved without verbal admission, falling back into my seat and folding my arms over my chest as I watched him sort the cards with his brows furrowed and his teeth sinking into his lower lip.

He would never be sexy, not in the classic, model sort of way. He was altogether too rough for that, too rugged and way too dominant. And yet as the sun set behind St. Louis Cathedral, its cream-plastered walls turning red and pink and yellow from the dipping sun, I couldn't look away from this man who I so wanted to hate.

"Turns out some of my rank didn't enjoy me coming to your rescue three weeks ago," he said, gently flipping over the tarot cards as his gaze tracked every minute detail of their illustrations.

My mouth dropped open. "They suspended you for *that?* You were helping me! And Casey, too."

Giving a curt nod, he turned over one last card, so that three were spread out before him. The rest he bundled up and slipped back into their velvet pouch, which had been resting next to the lit candle. "It was a use-of-force. I got a nice slap on the hand. They didn't want to piss off the kid's father, and I get it. Although I think it's safe to say that after recent events, me and Joshua Hampton won't be attending any crawfish boils together or anything like that."

Joshua Hampton? The kid who'd attacked us was Hampton's son?

I felt like a fish, my mouth snapping open and shut—or at least like a snapping turtle—but it was hard to digest all that information. If it had been Big Hampton's kid that night . . . "Was it staged?" I asked, already dreading the answer.

Blue eyes lifted to meet mine. "It wasn't staged by Hampton, if that's what you're wondering. Little Hampton showing up at the right time and the right place was just icing on the cake."

"Then by *who*?"

"That's who I came to talk to you about." Lips curling in a small grin, he gave a soft laugh that was so at odds with the harshness of his features. It lit me up like a match and kindling. "But, first, I'm gonna read your cards. Put you in the hot seat. What do you think about that?"

"I think the fist you took to the head the other day may have popped a screw loose." It wasn't at all what I wanted to say, but it sounded a lot more confident than the thoughts running on repeat in my head: *what are you doing here? Why are you being so* nice?

"You can learn anything off YouTube." Tapping the center of the first card with the tip of his finger, he dragged it close, shifting his big body so that he could get a good look at the illustration. "I spent a few hours today studying."

My mouth betrayed me by quirking up at the boyish way he confessed it all. "So, a few hours of YouTube later and you feel comfortable enough to read tarot?"

"Nah," he said with a shake of his head, "but I feel comfortable enough to read *yours*."

Something about that struck a chord, and I sucked in a sharp breath. If I let myself get lost in the tailspin of wondering *why* he was here reading my spread, I'd never venture up for air again.

Mentally, I shoved the *why*'s aside, sending them fluttering into the evening air.

"You're already off to a rough start." Wrapping a hand

around my mug of hot chocolate, I lifted it from the table to my lips, blowing away the steam. Asher's blue eyes tracked it all, but whatever emotions he felt weren't out for open season. He watched me steadily, carefully, but the heat I'd come to recognize from him was nowhere to be found.

Obviously, you idiot. Y'all aren't just strangers anymore.

The hot chocolate burned on the way down, its temperature a few degrees too hot. Coughing and swallowing happened all at once, and I cranked forward, hand to my throat, as I tried to catch my breath.

Asher's fingers went to my chin. "Look up. It'll help."

In between gusts of coughing, I croaked, "I thought that was just an old wives' tale."

His fingers didn't move away. Instead, he gently angled my chin so that my face tipped up, my gaze latching onto the darkening sky. Beyond the spire of the cathedral was a full moon in all of its glory.

My hand hooked onto his wrist, just as his deep voice rumbled, "Not sure about the old wives' tale, but it's what the nuns always told me."

The . . . *nuns*?

Tearing my gaze from the beauty above us, I fixed my attention on his face. "The nuns? Did you go to Catholic school?"

He pulled back, his touch leaving my skin bereft of his warmth, and he returned to the cards. "Nah, public," he finally answered. "But, before that, I was with the Ursulines for a time. I don't remember much."

Had Jay truly cast him aside at birth, just like that? It was beyond extreme, and until the day he'd ordered Momma's death, he'd never veered to the extremes. Even-keeled might as well have been his middle name.

Although it wouldn't be shocking to learn that all of that was just another lie.

"Did Jay . . ." How to even put this into a question that wasn't fully offensive? Swallowing, I tried again. "Were you ever close with him, at some point? I mean, with you growing up here in N'Orleans, you had to have seen him at some point, right?"

The following second felt as though it lasted months, and then Asher was sighing, dropping his elbows to his knees, lacing his fingers as he stared at our feet. "We're going to have this conversation right now, aren't we."

It wasn't a question.

Or, if it was, it'd totally been rhetorical.

"We don't have to," I murmured, and then risked another sip of my hot chocolate. *Mmm, much better*. "I mean, if you'd rather we discuss our meltdown from Thursday night, we can do that too."

His façade cracked, a grimace peeking through. "We both said some shit we didn't mean."

That wasn't true. "I meant every word I said."

Letting out a dry laugh, Asher lifted his head to meet my gaze. "I did, too. Should I be worried that you're gonna take that candle and shove it down my pants in retribution?"

"I'm not crass, Asher."

His arched brow was the only response he gave me.

Rolling my eyes, I crossed my right leg over the left. "All right, so I can be crass. Sometimes. Rarely." Uncomfortable under his astute gaze, I squirmed in my chair. Then reprimanded myself for acting like an immature brat who couldn't get comfortable. *Time to get this conversation back on track*. Hopefully.

"Go back to Jay." I tapped his shoe with mine. "What was he like?"

His big hands shifted over the cards once more, the pads of his fingers lazily tracing the illustrations while his gaze remained locked on my face. "We're going to do this the unconventional way," he said. "You good with that?"

"I don't even know what you're talking about."

Alongside my foot, his jumped into a small rhythm—like he couldn't keep his emotions in check. Or, maybe, it was actually his nerves.

"The unconventional thing is that I'm going to sit here and read you your cards. That work for you?"

I stared at him, refusing to show any hint of trepidation. He clearly had a plan with this tonight, and who was I to tell him to screw off without even allowing him the chance to give it a go? Maybe it'd be revelatory.

Or maybe he should learn that you aren't supposed to sift through the cards and pick the ones you want before a reading.

Maybe that was the case, but curiosity trumped every other emotion for me.

"Avery?"

A small nod tilted my head down. "Yeah, all right. It works for me."

A brief, grateful smile ghosted across his lips before he plucked the cards right off the table and clutched them in his big hands. Turning to me completely, his feet sandwiching mine and the table to his right, he flipped his pickings around, with only the first one showing.

The Three of Swords—Sorrow.

My nails dug into my palms as I noted the familiar card with its black and purple coloring, and a sword puncturing a rose. It wasn't a card I pulled often for myself, but it was nevertheless one that always made me feel a measure of sadness seep into my bones.

I pushed the question out: "What's that represent?"

Asher's lips parted on a short exhale. "This is your past."

The laugh that broke free from my chest was more air than joy. "Pretty accurate, I guess."

I don't know what I expected from this so-called reading. Perhaps for him to simply call the card out and move onto the next. Maybe for him to create a fanciful tale that was nothing more than unicorn bullshit, all gussied up with glitter and rainbows but containing little substance.

I'd expected those things, going so far as to gear myself up for them, but I couldn't have expected *this*.

"I never knew about you, you know." He set Sorrow to balance on my knee, forcing me to touch the card or see it teeter off and fall to the ground. "Until I was around twenty-five, I had no idea who my biological father was. I was given to the Ursulines at two. Dropped in foster care at three and stayed that way until I was a legal adult. Jay Foley never came around. Never showed his face." Blue eyes flicked up in my direction. "And when I finally met my mother, she never mentioned his name either."

Awkwardly, I shifted in my chair. "I . . . I don't know where you're going with this."

Clearly uncomfortable with the turn of the conversation, Asher raked his fingers through his messy hair. His hand hesitated at the back of his skull, forearm flexing as he studied me. Then, he spoke, that familiar husky timbre of his making me shift for an entirely different reason. "I was twenty-two when I heard about your suicide in the news."

In my head, I jumped up from my chair and stormed away, hands over my ears to stamp out the sounds of the words I didn't want to hear.

In reality, I didn't move a muscle.

"Foley was on the City Council at the time," Asher went on, hands linking together as his elbows went down on his knees. "And all I remember thinking as they showed your picture on the news was that you must have known so much love from your mom that it was impossible to live without her." A ragged laugh came from his mouth, and, as though embarrassed by the sound, he scrubbed a palm over his lips. "In that moment, I was jealous of your sorrow. Jealous that you'd loved and been loved, and all I knew was pain and disappointment."

Why was he telling me this?

The fact that he could sit down and tell me something like that was just—

"When Big Hampton dropped that little bomb," Asher said, cutting into my thoughts, "I realized you'd known a sorrow of a different kind." He nodded his chin in the direction of the card, which was still balanced on my knee. "You've been alone, isolated, and yet you still survived."

I had no other choice.

It was either survive or give up, and Momma had never raised me to roll over and take it. *Be brave*, she used to tell me, *and always be bold*. For years I'd repeated the words in my head, over and over again until it was either believe in what my Momma had preached or just accept that I'd been spoon-fed yet another lie.

Asher's foot nudged mine. "It wasn't true, what I said about you being a coward. I've known my handful of people who've pissed off Foley and they couldn't manage to do what you did. What you're continuing to do right now—live."

Every word that fell from his mouth pushed the blade of guilt yet another inch into my sternum. I wanted the anger from him. I wanted to feel that familiar fury swirling in my gut. I wanted, above all else, not to think of Lincoln Asher as anyone but a calculated killer who could snap my neck in two without remorse.

The words he spoke now didn't belong to a man who took lives apathetically.

And that . . . that only made me want to look closer and peer into his soul. Discover anything and everything I could learn about him.

Fingers pinching Sorrow, I positioned it on my thigh so it wouldn't fall off. "What did you pick for my present?"

With a quick glance in my direction, he revealed the next card that he held in his grasp.

Seven of Disks.

"Failure," I muttered, staring at the dark illustration with its Roman symbols embedded in what looked like a myriad of black feathers, but which were meant to represent dead vegetation. Forcing a smile, my teeth ground together. "How ironic."

Asher set Failure atop Sorrow on my leg, his fingers momentarily brushing the fabric of my black skirt. He sat back, arms on the flimsy armrests of his lawn chair. "You wanted to hide, Avery. You wanted to run from your past, and I brought you right back into it. That failure is mine."

But it wasn't, not really.

No matter the fact that Nat claimed to know him, she had followed *me* for years. I'd been in this mess for the long haul, no matter the fact that I hadn't even realized it all along. And it didn't help that he'd settled the card on my thigh with it reversed—in Thoth, Seven of Disks came with a darkness that always held light at the end of the tunnel. But if the card was drawn backward, and set down that way, that light was eclipsed. Negligent. The struggle never-ending.

I was so tired of fighting.

I set both Sorrow and Failure on the table, face down.

"Here's the third card I pulled," Asher murmured,

yanking me from my reverie. "Dominion. I'm no card reader, Avery, and that's something we both know. YouTube can't make you a pro, and I pulled cards that I thought resonated, but this . . ." He wiggled it back and forth in his hand. "This is gonna happen."

Plucking the card from his grasp, I stuck it back on the velvet-lined table, my palm echoing with a *thud* against the rickety frame. I should leave well enough alone. Accept that maybe he was trying to make amends after being an arrogant prick who thought he could say and do whatever he wanted.

But I couldn't leave well enough alone.

"What game are you playing at, Lincoln?"

His blue eyes never wavered from my face. "No games."

"I don't believe you."

"And why is that?" he asked, voice low. Behind him, the St. Louis Cathedral bells chimed the new hour, but he didn't so much as glance back. No, *I* was the center of his attention, and even though he sat in his chair and I sat in mine, I nevertheless felt crowded by his presence.

"Can we not—"

"We have to." His hands caught my wrists in a move so quick I barely had time to register it. And then he was tugging me forward until my hands were gripping his knees to stabilize my weight, and my butt was hovering inches off the fabric of my seat. "You don't know this world, this city, sweetheart, not the way you think you do." Thumbs caressing the delicate bones of my inner wrists, he met my gaze. "It was my failure that landed you in this mess, and I'll be damned if I let you get burned because of me."

"I can handle myself." Right? I'd done so, well enough this far, at any rate, and if push came to shove, I could carry on for another twelve years—if I wanted to. If Nat didn't flip the script on me and send her wolves sniffing at my ankles. If my stepfather didn't think back to our almost-meeting at the police station and wonder, *was that her*?

So many *if*s, but they were all I had.

The man holding my wrists was the biggest *if* of them all.

His lids fell shut, and I took the moment of solitude to study his features up close in a way that I hadn't had the chance to before, when we were too busy having sex in the dark. A thin, white scar marked his tan skin just above his left eyebrow. Dark stubble lined the lower half of his face, longer than it'd been when I'd first met him, but not yet a full beard. His scars—

I hated the way I ached for his pain. I wanted to keep my walls in check and my empathy at the bare minimum. I wanted, so very badly, to blame his dangerous life on the choices he'd made and the decisions that he'd set forth out of his own volition, and not as a consequence of anyone else's influence.

It was easier than facing and accepting the truth, and the truth was that I so desperately wanted to understand the inner workings of his mind. He'd saved me, at the Basement, when he could have so easily thrown me to the wolves. Even when it'd come to uncuffing us in that shack in the middle of nowhere, he'd demanded that I go first.

He wasn't a good man.

But he had a conscience, I had to believe that.

Once again it seemed like we were tethered together by a string because as I pulled from his grasp and laid one hand over the raised flesh of his scars, his lips parted to murmur, "Ask me what happened to my face."

10

LINCOLN

If Avery truly thought she could take on the likes of Foley, Ambideaux, and Big Hampton, then she'd be dead before she even had the chance to draw a breath to scream.

It was the reason I'd sought her out tonight.

The reason I was willing to share the one moment of my life that I'd vowed to carry to the grave, forever unspoken.

It's not the only reason.

No, I was a selfish bastard to my core. I craved her, even though I'd been a complete asshole when we'd last seen each other. I craved her, even though logic said she should be the last woman I should ever desire.

I didn't give a fuck about any of that.

There was something to be said about making amends —I could do that now, even though the ones of my past weren't so easy, or possible, to erase.

I opened my mouth, heard the words as they left—"Ask me about my face"—and then felt softness land on my cheek. My scarred cheek.

My heart lurched, the damn thing flopping around in

my chest like a beached fish desperate for water, for safety, for the familiarity of its everyday reality. Just like that, her gentle touch yanked me from my numb existence, like the flick of a switch, and emotion ricocheted through me.

We'd fucked, me and Avery.

But when was the last time anyone had ever touched me willingly outside of getting naked? When was the last time anyone had ever sought to soothe me or care enough to even try?

Never.

Not in any of the homes I'd lived in growing up.

Not Jason, and sure as hell not Nat.

Not my mother, who couldn't even bring herself to look at me.

If the Ursulines ever had, I'd been too young to carry the memories along with me into adulthood.

And, Christ, but the reality of my life hit me like a sledgehammer, pummeling my chest, forcing out a breath that echoed in my ears like a foghorn.

Words. I needed to speak, to say something so Avery didn't think I'd gone mute, but I found myself incapable of doing anything but soaking up the feeling of her hand against the ugliest part of me. I was ruined, as she'd told me when we'd first met, and she touched me now anyway.

Like I was someone worth her time and energy.

Like I wasn't a monster clothed in human skin.

"Lincoln."

Fuck, she could have lit a fire and told me to run through it, and I would have stripped naked to go the extra mile and then stood in the middle of the flames. Welcomed the heat. Welcomed the pain. If only I could pretend, if only for a second, that I was a man worth loving.

I blinked my eyes open.

She blinked down at me. "Where did you go?" she whispered, and I didn't even have to ask what she meant.

My throat constricted with a swallow. "To a place I generally like to pretend doesn't exist." In other words, my heart. My soul. Two things I'd thought were dormant until I'd found her in Jackson Square, exactly where we sat now. I reached up, hand circling her wrist, and startled even myself by settling her palm even more flatly against my cheek.

I waited for the disgust to twist her features, but it never did.

Instead, her hazel eyes went to our hands against my face and didn't flit away. "Tell me what happened."

Starting from the beginning wasn't an option, so I settled with the truths that could be told without landing her in even more hot water. "I worked for Nat's husband growing up. Jason Ambideaux."

Her features scrunched. "Like an intern sort of work?"

I wished. Maybe life would have played out differently if I was only one of the kids he hired from the local high schools to plan his social events and schedule his Facebook posts and coordinate his meetings in a fancy little calendar that cost more than my prized Glock 19. "No, not like an intern."

At the risk of seeing that disgust appear, I added, "I ran drugs for him, Ave. Murdered people."

Her nails scraped against my cheek, a gut reaction from her, I knew.

I plowed on—there was no other way.

"I told you that I don't know how many people I've killed, but that's not true. I know every person—their birthdate, their parents, their kids, if they had any." My chest would remain forever marked by their losses. A tattoo for every kill. Pain for pain, as the Romans would have once put it. My chest was covered, as were my upper arms. I was a walking tombstone, and I'd have it no other way. It was regret and shame that I carried on my shoulders alone, though, and it was the single reason I rarely removed my shirt in front of others.

I didn't want the questions, the curious glances.

They'd never understand, and it wasn't in me to try to explain what they would never, ever, comprehend. The ink was my penance alone.

"Jason had this . . . I hate to call him an enemy because it sounds so damn cheesy."

Avery hooked a foot around her chair and drew it forward, so that it was almost on top of mine, and then lowered herself onto it. She never tried to remove her hand from my face, simply angled her body so she could maintain contact. "He was an enemy," she said evenly, "just call it like it is."

My lungs squeezed with a heavy sigh. "Yeah, they were. They hated each other, for reasons that I still don't know, not then and not now either. Jason had learned something about Foley, though, and he called me in. He had something he wanted me to take care of, and I'd never told him no before. I was always the reliable one."

Her teeth sank into her bottom lip, and I could practically see the wheels spinning in her head. "Do you like . . .?"

Knowing the answer she wanted, I gave her my truth: "I'm good at it, but I've never taken pleasure in seeing someone die." No, I'd been worse. Indifferent. Resigned. Determined to please a man who wasn't my father but was the only person who even came close to filling the role. "Except then he'd told me the mark's identity, and I almost balked."

"Why?"

I met her gaze, and unraveled the words that I'd kept bottled up for so damn long. "The target was a kid," I said, pulling her hand away from my scars. As much as I wanted her touch, I didn't deserve her empathy with this story. I never would. "An innocent kid who'd done nothing but exist, but Jason wanted retaliation for something his so-called enemy had done."

Avery's gasp felt so very loud. *Just keep going. Get to the point of the story*. It was hard, so hard to know that my actions had set so much into motion.

"I agreed—"

Dark brows furrowing, Avery watched me carefully. "You said that you *almost* balked. Please—please tell me you didn't go through with it."

The weight of her quiet disappointment felt like chains circling my neck. I was going to hell, that was for sure. A first-class ticket engraved in gold, just for me.

"I agreed, at first. Ambid—Jason was like a father to me, and I hated the thought of disappointing him. But in the end, I couldn't go through with it. I went to Whiskey Bay, determined to get the fuck out of that life and confront him. He was waiting for me already, knew exactly how I'd failed to follow through."

My mind's eye brought forth a visual of Ambideaux waiting for me at the bottom of the stairs of the Basement, arms crossed over his broad chest. To say that he'd been pissed was an understatement. *Furious,* more like. I'd never seen him in such a rage before, and my gut had told me to whip around and get the hell out of dodge.

I'd stood my ground.

And he'd shot me in return.

My voice emerged like I'd been silent for years instead of seconds. "I told him he was a fucking predatory asshole for bringing a kid into the mess. I wanted out." Forcing the lingering panic away, I tucked my elbows on my knees and let my hands dangle between my legs. *Stay calm, man. Don't lose it.* "I remember turning away, and then feeling hot fire ripping through my right thigh. And, then, a split second later, more flames just above my knee."

Avery's eyes went wide, and her full lips parted like I'd ordered them open on my command. "He *shot* you?"

"Yes."

"What an *asshole,*" she ground out, as though horrified on my behalf. And, hell, but it felt good—even if her sympathy was all wrongly misplaced.

"I woke up in a car, blood all over me. We weren't in N'Orleans, and it was like some twisted sort of fate that I knew exactly where they were bringing me—Whiskey Bay." At her lifted brows, I corrected myself: "The Atchafalaya Basin. It's where we—*they*—brought the bodies we were dumping. The river would bring the dead straight out to the Gulf of Mexico, and if that failed, then they'd end up as food. I wasn't dead, and they knew that." But they'd stripped me of all my belongings—my ID, my guns, my sanity. "And before they threw me over, Jason made one last order."

"What else—" Breaking off with a low growl, Avery stared hard at my face. "Please tell me they didn't."

"Held me down." I could picture it all now, my limbs restrained as I tried to fight the fuckers off; the tip of the knife drawing first blood; my already tepid heart rate growing slower with extreme blood loss. "They carved my face with a *J*. One guy made the comment that he could see bone, and then they threw me in."

It should have warmed me to see the way Avery reacted, the utter shock that lined her delicate features as her hands went to her mouth to hold in a small cry. The chill was back in my limbs, though, the memories of that day still so vivid in my head that I could almost taste the bile that had stolen up my throat.

"How did you—" Shaking her head, Avery whispered, her eyes shimmering with unshed tears. "It doesn't look like . . ."

I laughed, but there wasn't a single ounce of joy in it. "Trust me, I wanted to die. There wasn't anything I wanted more. And I won't lie, I don't know what twist of fate had me washing up on a grassy bank like some sort of bastard prince, but there I was when some shrimpers were coming out to set some traps." Reaching up, I skimmed my palm over the jagged scars. I couldn't remember a time when they weren't there, but now, much like the tattoos, they were symbolic of my guilt. Visual suffering for all to see. Jaw unclenching, I said, "As for the scar, I fixed it."

Avery blinked. "You *fixed* it?"

I waited for the implication to sink in.

I didn't have to wait long—not even three seconds had passed before she was swallowing convulsively and tearing her gaze from my face, the first time she'd cut eye contact since sitting down. "Lincoln—"

"No one owns me, sweetheart. Not Jason, not Foley, not Hampton. I would rather have a face that scares kids for the rest of my life than live a single day with that asshole's initial etched into me."

"I-I don't even know what to say. He's awful—and awful isn't even a good enough word for it at all. You shouldn't have had to suffer like that, just for wanting to do the right thing. The *noble* thing. It's not okay. None of it is okay, and I can't even imagine what that must have felt like, having your—"

"There's nothing to say. That was my reality and so I

walked out. I'm a damn lucky bastard, but that's not the point to why I brought up all this up." I picked up the card that I'd selected for her future while stalking the internet for any and all understanding of tarot. Dominion had fit for what I wanted for Avery, according to the website I'd found. Illustrated with yellow and orange swords and flames, the card was supposed to represent boldness and courage. Something about the spirit rebelling against boundaries in order to find a resolution.

What it meant besides that—or, hell, if that meaning was completely wrong in the first place—I had no idea.

Guns were my area of expertise, not fortune-telling.

Twirling the card between my index finger and thumb, I husked out, "My point is, Avery, I don't want that for you." I tapped the corner of the card to my face, just below the raised flesh. "*This* is not going to be your future. I'll be dead before I let them touch you. So everything we said the other night, all those bitter feelings? We're squashing the fuck out of them right now. You need me, I'm here. You *don't* need me, I'm still gonna be right here, waiting."

Looking shaken up, Avery licked her lips. "You could be waiting forever. I highly doubt anyone is looking for me."

"You don't think Foley will be if he finds out?

Her hazel eyes squeezed shut. "I don't know. I hope not."

He might not be right now, but he would be soon. If Hampton was stirring the pot, and so was Ambideaux, it was only a matter of time before Foley caught wind and started paying notice to everything around him.

My father had grown comfortable during his term as mayor—it wasn't a secret. But shit was changing, and one wrong move could land Avery back on his radar.

Unless I stepped in and watched her back. I was a glorified hitman with a suspended badge, not a bodyguard. *You can't walk away—not again.*

Not from her, Avery.

Laurel Peyton.

The reason for the scar on my face and the age-old pain in my right leg.

She was the kid I'd been sent to take out. Only, I'd never made it past the front lawn of Foley's mansion. A visual of her running from the house and falling to her knees stained my retina. I recalled her vomiting, her young face inches from the grass, her long, blond hair brushing the ground, as I heard a gun fire from the grand mansion.

I'd assumed Ambideaux had sent someone else after sensing my hesitation.

Who Foley was to Jason, I'd never known. Who he was to me, well, I hadn't discovered that until much later.

But I'd failed her that night. Heartless to the very end as I'd left and climbed back into my car. At any point, I could have warned Foley about Ambideaux's plans. What man wouldn't want to know that his family was being targeted? And yet, I'd left, all the while knowing that someone else could be sent in my place to do the job I couldn't carry out.

A year later, when I'd heard of her suicide on the news, I'd vomited just as she had—on my knees, stomach roiling from pent-up guilt and self-disgust. I may not have been the direct reason for why she was dead, but I'd felt responsible nonetheless. And, beneath it all, her death was a reflection of how far I'd sunk: stealing lives was never honorable, but to even consider killing someone so young? There was nothing worse. Nothing more disgusting or deplorable.

I settled a hand over my heart now, my fingers brushing my sweater, right over where I'd tattooed her number on my chest.

47.

I may not have made her take those pills, but the way I'd looked at it back then, I'd had a direct hand in her death anyhow.

Except she wasn't dead.

She was alive, breathing, and thriving just in front of me, and I was stuck in limbo, wanting to capture her lips with mine and beg for forgiveness while simultaneously wanting to keep our relationship strictly professional.

Hampton's little bombshell had thrown me for a loop, for more reasons than one.

I was the sinner.

The executioner.

The man who belonged in every circle of hell.

With my hand over my heart, I met Avery's gaze and dropped my voice to a low murmur. "Let me be there for you."

Let me find some sort of atonement.

Her lips parted on an inhale. "Okay," she whispered, "okay."

11

AVERY

"Soooo, how long exactly are we going to pretend that Mr. Hot Cop himself isn't downstairs and acting like our very own Captain America, all chivalrous and gentlemanly?"

Dammit. Clearly, today wasn't going to be the day that Katie suddenly learned not to pry into everyone else's business.

I shoved a pillow under my arm just as the front door clicked shut behind her. "He doesn't have a shield," I said, turning to face my roommate and best friend, "so Captain America probably isn't the best comparison."

Dropping her work bag by our tiny entryway table, Katie gave me a crooked grin. "Ave, let's get this settled." She jerked her thumb over her shoulder at the door. "A man like that doesn't *need* a shield. He looks like he breaks bones for a living and takes names."

Andddd, we've officially gotten too close for comfort now.

Even after telling Lincoln that I didn't need him hanging out in front of my apartment building tonight, he'd refused to listen to reason.

"What are you going to do if someone shows up looking for you?" he'd demanded, arms over his wide chest, jaw working tightly as he stared down at me. *"You're already out one taser, sweetheart. I'm the next best thing."*

The way I looked at it—he was selling himself short. He was way more capable than the taser would be, electroshock prongs and all.

Plus, the stubborn man was the reason I was "out" one taser in the first place.

Clamping the pillow beneath my arm so I had a good grip on it, I slung a blanket over my forearm, and then dipped low to grab the assortment of snacks I'd picked up earlier on the way back from Flambeaux. For the first time in years, I was thankful for having interacted with one of Pete's employees and not Pete himself—not with Lincoln Asher waiting just outside on the street. I could only imagine what sort of questions that would bring up.

"Oh, Ave."

Hearing the plaintive note in her voice, I lifted my gaze to meet Katie's. "What?"

She gestured at all the items in my arms. "Girl, you're nesting."

Wide-eyed, I glanced down at the weight in my arms and shook my head. "False. I'm just bringing him—"

"You're nesting." Without giving me the chance to protest, she stole the yellow package of M&M's from the plastic sack hanging from my index finger. Ripping it open like a savage, she popped a red M&M into her mouth, molars grinding as she crunched away. "Let me ask you this," she said, "*why* is Mr. Hot Cop down in his SUV right now, hanging around?"

Another M&M went into her mouth as I stood there and contemplated my next move.

Finally, I muttered, "How did you even know he was there?"

"His face. Totally dream-worthy. It's the kind that's totally hard to forget."

I highly doubted that "dream-worthy" was a name that Lincoln Asher heard frequently about his looks. Gritty. Powerful. Raw. Those seemed undeniably more appropriate.

Then again, when he actually allowed himself to wear his heart on his sleeve, as he had earlier tonight, then, yes, "dream-worthy" was actually a perfect description.

"Avery."

Jeez, she wasn't shaking the claws off tonight.

"Have you ever found yourself drawn to someone who wasn't any good for you?" Rolling my shoulders, I awkwardly gestured for her to return the M&M's to the bag. "And I'm not just saying they're a night owl and you love waking up at the crack of dawn."

Kate's gaze skirted away, landing everywhere but on me. "Oh, you know," she murmured in a blithe tone, "just like every relationship I've ever had."

Right. Somehow, I didn't think it was exactly the same thing.

Katie might love getting outrageous in the bedroom, but her relationships were frequently much more conservative. She fell for the rich types who strolled into the club on a weekly basis. The sort of men who were in town on business, and who felt the inexplicable need to party it up like they were in their twenties.

How many times had Katie come home heartbroken when yet another jerk dumped her three months after his visit to New Orleans?

It was a vicious cycle, one sporadically broken up by hot sex with whoever she fancied at the moment, but was still, in no way, the same as the situation I'd found myself in.

"Asher is trouble," I said, struggling to maintain a neutral expression.

Blue eyes flicked down to my armful. "Then why are you bothering to go downstairs at all?"

Because I can't stop myself.

I hadn't asked him to stay, but now that he was here, I couldn't stand the idea of him sitting in his SUV alone all night without a single creature comfort. No matter the fact that he probably did this sort of stake-out for a living. Just because he was *accustomed* to it, didn't mean that I wouldn't worry.

My forced smile slipped a notch. "No questions tonight. Please."

Katie's blond ponytail swung sharply as she shook her head. "After years of listening to you go on and on about how you didn't need a man, you've made a real quick turn-around." She tapped her chin, lips pursing. "Is this when I tell you that I told you so?"

I grimaced. "Maybe a little too soon?"

"Nah, never." Grinning, Katie surprised me by pulling the pillow from my grasp along with the snacks. "C'mon, I want a formal introduction."

A formal . . .

"Wait!"

Katie waved an arm up above her head, the plastic bag of goodies dangling from her index finger as she turned on her heel and headed for the front door. "Come along, Ave. I don't want to look like an idiot when I knock on his window."

A visual of Katie startling Lincoln—and, naturally, him reacting aggressively—shot me into motion. My legs churned toward the door, blanket in disarray within my arms. "Really," I muttered, slipping out of our apartment to tail Katie down the wooden stairwell, "we don't need to make this a whole big *thing*."

"Who else is going to make it a thing for you? A grandma? An aunt? You have me, Ave. Just me."

"*And?*" Never had I been more thankful to be rocking my solo life than in this moment. "I'm perfectly okay with that."

With her back to me, and her feet making headway down the last flight of stairs, Katie announced, "Listen, girl. Not once in all the time we've lived together have you ever even *flirted* with a guy. So, this sergeant? It's big news. Before you throw your heart into it all, I just want to do a little reconnaissance to make sure he's up to speed on how everything goes down."

"Reconnaissance? I thought you stopped watching *CSI*." Confusion splintered the fog of my thoughts. "And how *what* goes does down?"

"He screws with you, and he'll hear about it from me."

The front door cracked open, and Katie spilled out onto our front stoop. She barely waited for me to appear at her side before she was stepping out onto the cracked sidewalk and glancing from right to left before ambling across the one-way street, calm as can be.

"Katie," I bit out, trailing after her, "seriously, please don't embarrass me."

Her laughter was all I heard. And then, "Don't worry, I'll keep the good stuff to myself. For now. Oh, look! Here he is." She flashed a smile in my direction, and then, with typical Katie-flair, simply knocked on the SUV's window with full-on confidence.

Hurrying toward her, tripping on a corner of the blanket,

I yanked the material out from between my legs and picked up my pace. "Katie, c'mon—"

I watched her spine snap straight, the plastic bag falling to the cement.

Oh, crap.

Then, sounding like she was being strangled, my best friend coughed out an awkward laugh and said, "Captain America is packing, Ave. You're right—I would've preferred the shield."

12

LINCOLN

I stared at the blonde outside my window, watching her from the interior of my SUV as she mouthed something that looked a hell of a lot like "Captain America."

Before I even had the chance to make sense of that, she was being bulldozed to the side by a woman who looked eerily similar to Avery.

My eyes narrowed.

Fuck. It *was* Avery.

Flinging the door open, my feet hit the concrete just as Avery's dark head whipped in my direction from where she stood, body angled in front of the blonde. "Gun down, Sergeant."

My empty hands flexed at my sides, and I felt the absurd urge to lift them and wriggle my fingers. Just to show that I wasn't a complete savage. "Gun's not out, *Avery*."

Behind her, the blonde piped up. "Why are we talking about guns?"

Glancing behind her, Avery let out a very strangled sounding, "You said he was *packing*."

"Oh, right." She stepped out from around Avery, then

tacked on, "I was making a joke. He was . . . well, he was eating a po'boy."

Satisfaction sliced through me as I watched the reality of the situation hit Avery. Her lips parted and her cheeks turned a pretty blush shade and I was just enough of a bastard to murmur, "Fried catfish, in case that was in question, too."

The blonde let out a boisterous laugh.

Avery looked like she was just hoping for the ground to swallow her whole.

And that's when I noticed it.

All of it.

The pillow clutched to the blonde's chest; the blanket half-tangled around Avery's legs. A plastic bag lay torn on the cement, its contents spilling out.

Peanut M&M's.

A bag of chips.

Two triangular sandwiches still tucked safely in their plastic containers.

One bottle of water.

A sensation I didn't recognize pulled low at my gut, warm and completely foreign. My gaze inched up, over Avery's baggy sweatpants to the Saints T-shirt she'd pulled over her head. She looked like she was ready for bed. Rumpled. Sexy. So damn off-limits.

Voice husky, I asked, "What's all this?"

The blonde answered in Avery's stead, striding toward me with her hand outreached. "I like to think that I'm watching my best friend finally fall. Anyway, I'm Katie! Avery's roommate, friend, sister from another mother. And you're Captain America."

"Oh my God, Katie, please stop talking."

Laughter rumbled in my throat at Avery's miserable-sounding tone. I couldn't resist getting under her skin. "You give me that nickname?" I asked her, altogether enjoying the way she bit down on her bottom lip in clear consternation.

Her mouth dropped open. "No—"

"She totally did," Katie interjected, her expression one of pure joy. "She's just feeling a little embarrassed that I've called her out on it. She thinks the *highest* of you." Ducking down, she grabbed the plastic bag and shoved the food right back into it. "Which is why she planned this picnic for the two of you."

Christ, I knew I shouldn't find it funny.

But in the grand scheme of competing politicians and rising death tolls, this was the highlight of my week.

If we didn't count me having sex with Avery, obviously.

Mirroring the roommate, I crouched down and grabbed the water bottle from where it'd rolled right next to my tire. Gently pulled the pillow from Katie's grasp and then did the same to the blanket wrapped around Avery's legs. To Avery, I said, "You know of somewhere we can go to enjoy the spread?"

That seemed to startle her out of whatever trance she'd been in.

Hazel eyes blinked at me, and then lowered to the goods. "I thought you said we needed to stay local?"

Yeah, it was probably best—only, I wanted to feel again, just like I had at Jackson Square earlier. Would we be making a major mistake by leaving home base? Only one way to find out.

Opening the back door, I set the pillow and blanket down on the leather seat. Then, motioning to Katie for everything else, I tied off the top of the plastic bag, so shit wouldn't get loose again, and placed it on top of the blanket.

Somedays you just had to take the risk and hope you didn't get scarred in the process.

I turned toward the women and gave a quick nod in the blonde's direction. "It was nice meeting you, Katie."

"You, too, Cap'."

I almost laughed. She was a nut—the perfect balance to Avery's more somber outlook on life.

An outlook, I reminded myself, that she had every right to.

Guilt slithered up my legs like overgrown, wild vines.

Hand curving over the top of the door, I fixed my attention on the woman I wanted with every fiber of my being. "Get in the car, Ave. I've got the perfect place for our picnic."

A picnic at almost midnight.

If my heart hadn't been thundering with anticipation, sending blood pumping to two different hemispheres of my body, I would have questioned my own sanity. *Why the hell are you going out of your way to make this happen?*

Without a glance in the direction of her roommate, Avery closed the distance between us. Her hand landed on the door frame next to mine, our pinkies tangling like we were high schoolers feeling each other out for the first time.

It wasn't enough, not for me.

My hand covered hers, our fingers interlacing, my breath catching the loose tendrils at her hairline when I leaned down.

Chin tipping up, she met my gaze and said the words that stole the proverbial rug out from under my feet: "I need this."

I needed it, too.

Her heat.

Her slow smile.

Her dry wit that challenged mine.

I squeezed her hand and stepped back. "Get in the car. We're going for a ride."

⚜

I TOOK HER ACROSS THE MISSISSIPPI RIVER TO ALGIERS POINT, a cornerstone of New Orleans that rivaled the French Quarter when it came down to quaint, nineteenth-century character. The historical neighborhood sat directly opposite the Quarter and the downtown Central Business District, and its views were ones for the record books.

And for dates.

If this *was* a date, which logic told me it wasn't.

There was too much convoluted drama surrounding us, threatening to drag us under, but I couldn't—for the life of me—walk away from how I felt around her. Alive. Human. A numbed man finally unthawing to the world.

Putting the SUV in park, I glanced over at her. "Have you ever been to this side of the river before?"

"Once." Staring straight ahead at the tops of the high-rises peeping out over the twelve-foot tall grassy levees, she added, "He brought us here for a dinner. One of those fancy parties where I was shoved into a dress with sequins at the age of eight, and my tight shoes pinched my toes for the entire night. All I remember beyond that is the amount of food that covered the dining table. It could have fed my entire grade at school, including the teachers."

A party like the sort Ambideaux had held all the time—the kind I'd watched from outside the windows, a silent voyeur to a life I'd never even dreamed of having.

Swallowing past the lump in my throat, I turned off the car and waited for the quiet hum of the engine to settle down. "Ready to go up? I promise the view's even better at the top."

"Yeah, let's do it."

We gathered the goods, me with the pillow and the blanket, and her with the food. The levee was a steep climb, a modern-day outer wall to protect the neighborhood from any flooding. Algiers Point was quiet at this time of night—a bar down the road had old blues playing, and there was some laughter and music emerging from the two restaurants just behind us.

Otherwise, it was just the sound of our shoes crunching over grass as we rounded to the top of the levee, where a concrete path was located for cyclers and walkers.

I nudged Avery in the arm, gathering her attention. "Wanna live life on the edge?"

A soft laugh escaped her, and in it I heard all of the longtime exhaustion of actually existing on that cusp of no-return. "Why not?" she said, lips turned up in a smile. "Might as well go all out."

"Brave girl."

Her shoulders jerked, and the plastic bag tangled in her hands whipped to the right as she twisted to face me. "That's the second time you've said that to me. You say it like you admire me."

I didn't want to lie but given recent news about our respective connections to Jay Foley, I didn't want to make her feel uncomfortable either. Over the years, I'd learned that if I wanted something, no one would ever be there to offer it to me.

I took, or the opportunity passed me by without a second chance.

With Avery—*Laurel*—it had to be a two-way street. I couldn't take without her giving approval first that she wanted me in return, and I couldn't assume that we were both on the same page.

"You're a force to be reckoned with," I finally said, meeting her gaze without hesitation. "I'd be an idiot if I didn't admire that."

She chewed on that, literally biting down on her lower lip as she gave me a onceover that had my cock hardening in my pants. "I can't imagine Captain America ever being an idiot." With a wink and a smile, she turned away, her long ponytail swooshing with the movement. "Now where are we going? I'm ready to take a risk. You've convinced me."

My feet were rooted to the concrete.

And, for the first time in my life, I wished for something other than death.

If I closed my eyes, I could almost pretend that *this* was my life—having a midnight picnic up on a levee with a beautiful woman who made my cock hard and my heart warm, and who made me want to toss her over my shoulder, just to hear the sound of her laughter as I teased her with the possibility of throwing her right into the water.

The reverie got away from me, and then it wasn't just Avery and me here at the riverfront, but also a dog pouncing around after a tennis ball. He'd be muddy, feet dancing with the water, before tromping back and shaking himself dry at our side while I wrapped him up in a towel and looked to Avery. Her dark hair draped over one shoulder; her face glowing with happiness; her one hand settled over the curve of her pregnant belly.

"Lincoln! Are you coming?"

Just like that, the vivid visual dissipated like mist on a hot, sunny day.

The chill coming off the Mississippi River cooled my

racing heart, even if it did nothing for the hard-on I was now sporting below the belt.

"Yeah," I muttered, my voice rusty with want, "follow me."

Just like we'd climbed up the levee, I led her down the other side of it, toward the water. We'd had weeks without rain, which meant that the river was lower than usual and grassy banks had popped up along the waterfront. One glance at the exposed knees of the cypress trees was enough to tell me that we didn't have to worry about the river's current coming this way—they were as dry as the Sahara.

I picked a spot with a view of the skyline and the GNO Bridge we'd taken to drive over to Algiers Point. Down here on the banks, with the lights from the Point eclipsed by the height of the levees, there wasn't a chance that anyone would spot us if they happened to be meandering down the bike path.

"It's gorgeous," Avery murmured, as I laid out the blanket for us to sit on. "I was so young when I came here last, I don't even think I paid any attention to a view like this."

Sitting down, I patted the empty spot next to me. "At home, I've got a picture frame up with this view. I got it down on Royal—someone was selling artwork on the street and I had to have it."

"And Sergeant Asher always gets what he wants."

She said it in a teasing tone, but it rubbed me raw, anyway. "Sometimes you learn the hard way that no one is out there handing you freebies just for breathing."

That made her laugh. Picking up one of the sandwich containers, she popped it open and handed it over. I took it with a husky *thank-you* and waited until she'd done the same to her own sandwich before taking a bite into mine. Chicken salad on rye bread—not bad.

"We're such a jaded pair," she said after washing down a bite with a swish of water. "Katie likes to joke around that I'm too wound up, but I just . . . I don't know how to let my guard down. After my momma . . ."

Rumors circulated enough in the underbelly of New Orleans that I'd always suspected Foley had done away with his wife the same way I'd been sent to do away with Avery. At the time, though, I'd selfishly only thought about my life and wanting out of it.

Sandwich clasped in my right hand, my knee bounced under the weight of my elbow. *Tell her everything. Own up to it.*

My mouth opened, and an apology wasn't what emerged: "Go on. I'm not going to repeat what you say to anyone."

"And I should trust you . . . why?"

You shouldn't trust me. I didn't say that either.

I tapped her knee with the back of my hand, the one holding the sandwich. "Thought you said you wanted to take a risk."

"I do."

"Then lower your guard," I said, hating myself with every word for not doing what I preached, "and let me in. No tarot cards, this time—just me and you."

She treated me to her profile as she glanced out across the river. In the dark of night, the water appeared almost black, though the lights from the CBD and Quarter reflected off its swirling currents. She huffed out a soft laugh. "Funny how sitting on this side of the Mississippi makes me feel like I've got an entirely different perspective on life."

Someone could have held me at gunpoint, and I still

wouldn't have wrenched my gaze away from her face. Moonlight kissed the crooked slant of her nose, caressed the crests of her cheekbones, highlighted the length of her neck.

"Tell me why," I rasped.

"Give me your guns."

Incredulous laughter climbed my throat and bubbled out. Only, she didn't laugh with me. Chest tightening, I stared at her. "You're not fuckin' with me right now, are you."

It wasn't a question.

She only patted the empty space between us, much like I had, the palm of her hand landing on the chip bag and making it crinkle. "I'm evening out the playing field. You want me to trust you? Then I want you to lower your guard, too." Her mouth quirked up. "Unless you're too much of a chicken to do as you preach?"

Do as you preach . . .

Christ, she didn't pull any punches.

Flicking my gaze up to the levee, I submitted. Not that I was happy about it. "Hold my sandwich," I grunted, already questioning my sanity as I passed the damn thing over and bent one leg. Lifting the hem of my pants, I unholstered my sidearm and placed it on the corner of the blanket. Still in reach if we needed it, but far enough to make a point.

I was lowering my guard—literally.

Only for her.

After repeating the process with the gun at my hip, I motioned for her to give me back the sandwich. It wasn't that great, but eating it beat worrying about the fact that I was unarmed—

"Other gun, too."

I lifted my arms, my brow raised. "All out of guns to give up, sweetheart."

Her gaze roved over my torso, then paused and cocked her head. "Anything else you want to put in the pile?"

Fuck, but she was pushy.

Popping the rest of the chicken salad sandwich into my mouth, I chewed, frustrated, and then lifted the hem of my shirt. From its leather band, just behind the holster for my gun, I withdrew my trench knife and dropped it next to the firearms. "Happy?"

She chewed on a bite from her sandwich. Swallowed. "Feeling naked, Cap?"

I was feeling *something* all right, but it was probably for the best that I kept all grumbling to myself. "The captain thing isn't going away anytime soon, is it?"

"I like it."

"I'm not a hero, Avery. We both know that."

"Maybe not, but how about, for tonight, we both pretend to be something we're not?"

My mouth went dry. And my hand went to my chest, right over where her number was inked into my skin, and then I voluntarily stepped in front of the proverbial bullet: "What're you pretending to be?"

"Yours."

13

AVERY

I was playing with fire.

And there was not a damn thing I could do to stop myself.

Sitting here in the calm of the night, away from the bustle of the city, made me feel like anything was possible. For the first time in years, my head felt clear. There was no Jay, no fear, no need to be brave for the sake of survival.

What had that lady said at my table in the square some weeks back?

I want to be wanted.

It felt like some odd twist of fate that Lincoln had walked into my life that night. Here I was, three weeks later, almost to the day, and I was just like that woman, smoking a cigarette, hoping beyond hope that all would be well in the end.

I wanted to be wanted—by no one else but him, the man who was wrong for me on every level.

"Avery."

He said my name like it was the last word he'd ever utter, and I took the opportunity to appreciate the way the moonlight glossed over him. He was on his knees, hands on his belt, and I took the plunge.

"Ask me whatever question you want, and I'll answer." I eyed his shirt, the way it flirted with his pants. God, I wanted to strip it off him and finally see *all* of him. "I'll do the same in return."

His face turned away, toward the river, exposing the unmarred side of his face. Sinful. He looked downright sinful with his big muscles playing under the fabric of his shirt, and the messy way his dark hair fell over his brow. He needed a cut, just like he needed a shave, and yet I didn't want him to do either one.

One hand lifted to scrub over the lower half of his face. "I need two questions."

"That's being greedy."

He flashed me a wicked grin, his teeth appearing extra white in the evening light. "Put it this way—one question is for me and the other is for *us*."

Us.

Two little letters and yet they warmed my heart like no other.

"You push a hard bargain," I said, trying to sound playful and not nervous, "but I accept."

Sitting back on his heels, his hands went to his thighs. "Tell me what happened to your mom."

Murdered. Brutally so.

In theory, it should have been as easy as that to admit. It wasn't like it was the first time I was telling someone—Katie knew. And yet, my tongue felt swollen as I sat there, fingers reaching for the water bottle to quench my sudden thirst.

He was patient in waiting, expression solemn, body completely still.

Just say it.

I took a sharp breath. Clenched the water bottle in a tight fist. Forced the words out: "He killed her. The one man who the whole world of N'Orleans has put on a pedestal. He . . ." My throat closed with anger, and I swallowed a fistful of water. "He hired someone—I don't know who he was—and that man shot her. I-I heard it all."

Lincoln let loose a volatile curse, and then he was shifting forward and wrapping his big arms around me. "Don't cry, sweetheart," he said into my hair, "fuck, don't cry."

I wasn't crying.

I hadn't cried in *years*.

But as he rocked me in his large embrace, I touched a finger to my cheek and was startled to find it damp.

Crap. I *was* crying.

"He's a bastard." Lincoln cupped the back of my head, cradling it as he encouraged me to look up and meet his gaze. My heart went into triple-time at the strained set to his face—he looked ready to commit murder, and I had a sneaking suspicion who the mark was in this case.

And it wasn't me.

As though he'd opened the dams, I couldn't lock them back up. The words flooded forward, a tangled mess of things better left unsaid. "I hate him. Every day I wake up and I"—my hands flexed against the strong muscles of his biceps—"I think about how much he took from me that night. My mother, my identity. I'm *no* one, and there is nothing—nothing—more that I want than to return that favor."

Lincoln's body froze against mine. "You can't."

Can't?

Pushing backward, I landed on my ass—and the chip bag. With a *pop!* it wheezed out air. I swatted it to the side, frustration sharpening my motions. It made my voice even sharper. "What? You don't think I can do it? I'm not a kid, Lincoln. If I wanted to kill him, which I do, I would have no trouble—"

Strong hands wrapped around my wrists. "Stop," he growled when I tried to twist away, "just stop and look at me."

Perhaps it was the imploring note in his baritone voice, but I gave in. Just like that, the struggle fled my frame.

"Look at me, Ave. Fucking look at me."

I looked.

And suddenly wished I hadn't.

His blue eyes were eerily intense in the sporadic light that slashed across his face, and there was something almost ruined in the way his gaze searched my face. "You asked, once, if I knew how many people I've killed. I told you tonight that I did." His hands tightened around mine. "Sixty-one. Sixty-one people I've looked in the face like I'm doing to you now and betrayed them in the next breath." Breath drawn in tight, he blew it out like a gust of wind. "There's no pleasure in it."

"I'm not doing it for *pleasure*, I want to do it—"

"For vengeance," he finished for me with a quick shake of his head. "You asked me if I killed Tom Townsend. You were so determined to know if I had or not. So, ask me again."

My stomach turned over. "Lincoln . . ."

"I won't bite. Ask me the question."

God, it wasn't supposed to be like this. He wasn't supposed to make me question myself. For years, beating Jay Foley at his own game had been all I'd ever wanted. And here was his son, trying to convince me otherwise. The irony was almost painful.

Bitterly, I bit out, "Maybe you just want to change my mind so I don't hurt your precious dad."

A half-second later, I found myself on my back, Lincoln's body pressing me into the blanket. I gasped for air, sucking it down into my lungs.

Our legs tangled. His elbows planted themselves on either side of my face.

His lips—oh man, they were temptation at its finest, just inches away from my own.

"Let's get this straight," he rumbled, his chest reverberating against mine. "I don't give a fuck about Foley, but I'll be damned if I have you ending up just like me."

"There's nothing wrong with you—"

He tossed his head back with a harsh laugh. "Don't lie, sweetheart. You called it like it is in that damn motel room. I'm a killer. Coldhearted to the very end. *You don't want to be me*. Don't you get it? I'm fucked up. I don't sleep. I walk around like a fucking armory. Given the opportunity, half this city would take me out." His breath wafted over my face as my breasts rubbed up against his hard chest. It wasn't intentional, but that didn't stop the two of us from groaning at the contact.

His arm muscles flexed by my face. "You think you know what it's like to walk around with a target on your back, but I can promise you"—he lowered his face, our noses almost touching—"you don't want to find out."

"What did you do to Townsend?" I didn't want to know the answer, not truthfully, but it felt like it was something I needed to hear. Maybe hearing the graphicness of it all would slap me back to reality, back to a place where I was perfectly content getting on one of those MegaBuses down at North Claiborne and Elysian Fields and leaving the state.

Blue eyes never wavered from my face. "I put a bullet in his skull and left him in the Atchafalaya."

I wanted to vomit at the visual, as well as the senseless loss of life.

And then I wanted to punch Lincoln for being so blunt, as though he knew that if he said it all matter-of-factly I'd wobble in my decision.

My neck strained as I glanced up at the sky. "Will you kill Tabitha?"

"Tabitha Thibadeaux? No. I walked out on the job. Jason—Nat's ex-husband—didn't take it lightly. They all . . . shit, how do I say this?" He coughed awkwardly, and then rolled to his side, resting on his elbow as he kept his gaze locked on my face. "Your girl got herself mixed up with the wrong crowd."

"How do you know that?"

He blindly reached for my hand and then lifted it, curling my fingers so that they brushed through the dark strands of his hair. Until my middle finger was pressed to a spot at the base of his skull.

"I don't understand."

"Jason's got a superiority complex. He brands those who work for him—I have one here, where you're touching me now. Didn't you ever get curious about your friend's tattoo on her forehead?"

"She said she got it on a whim."

"Not the way it works." Dropping my hand, he added, "She worked for him—who knows for how long—and at some point she decided to work for Nat instead. Jason took exception. Hence, the bodies of Banterelli and Welsh, who also ditched him. And, no, I had nothing to do with them two."

It just didn't seem possible that Tabby would be working

for any of that. And yet, Lincoln had no reason to lie to me about her either. Hell, he'd been sent to *kill* her, which said it all, really.

She was still breathing, which meant she was just fine. For now.

I pushed up onto my elbows, my gaze landing on the cityscape just across the river. "We both know why I'm still here in N'Orleans. Why are you?"

"Too many connections," came his low response. "You can't leave a city when you've got unfinished business."

Intriguing. My thumb drummed a steady tempo against the rumpled blanket beneath me. "And when that business is done, you're going to leave?"

"Never let myself think that far."

"Because you don't think you'll ever take that step?"

He paused, the silence drawing out. And then, "Because I never really believed I'd be alive long enough to make a decision like that."

14

AVERY

My stomach dropped at his gritty confession.

"Cap," I whispered, trying to stifle the horror in my tone, "don't talk like that. You're invincible."

He chuckled. "No one's invincible, sweetheart. Not even me."

Sweetheart.

Lids squeezing shut, I edged out, "It's my turn. Let me ask my question."

There was the soft ruffling as though he were repositioning himself, and then, "Shoot."

Dammit. Did he *always* have to bring me back to that? The man liked his guns—a fact I knew pretty well by now. Rolling up onto my shins, I set my hands on my baggy sweatpants at the knees. It was now or never.

You can do it.

I reached up to tighten my ponytail, just to buy myself time. A second trickled past, and then another. Swallowing hard, my chest heaved with courage. Fake courage, but courage nonetheless.

"I want you." *Keep going.* I squeezed the band of my

ponytail loop again. "I know I shouldn't. I mean, for one, we're all wrong for each other. And second . . . about what Big Hampton told us—"

"I don't give a fuck what he said."

I blinked, startled. Glanced behind me in case he was actually talking to someone else. "I'm sorry," I said, "what?"

Lincoln's hands touched mine, lowering them from my ponytail and setting them on the hard planes of his chest. "I don't give a fuck what he said. You and me? Strangers until three weeks ago. I didn't know you. You didn't know me. If anyone has something to say—and why the hell would they when you don't even go by your legal name?—then that's on them."

Laughter warmed my chest. "You make it sound so easy."

"It is that easy." With a gentleness I didn't anticipate, he cupped my cheeks, his thumbs brushing over cheekbones. "I admire you. You admire me—"

"Don't push it, buddy," I muttered, though I was sure my smile belied my short tone.

He continued on as though I hadn't interrupted him at all. "You admire me, Ave. It might just be for my cock, but hell, I'll take it."

I set my hands on his knees, nails digging in as I waited for him to make a move. Although I'd never go so far as to say that I was submissive, by any means, he was the aggressor in our relationship. The one who'd pushed me up a wall and made me pant into the curve of my arm. The one, when seated in a room of people all having sex, who tore my panties straight off my hips and proceeded to make me come with his tongue and his fingers.

He pushed and I gave back, tenfold.

It was our thing.

But as I sat there with his thumbs caressing my cheeks

and my hands on his knees . . . he did nothing but watch me. Haint-blue eyes tracking my face, dipping down to my neck, but he never moved closer. Never crashed his lips down on mine and made me beg for more.

A minute passed.

Then a second.

And all the while, my core tightened and my toes flexed in my shoes and my breathing grew more erratic as I wondered when he'd push me back and stake his claim.

"Take what you want."

My gaze snapped up to his. "What?"

His head dipped, mouth finding the curve of my ear to nibble on the flesh, and *oh God,* but that felt good. Mouth rasping against my skin, he murmured, "I'm teaching you a lesson." Another sharp bite at my ear, and then his tongue smoothed away the sting. "I told you—sometimes you gotta take what you want or you'll end up with nothing."

"What are you saying?"

"Don't be coy, that's our first rule." His hands fell from my face and he sat back, so that my fingers slipped off his knees.

"And our second?" God help me, but I already sounded turned on. I squeezed my knees together, but the pressure did nothing to alleviate the way my core pulsed.

Lincoln shook his head. "Tell me, Ave, what did you like about the times we hooked up?"

I laughed nervously. Reached up to tug at the neck of my T-shirt and pull it away from my skin. "It, ah, felt good."

"Goes without saying," he said, "but that's not what I mean. What did you like about it all? What made you go from, *I want to smash this guy over the head* to *I just want to fuck him?*"

Oh. That.

Shifting my weight farther back on my heels, I mustered up the confidence to get the words out. To really *think* about what it was that sent me from zero to one hundred in under a second. "I . . . I liked—" Jeez, this was not easy. I wet my bottom lip, then swung my gaze over to the brightly lit downtown area. "I liked—"

Without waiting for me to finish my sentence, Lincoln stood. He let out a low groan when his right knee straightened, and I grimaced in sympathy. No doubt he was still feeling the pain from Big Hampton's asshole lackeys.

My gaze trailed him as he moved the food off the blanket, and then as he circled around me to stand at my back. He kneeled there, my lower body sandwiched between his legs. The unexpected close contact made me jump, but I settled down as soon as his hands fitted themselves at my hips.

"I'm gonna tell you exactly what I liked."

Oh, God.

A shiver carved down my spine at his deep baritone by my ear, rustling the baby-hairs that hadn't made it into my ponytail. "All right," I managed to get out, wondering what protocol was when it came to my hands. Should I put them on his arms? Let them hang by my sides? Tangle them in his hair?

In the end, it didn't matter.

Not when he spoke as though the words were a piece of his soul, selected and chosen just for me. "I like the way you fit against me." His hands swept up my sides, following the indent of my waist to the slight weight of my breasts. "I noticed these first, how perfect you were on top."

Small as my breasts were, I still gasped when he pinched my nipple over the fabric of my T-shirt, pelvis bucking unintentionally.

"I like that too." His mouth dropped to my jaw, and he pressed a kiss there. "For a woman, your voice is so unique. Throaty, I thought once. But that's not the way you sound when you're in my arms. Your gasps"—he slipped his hand under my shirt—"make me hard in an instant. Your cries"—*please,* I thought, as he circled my nipple and tugged, hard—"are addictive enough that you've ruined me forever."

"Lincoln—"

His other hand went to the center of my back and gave a gentle push. It caught me off guard, and I went down willingly, landing on all fours as I twisted my head to try to look back at him.

"I like this, too," he growled, that big palm of his sliding down, down, down the ridges of my spine until it rested over the crevice of my butt. "I like how quick you are to put someone in their place, but with me, all you want is pleasure."

I want to be wanted.

"You look gorgeous, but I think . . ."

I waited for him to finish that thought, my ass suspended in the air, my braless breasts loose beneath my shirt. My neck strained as I held the position, my arms quivering with every effort it took not to turn around and demand to know why he'd stopped.

But then I felt a rush of cool air on my backend, and—

Oh. My. God.

He'd tugged down my sweats until they were pooled at my bent knees.

Thighs squeezing, I slammed my eyes shut. I should argue. Tell him to cut the shit and then yank the material right back into place.

"Spread your legs for me, sweetheart."

Cutting a glance through the darkness to the levee, I did

as he ordered. There was no one around. Just him and me, *us*, with a Louis Armstrong song playing off in the distance and the quiet hum of cars as they drove along the other side of the levee.

At the barest touch of his finger to my inner thigh, my head dropped and my fingers curled into the blanket beneath me.

"You know what else I like?"

The pad of his finger hit home base, circling my clit with the slightest hint of pressure, wrenching a sob from my mouth. He pressed down on the sensitive nub, brought another finger into play, circling and circling and circling until my voice cracked out his name.

His low chuckle echoed in my ears. "I love how wet you are. How eagerly your pussy drips for me. How just being out here, with the possibility of anyone seeing us, turns you on so much that you're already shaking." He thrust two fingers inside me, curling them just right, right off the get-go, so that my spine arched and my core squeezed around him.

"Why is that?" he demanded, and then my ponytail was lifting off my shoulder and being wrapped around a masculine fist. "Don't be coy."

His first rule.

His *only* rule.

The truth hovered on my tongue, but his thrusting fingers stole my attention. Greedily, I sank my hips back, seeking more of that deliciousness. God, it felt so good. I wanted more of that pressure, more of that friction that only he could give me—

He pulled on my ponytail, and my teeth cracked together.

Like he'd flicked a switch, the words spilled from me on

a harsh gasp: "I'm tired of hiding." His hold on my hair loosened and I immediately missed the contact, however wrong that was. "I want to feel alive. I—Lincoln, *please.* Yes, *yes,* just like that."

He worked another finger into me, that sensuous slide feeling that much tighter. It was almost too tight, but I knew —oh, I knew, that his cock was bigger. Thicker. Sweat beading on my forehead, I bared my soul and whispered, "I want to be loved. I don't care who knows. I want to scream it from the rooftops, and not care who sees me, *us*."

"*Fuck.*"

As his fingers slipped from my core, I bunched the blankets in my fists and prayed that I hadn't just made the biggest mistake of my life. But I wouldn't hide—he'd asked for my truth, hadn't he? He'd asked me what I liked.

I'd be damned if I apologized for any of it.

"The next time we do this," came Lincoln's hard voice, "it's gonna be somewhere private. Iron bars sort of private. But there's not a chance in hell that I can . . . Christ, you're beautiful. Turn over onto your back, Avery. I want to see your face when I sink into your body."

I flipped over—like there was really any other choice.

There wasn't.

For some reason, Lincoln had walked into my life. I wasn't a huge believer in fate, despite the fact that I read tarot cards for a living.

And yet, it seemed like fate had a hand in tonight. Not a single soul walked past up on the levee. It was just me and Lincoln, and when he reached down to pull off his shirt, I felt myself grow warm. Or warm*er*, as the case might be.

"Cap," I said, almost reverently, kicking my sweatpants and underwear off completely, "you've got some ink on you."

It was too dark to make out the details, but there was

enough light to note the dark tattoos covering his chest and the upper parts of his arms. His shoulders were big, biceps even more powerful. Unable to stop myself, I propped myself up on one elbow and traced the hard ridges of his abdomen with my other hand.

He was . . . godlike.

"Thor."

I felt him tense. "What?"

"I think that"—oh man, now was *not* the time to begin suffering from verbal diarrhea—"Katie may have been mistaken in calling you Captain America. Thor might be more . . . appropriate."

There was a minute pause, in which I ran over every other idiotic thing that could possibly come out of my mouth, and then his hand was pressing me down into the blanket before sweeping it over my body to cup me between my legs.

A hiss escaped me, to which he only let out a dark laugh. "Good thing I come equipped with a hammer."

He slipped a finger into my pussy, and I didn't know whether to moan or laugh, it felt so sinfully good. The sound that *did* emerge was strangled. "Put the hammer to good use, please."

"Take off your shirt and I will."

He didn't have to ask me twice.

I whipped that bad boy off in the next breath, then used the fabric to hook around the back of his neck and pull him down onto me.

He caught his weight on his palms and didn't waste another second before claiming my lips. The kiss was obsession personified—needy, raw, demanding. His tongue swept along the cushion of my lower lip, and I opened to him. Giving him anything and everything he wanted.

And he took, like he'd taught me to do.

But I'd learned the same tonight.

Letting go of one side of the T-shirt, I skirted my hand down over his chest, his abs, and then circled his cock with a tight grip.

"Not tonight," he grunted, trying to bat my hand away. "I'm two seconds away from fucking you."

I nipped at his jaw. "Then I have two seconds to make you lose your mind this way."

I made good on that vow, swallowing his dick with my fist. Squeezing tight on the ride up to the head, twisting at the crown the way he'd enjoyed when it'd been my mouth doing the work at the Basement, and then diving back down to the thick base. Over and over again, until his mouth was open, and his eyes were shut, and he was cursing me and praising me all in the same breath.

Only then did he shove my hand away and reach for his wallet. There was the telltale sound of a condom wrapper being torn open, and then my legs were being pushed wide and I didn't even have the chance to prepare because—

"Oh!"

He buried himself to the hilt, pausing only long enough to mutter, "Feel free to shout how you're feeling to the rooftops," before he pulled out and thrust back in.

Forget shouting from the rooftops.

If I didn't hold on, I'd be shoved all the way out into the Mississippi River.

Wrapping my legs around his waist and clutching his inked shoulders, I looked up at the man whose soul, he claimed, was as dark as the devil's. But that wasn't true—he'd let his guard down tonight, peeling back his layers until he'd been completely exposed.

Neck muscles straining, he angled his hips differently.

With every thrust, his pelvis ground against my clit, and it was too much. My head thrashed to the side, and as Lincoln dominated my body, I caught sight of the city that had buried me in the underworld of New Orleans.

If it weren't for my past, I wouldn't be here now.

Clinging to a man who could pass for a Norse god.

Moaning his name like I'd never get enough of him.

Rubbing my hands along his inked skin.

This close, I could make out that the tattoos were of numbers. They weren't in a line. They weren't in order. And in the back of my head, I realized what they had to be.

His kills.

Each and every one.

My breath caught, and he leaned down to capture my lips with his, tangling our tongues together.

He was powerful. He was deadly.

"More," I whispered, one hand landing directly over his heart, "don't hold anything back."

Lincoln cursed, his hips momentarily pausing, before continuing the pace that sent my toes curling and my heart thudding. "You were made for me, Avery," he whispered back, his breath harsh as he took me, "everything that you are . . . was made for *me*."

He reached down, one finger landing on my clit, and that was all I needed to go over the edge. I came, calling out his name, and he followed a moment later, back strained, mouth pressed in a firm line, blue eyes focused solidly on my face. Like he never wanted to forget a thing about this night.

He was powerful. He was deadly. And for tonight, he was mine.

15

AVERY

We fell asleep on that blanket, our discarded food scattered around us, the horizon turning into a smattering of orange and yellow and pink.

Lincoln had mentioned that he rarely slept, but his chest lifted and fell evenly under my cheek.

With the sun rising like a spotlight on my sins, I gently pulled out from his embrace and righted my tangled T-shirt. Like any other stubborn man, Lincoln had foregone wearing his shirt when we passed out, and I took the opportunity now to study the tattoos inked into his tan skin.

Numbers.

So many numbers.

Some were single digit, others two digits, some marked as though they were birthdates. In the early morning glow, it was easy to see that he'd sought to give his kills some sort of haven. Angel wings stretched across his chest, and the numbers were seemingly "stitched" into the feathers themselves.

He'd called himself a sinner.

And me a saint.

But he had it all wrong.

My gaze latched onto the firearms I'd urged him to remove last night. They lay exactly where he'd set them, and, on silent feet, I moved to that corner of the blanket and dropped to my knees. Picked up the knife that looked like something out of an action movie. Tested its weight in my grip, and then glanced back at the man who'd rocked my world for hours without tiring.

One expertly placed thrust of the knife and I could have everything I'd ever wanted. Jay Foley dead, at my hand. My freedom, finally.

Be brave.

Be bold.

Blood thundered in my ears, as loud as the tugboat foghorns we'd heard late into the night as they powered down the mighty Mississippi.

I readjusted my grip on the knife, twisting my head so I could look at Lincoln again. He shifted in his sleep, arms reaching out as though missing my heat pressed against him.

Yeah, he had it all wrong.

I was the saint, the sinner, and at the end of the day, I was the one who bled vengeance.

16

LINCOLN

There was something to be said about waiting for your boss to show up when your ass was already on the bench—especially when you had news that could potentially change the game.

"Next!"

I stepped up to the counter at Café Vieux Carre, and promptly swallowed a groan when I saw it was Sarah at the register. Her eyes were bloodshot—tears, not weed, if I had to guess—and she looked like she'd just rolled straight out of bed.

Putting it bluntly, she looked like hell.

"Mornin', Sarah." I paused, waiting for her usual flirtatious greeting and, because I was still riding on the high of sex with Avery all night, tried to be nice. "You doing okay?"

Her ponytail slashed through the air as she angrily twisted around, already grabbing a Styrofoam cup from its stack. "I'm just *fine*."

Oh, Jesus.

Even I knew what "fine" meant—as did the guy behind me in line. He muttered something that sounded suspiciously like, "Fuck that," and then hightailed it out the front door. Smart man. If I didn't have to be here this morning, I'd do the same thing.

With a hard *clang!* Sarah dumped new coffee grinds into the machine, and then shoved the cup into the appropriate spot. "Milk?" she snapped, hand on her hip as she faced me.

"Uh . . ." My gaze darted to the left and then to the right. No one seemed to be noticing the café's barista having a meltdown. Either they were oblivious or had already received her special treatment for the day and were determined to keep their heads down and out of sight. *Wish I could do the same.* "Yeah, milk's great. I'll take the usual."

As if I ever chose something else besides a *café au lait.*

Bending at the waist, Sarah flashed me her jean-clad ass and yanked open the mini-fridge.

Yup, something bad was about to happen, and I checked behind me and counted the number of steps it'd take for me to escape. Six. But only if I wasn't running.

"Here's your milk, *Sergeant.*"

I whipped around just in time to see her pour soy milk into my coffee. My eyes went wide when she didn't stop pouring, and the coffee that should have been toffee in color was suddenly looking like shit that had just been pumped out of a cow's udder.

She slammed the carton down on the counter, and the coffee splattered over the lip of the cup. Palm out for my debit card, she said, "I hope it's as weak as Marco's dick."

Halfway wanting to protest paying for what had to be the shittiest coffee in the city, I pulled out my wallet and handed over the card anyway. "Guessin' y'all went on a date and it didn't go well?"

"*Didn't go well?*" Sarah's brows furrowed together. "His

dick was as big as this straw." She pointed to the straw in question, and I winced.

I opened my mouth. "Not everyone can be—"

"He's overcompensating. *Five* daiquiri shops. Literally, who the hell needs *five*? You try one slushy, you've tried them all."

It probably wasn't the best time to tell her that the daiquiri shops were just a front for passing drugs through the city. She waved her hand around as she continued her rant, my debit card clutched between her fingers, and I made a quick dodge of my hand to snap it out of her grasp.

I missed the first time. Snagged it on the second.

Shoved the bastard into my wallet and picked up my mutilated coffee.

"You have a good day now, Sarah."

"I bet you have a small dick, too, if you're friends with him!" she shouted at my back. "It's the small dicks club!"

"What the hell have you been joining since I suspended you, Ash?"

Fuck. As if the morning wasn't going just fantastically shitty already.

Swinging my head toward the direction of my lieutenant's voice, I watched his approach with a sip of my coffee. Nearly came up choking when I tasted how awful it was.

When Stefan Delery was less than a foot away, I muttered, "How badly do you feel about booting me off the force?"

His mustache twitched. "First," he grunted, "you're *suspended,* not fired. I'm not interested in getting the union involved in this shit. Second, not bad at all. It's been fucking sunshine and rainbows showing up to work without having to see your mean mug."

Yeah, I was going to ignore all of that. "Great. For the greater cause, get me something else." I dumped the cup into the closest garbage can. "You don't want me having this conversation without coffee, and I sure as hell can't go up there again."

He glanced past me toward the register. "Don't tell me you fucked her, man."

I'd been coming here for years and had never given her a second glance. And now that I was all wrapped up—literally—in Avery . . . yeah, that ship was never sailing. Not a chance in hell.

"Nah. Set her up on a date with Marco Carvino. Turns out the man's loaded in every place but his pants."

"That's unfortunate."

"So's my coffee that was just subjected to soy milk." I clapped him on the shoulder. "*Café au lait,* large. I'll even smile for you when you hand it over."

Not wanting to give him the chance to turn me down, I was out the front door in six steps and taking a seat at one of the outdoor picnic tables in ten. My back to the café, I slipped my sunglasses on my face and watched the street. If I'd had the opportunity to have this conversation at the station, I would have, but with my suspension still looming over my head, there wasn't any other choice.

L-T was weird about meeting at people's apartments, and rarely—aka never—allowed others to visit his house.

So, we were doing this shit here, and all I could do was hope that no one overheard.

The door to the coffee shop swung open, and Delery ambled over, two coffee cups in hand. He slid one over to me with a dry, "Soy for you," and didn't even blink twice when I flashed him the bird and took a small sip.

It went down smoothly, albeit scorching its way down my throat, and I nodded in satisfaction.

"What're we doing here?" Delery took the bench opposite mine and clasped his cup between his hands. "You know we're not even supposed to be talking right now."

We both knew I had the upper hand in this situation. Maybe in the walls of the precinct, Stefan Delery reigned superior, but we weren't on NOPD property. And the shit I had for him was completely off the books anyway.

Months of work in the making.

Years, if you counted the time that I'd been making moves without the New Orleans Police Department behind me—and even when they had, I'd always skirted the line of illegal. Rank like Delery turned a blind eye when I got them the results they wanted. But this sort of break . . . it could change things. Hell, it could change *everything*.

And then Avery would be free.

She hadn't asked for a savior, and it wasn't like I had a damn halo above my head—but involving her in this would mean setting aside years of my life and taking a damn breath of my own.

Just like her, I was ready to live.

Reaching into the inner pocket of my jacket, I cast another glance toward the street and then slipped a small notebook from its sleeve. I dropped it on the table, thumbing it open to reveal a folded sheet of paper.

"Look at that," I said, then took another pull of my drink.

I waited, stomach clenched, for my lieutenant to palm it flat.

His surprise registered in the twitch of his mustache. "You have a point in showing me the obituary for the mayor's stepdaughter?" He rubbed his jawline. Tugged on his right ear. "Jesus, that was some sad shit."

Guilt thrived in my veins like I'd taken a shot of a depressant, and I purposely distracted myself by flipping to the next page of the notebook. Withdrawing the ID from where I'd quickly stashed it this morning, I slid it over to Delery. "Notice anything?"

Fingers to the laminated plastic, my lieutenant dragged the ID closer and peered down at it. "Avery Washington." He glanced up at me. "Am I supposed to recognize her name?"

My gut told me I was overstepping boundaries here. Not even overstepping—*leaping*.

You have the chance to save her while keeping her safe.

Up until three weeks ago, I wouldn't have questioned my decision. When you cared for little, not a damn thing mattered. I did my job, just like I had, once, for Ambideaux. At least this one was closer to the state line of being legal. But with Avery to consider . . . shit, no more second-guessing.

It was the right move.

It *had* to be the right move.

Clearing my throat, I nodded my head toward the ID. "It's one of Rafael's," I muttered, referring to the tech whiz over on Basin who was known for making fake ID's, to say nothing of the crazy sort of magic he wielded over the internet. "You stare at enough of those like I have in the past, and you start to recognize the small details."

Like the extra space he added after the person's birthdate.

And the hologram that was a damn near replica to the real Louisiana ID but was off . . . just enough for someone like me to notice.

"Ignore the dark hair, Stefan. Look at her face."

Sitting in my SUV after commandeering one of Avery's "spare" ID's from her wallet, and dropping her off at her apartment, it was hard to believe I'd been such an idiot. How had I not spotted the similarities before? The green ring around her hazel eyes and the defiant set to her chin, and a myriad of other small quirks that were intrinsically *hers*.

Maybe because you didn't want to.

Delery's mouth dropped open. "Ash, you're not saying that..."

Don't do this to her. Don't expose her.

I swatted the thoughts away like a fly getting smacked into nonexistence.

Elbows on the table, I spoke, voice low. "It's her. I know it's her, which means this shit with Foley can finally be put to rest."

Delery's gaze went back and forth between the obituary picture and then the ID. "You think she'll testify?"

"To the fact that her stepfather has got a sick fetish for underage girls? Why the fuck *wouldn't* she testify?"

It was the reason Ambideaux had sent me to murder her, after all. What better way to strike back than to take out the one person your enemy prized most of all? There *was* no better way. Me going after Avery at thirteen was like cutting Foley off at the knees. If any of my investigations over the last few years had proven anything, it was that he liked them young and innocent. Avery had been that way, perfect pickings for a man like the mayor.

And it was the reason I'd spent the last number of years working underground in this city I called home. Tailing leads, talking to all manner of girls who'd found themselves connected to my bastard father in some way.

And sometimes, the rage got a little too much to handle. Sometimes it wasn't Foley's victims I came across but other juveniles who'd been dealt an unlucky hand of fate. And, sometimes, I voluntarily chose to do what I do best and take out the predators—I wasn't a modern-day Robin Hood by any stretch of the imagination. Had never wished to be someone else's hero.

But when you split your time between working the beat with your coworkers and then living in the trenches with the vilest humans the world had to offer, being a little trigger-happy wasn't necessarily a bad thing.

Not if it let someone else breathe a little easier when they went to sleep at night.

And even if it carved another sin into my rapidly growing tally.

Delery sat back, the ID in one hand and the obituary in the other. "I'm not going to lie to you, Ash. If this . . . Miss *Washington* doesn't come forward with solid proof, I'm not sure how much longer the NOPD can have your back on this."

My mouth curled in a sneer. "Christ, do you *hear* yourself, Stefan?" I planted a hand down on the notebook. "Don't be like every other pussy in this department, bending over to take it up the ass. He's a mayor. He's not fucking *God*."

My lieutenant swallowed. "You know Harlonne's in his back pocket. You *know* how hard it's been for me to keep this on the down low when no one's willing to go against the prick—at least, not until he's out of office."

Fury boiled deep in my gut as I pushed my chair onto its hind legs and tried to rein in my temper. Exploding on my boss wouldn't do me any good—not for keeping my job and absolutely not for landing Foley in prison. Let him be someone else's bitch and see how much he liked it.

Air pumped into my lungs as I inhaled deep. *Be calm, man.*

"So, what you're saying is, I can either convince Avery to

testify or I'm shit out of luck on this. Even with all the other evidence I've gathered."

"You don't have evidence when those girls won't repeat to a judge what they told you. What they wouldn't even tell you over a damn *audio* recorder because they're terrified of the consequences. You've got stories, Sergeant. Grotesque, ugly stories told to you on street corners in the dead of night, but nothing more."

It all boiled down to Avery, and wasn't that the true irony in this situation?

When she'd spoken of Foley, she hadn't mentioned abuse. It was possible he hadn't messed with her yet, just biding his time until she was ripe enough to pluck off the proverbial tree branch.

And she'd been a virgin . . . until you.

Delery sipped his coffee, then wiped a hand across his mouth. "You've been a cop for a real long time, Lincoln. You're a good one. A damn good one. But you know what'll work and what won't. You're too close to this case to even be remotely objective anymore. *There's not enough evidence.*"

Head pounding with undiluted frustration, I slammed the notebook shut. "Sometimes, I think the reason this 'case' hasn't gone anywhere is because none of you want it to."

My lieutenant slid the obituary and ID across the table. "For whatever reason, you've got a vendetta against the man. I don't like him—never have. But I know my place and I like my job. Not everyone's you, Sergeant. Not everyone cares."

He made it sound like I wore my heart on my sleeve.

That couldn't be further from the truth. Hell, the only person I'd even come close to sharing any part of myself with was Avery, the one woman I had to convince to come clean and *not* kill her stepfather, so that all the work I'd done for years could finally be done.

She wasn't the only one running.

She wasn't the only one whose life had been brutally torn in half by the man running this city.

But she was the only one who had complete power to end it all—for good.

17

AVERY

University students were everywhere—and I did mean *everywhere.*

The good news: Pershing University was equipped with maps throughout the campus, which meant that it *should* be easy to navigate my way to the head administration building.

The bad news: there was some sort of sporting event happening today. I'd never seen so many bare chests with letters painted in green across their lanky forms.

A P stumbled his way into my line of sight, the paint on his chest half washed away as he shook a water bottle then dumped it over the top of his head. "Fuck yeah!" he hollered, throwing the bottle into the crowd.

It bounced off a girl's head some seven feet away.

I'd always thought I'd missed out on the whole college experience, but one glance at the chaos around me told me maybe *I* was the one who'd ended up getting lucky.

You're way too old for this.

In terms of years, maybe not so much.

Based on life experience, I might as well have arthritis, a

cane, and a tomb picked out at one of the city's notorious aboveground cemeteries.

"Excuse me," I muttered, giving up all pretense of playing nice. I palmed a guy's shoulder and shoved him roughly to the side. Slipped into the next open pocket within the crowd—and then repeated the process until I was nose-to-one-of-the-campus-maps, trying to determine exactly where I stood in relation to the admin offices.

Pershing University was seated in the center of New Orleans' Uptown neighborhood, right on the streetcar line that started in the French Quarter and cut through the city. Unlike the campuses I saw on TV, Pershing wasn't massive in acreage but more jam-packed into a centralized area, its perimeter flirting with surrounding residential homes.

My gaze tracked my location—the quad by the main dining hall—and then followed through to my end destination. Not far, maybe a five minute walk.

With one glance at the mayhem happening on the quad, I turned my back on the campus party and stepped on the pebbled pathway. Limestone buildings reached toward the sky on my left, and what had to be the smoothest street in the city graced my right.

Pershing was beautiful—if only its president wasn't a total kidnapping prick.

By the time I climbed up the front steps and then rode the elevator to the third floor, I was sweating under my armpits, and the unease once again began to cling to my confidence. Visiting Big Hampton was a bold move, albeit an unexpected one. I hoped.

A bell jangled up above as I pushed open the glass door and stepped into the seating room. Luxurious artwork covered the walls, and potted plants sat atop every small table.

The receptionist's head jerked up at my entrance, and a wide smile spread across her face. "Oh! Hello, dear." She pushed the glasses that were perched on her nose up to the top of her head. "Do you have an appointment with one of our counselors?"

Luckily, I'd thought ahead.

Closing the distance from the door to the front desk, I smiled down at the woman, taking note of her nametag. "Hi there, Ms. Betty. I actually called earlier this morning? About the article that I'm doing for the *Times-Picayune*?"

Snapping her fingers, she exclaimed, "Ah, right! Yes, yes. Ms. Samantha Lovelace. Yes, I'm so sorry. I've got you all marked down for your appointment with Mr. Hampton." She tapped a finger to her nose, staring at the expanse of her messy desk, and then snapped up a sheet from the far-right corner. "Here we go. He's expecting you—2 p.m., right on the dot."

I forced a smile. "Sorry I didn't get here a little earlier, as promised. I wasn't expecting the campus to be so busy today."

"Oh, you're just *fine*, dear. It's Pershing's one-hundred-year-old anniversary this week, so there is celebration aplenty." Beneath her breath, she muttered something that sounded very much like, "and so much booze."

My fake smile flirted with a real one. "So long as Mr. Hampton still has room for me today, I think we can include something about the anniversary along with my article."

Green eyes blinked up at me. "He would *love* that. Good press is the best kind of press."

I was pretty sure that the saying went "any kind of press was good press," but I wasn't about to correct her.

"Why don't you follow me?" She pushed back her chair and came around the corner of the desk, gesturing for me to step ahead of her. Clamping my purse close to my side, I held my chin up and kept my shoulders pressed back.

Act like you belong here.

"Coming here today, I can't believe I chose to go to Loyola University instead." The lie nearly made me grin, and because Samantha Lovelace had always been a more naïve version of myself, I blithely added, "It's just so *beautiful* here. Oh my God, the campus is like something out of a fairy tale."

"Isn't it?" Betty patted me on the shoulder like I was a good dog. "Don't worry, dear, we won't hold it against you that you went to *that* school over Pershing."

That school.

Wouldn't she die a little inside if she knew I'd never even graduated high school?

One day I would, though. I'd get my GED and then my college degree. And maybe, when all this had blown over, I'd apply to vet school, just to see.

I was one step closer to freedom, but first Joshua Hampton had to get me there.

Betty knocked, twice, and then at a booming masculine voice calling out "enter!" she edged the door open and popped her head in. "You all ready for your two o' clock? Ms. Lovelace is here."

"What the hell kind of name is *Lovelace*?"

A fake one. Definitely a fake one.

Not to mention I'd come up with it when I was thirteen—no one should judge a girl that age.

"Is that a yes, Josh?" Betty asked.

"Send her in."

Facing me again, good old Betty gave me an encouraging grin that could have read anywhere between *go get 'em tiger* and *bless your heart*.

One quick nod of appreciation later and I was in the office, the door shut behind me, as I looked to the man of the hour behind his desk.

His eyes narrowed. "*You.*"

Time to make the magic happen.

Perky smile on my face, I took the available seat across from him, purse in my lap. "How amazing to see you again, Mr. Hampton. It's been what . . . three, maybe four days since you held me at gunpoint?"

He blanched, gaze skirting behind me to stare at the door. "What are you doing here, Ms. *Lovelace*?"

"What? No small talk?"

"My secretary said you were here for an article about the mayoral race."

My lips quirked. "I am. Unfortunately, the information will go no further than me, but I can't imagine how you'd have a problem with that." I leaned in to whisper, "I mean, no offense, but considering recent behavior, you'd have a lawsuit on your hands if word got out about your ventures in kidnapping."

"My . . ." His brows went high, and his hand, which had been balled into a fist, smoothed out over the desk. "I'm not going to repeat myself again—what do you want?"

I gave a small shrug. "I want what *you* want—Foley dead. Although I'm going to harbor a guess that our reasons for why we're praying for a miracle that our lovely mayor drops dead are for two different reasons." Reaching into my purse, I pulled out a manila folder and propped it open on the desk. "You tell me what you know, and I'll do the same. I think you'll find that we're both reaching for the same outcome."

An outcome that didn't include Lincoln Asher dead.

My heart twisted at just the thought of it alone, and I

suppressed the emotion for the sake of staying on my toes. I couldn't allow myself to dwell too deeply on him—not right now. Not when this was a life or death situation, literally.

At Hampton's stubborn silence, I sifted through the leaflets of paper I'd brought along. The copious notes I'd taken over the years were finally paying off. Although if Hampton failed to cooperate with the plan I had in mind, it wouldn't matter what I said today.

"How did you meet Nat?" I asked casually, hand coming down to rest on the final sheet of paper in the bunch.

Hampton stared at me. "What does that have to do with anything?"

I met his gaze unflinchingly. "Haven't you ever wondered how she's so wrapped up in the politics of this city? She married Ambideaux, worked on her back for my stepfather, and now"—I offered a little smile—"she's fucking *you*. The richest man in the city, the mayor, and an esteemed university president like yourself. Why?"

"Maybe she's got good taste."

Doubtful. All three of them were creeps of the first order.

Shaking my head ruefully, I murmured, "Or maybe she's got an ulterior motive."

He barked out a laugh at that. "Of course she's got an ulterior motive. She's a hustler, Ms. *Lovelace,* and that's what hustlers do. They'll social climb until they're either dead, in jail, or living under a fake name in Mexico. I have absolutely *no* delusions that she wants me for anything but my money and my status."

Jeez, he was a cocky bastard.

Not that I'd expected anything else.

Drumming my fingers on the desk, I drew out the

silence until his cheeks began to redden with impatience. Then, "And why do you want her?"

His stance stiffened, mouth going flat as he stared at me. "She has a great rack and an even better pussy. Does that answer your question?"

"Not even close, but the sarcasm is appreciated."

His molars ground together and he shoved away from the desk, chair nearly toppling over until he caught the back. "This *appointment* is getting old. I have no interest in playing games. Either say what you came to say or get out of my office."

The sweat that kicked off its marathon under my armpits spread to my chest, between my breasts. It'd be so easy to succumb to the fear and the nerves, but neither fear nor nerves would get me out of this mess.

"I don't believe you're a bad man," I murmured, dragging my folder close and flipping to the front of the stack. "Sometimes good people do bad things." *Like me right now*. "Sometimes"—I flicked my gaze up to check out Hampton's expression—"you find yourself in a tough position. Right or wrong, good or bad. You can only do what you think is right."

His eyes narrowed into slits. "How lovely to know that you don't believe me to be an asshole."

Pretentious asshole, more like it.

Shrugging off his bad attitude, I returned my attention to the folder before me and to the notes that I'd faked just this morning. *Sometimes good people do bad things*. My new motto—for better or for worse.

"Nat's come to visit me for years in Jackson Square, Mr. Hampton. I've read her cards enough to think I know her reasonably well."

"No one knows Nat well. Not you, not me, not her damn ex-husband. *No one.*"

My plan was risky, and there was a good chance Big Hampton would laugh in my face. But if there was anything I'd learned from watching the world behind the curtain of reading cards, it was that there was nothing more destructive—nothing more *implosive*—than pitting two self-centered people against each other and watching the sparks fly.

Flexing my fingers to subtly shake out the nerves, I pulled out the three tarot cards I'd layered at the back of the folder. "Tell me, have you ever had your tarot cards read?"

Mouth curling in disgust, Hampton snapped, "Do I look like someone who believes in that shit?"

Judgmental jerk. I wouldn't even deign him a response for that one—although it did make me feel better for what I was about to do. One by one, I laid out the three cards before me on the oak desk, pushing my chair back with the hope that curiosity would bite Joshua Hampton in the ass and propel him to see the cards I'd pulled.

"The thing is," I drawled, dropping the pitch of my voice to match the throaty tenor I always used in the square, "tarot is a lot like Murphy's Law, Mr. Hampton. If you believe something *will* go wrong, it no doubt will. But within tarot, I like to think of it like . . . if your mind is constantly obsessing over one thought or idea, it'll naturally manifest in the cards you pull."

From my jacket I pulled my velvet pouch where I stored my cards. Emptying them out, I set the deck on the desk, to the left of the three splayed cards. With my palm, I rolled the deck out, so that they formed a shallow arc.

Stepping back, I met Hampton's gaze. "Humor me, sir. Why don't you pick a card?"

Jaw clenching, he looked from me to the desk and then back again. "Nat does this?" he asked, and there was no denying the hesitation coating his tone.

My lips turned up in a smile. "Weekly. She's quite the *fanatic* about coming to see me."

Indecision danced across his features.

The seconds dragged on. I refused to let my smile dip, refused to holler like a maniac when he caved and approached the desk like he had chains locked around his ankles.

"I can pick any card?" he asked, sounding doubtful.

"Whatever card speaks to you."

Please let this work.

I was desperate to fiddle with something, just to work out the excess nerves, but I forced my hands to my sides.

His hand hesitated over the middle of the arc, hovering. He glanced at me over his shoulder, scrutinizing me with narrowed eyes, and it took everything in my power to keep my expression passive . . . even though, on the inside, I was dying for him to make a pick.

Over the years, it wasn't only people's stories I'd recorded, but the cards they typically picked from the spread—and which number they were in a lineup. Confident people tended to pick from the front end of the deck, as though assuming that even in their readings, they were always ahead. Those who were more sensitive chose from the middle, like they were shoving through the murky in-between and looking for some kind of guidance.

Joshua Hampton was a confident man.

A man who didn't believe in the art of tarot or anything that he couldn't touch tangibly.

It was obvious that he wanted power and money. Even more obvious that the only thing he despised more than someone messing with his kid was a person who threatened his power *or* his money.

His fingertips flirted with the very first card in the spread, and then, turning his body to face me, he selected the second card.

Pulled it from its spot.

Turned it over and squinted at the words at the bottom of the card.

He cleared his throat. "Four of Disks."

Also known as Power, the card I'd placed in that exact spot for him to select, knowing that it would stroke his ego and make him more malleable. *Thank you, Lincoln, for showing me the way to* not *read tarot properly.* After all, if he hadn't decided to teach himself to read tarot, by picking my cards in advance, I would never have even given thought to doing the same to Hampton now.

Only, unlike Lincoln, I had no plans to tell the university president that I'd had a hand in anything at all.

"How interesting," I purred, stepping close to make a show of craning my neck to see the card he held in his hand. "And how appropriate."

"Yeah?"

I tapped my temple then pointed my finger at him. "I was under the impression you wanted to be mayor."

He frowned, staring down at me. "I do."

Without giving him the chance to protest, I plucked the card from his grasp. "Then there's no better card to pull. Being mayor is like being the most powerful man in N'Orleans. Seems like you've been thinking real hard about this, Mr. Hampton."

"I think of nothing else."

"No?" I gestured to the spread again. "Why don't you

pick another card? See if Murphy's Law is working in your favor again—the tarot version of the law, I mean."

His Adam's apple bobbed down the length of his neck, but unlike with his first selection, he wasted no time in reaching for the cards again. Palm open, he waved his hand from the front to the back, hesitated, and then his fingers were pushing at the third to last card, removing it from its pack.

I stifled a sigh of relief.

I'd put three possible cards for him at the back, but my first choice was the one he'd gone for.

Must be my lucky day.

He flipped it over and immediately held it up for me to view. "Six of Disks."

Success—literally. I gave him a bright smile. "Looks like your path to mayor will be greeted with success. How fortunate."

"Yeah?" He pulled back his arm to stare down at the card. "Just like that?"

I shrugged. "Nothing is guaranteed, and free will can change anything."

With another glance down at Success, he set it down, and promptly let curiosity bite him in the ass—just like I'd hoped it would.

Knuckles pressed into the desk, Hampton leaned his body toward the three cards I'd first laid out. "Are these for you?" he asked.

Not even close.

Twisting around, I leaned up against the desk and folded my arms over my chest. "Those?" I shook my head. "Unfortunately, those were the last cards I picked for Nat."

Hampton jerked in my direction. "Why are you showing them to me?"

Because I'm hoping you're dumb enough to fall right into the trap.

And then, like I was putting on a stage performance on Broadway, my tone hardened as I murmured, "Honestly, after what you did to Lincoln and me, I had no desire to help you whatsoever. For all I care, you could rot in hell. The hotter the flames, the more satisfied I'll be."

His nostrils flared. "And yet here you are."

"And yet here I am." Reaching over, I tugged the three cards close to me. "You see, Mr. Hampton, I'm the type of person who'll stop a group of idiot boys from assaulting a young woman." If he caught my reference, his expression didn't even twitch in acknowledgment. I pressed on. "For all I've been through, I just want to help people. Nat's been coming to me for years now, and I've read cards for her at every stage of her life."

I lifted my gaze, climbed the tight fit of the man's suit, and fixed my attention on his face. "I would love to let this go. The idea of helping *you* of all people turns my stomach, but here I am, once again playing the saint because I just can't help myself."

Voice tight, he bit out, "And your point is?"

"Here are the cards that I last pulled for Nat. Read them to me."

Hand balling into a fist, he dropped it to the desk and leaned forward to look at the first card. "Eight of Swords."

I swallowed a smile. "That'd be Interference."

He visibly stiffened.

"Read the next, sir."

Free hand coming up to run the course along his jawline, he looked to the next card. "Death."

Wincing for dramatic effect, I placed my hand to my chest. "How unfortunate."

This time, I didn't even need to prod him into telling me the next and final card. He stared down at it, his cheeks turning red from what could only be rage or embarrassment.

"It's The Emperor," he breathed out, turning to me. "What does this even mean? Is this about Whiskey Bay?"

Sometimes good people do bad things.

I took the card from him, drew in a deep breath, and then lied. "It's about you, Mr. Hampton. She came to me wanting to talk about a love interest, and then . . ." I shrugged. "Well, I saw the way you acted toward her the other night, and as much as I'd *love* to see you go down in flames—"

"Yes," he ground out, cutting me off, "you mentioned that."

"—it seemed only fair that I tell you what she told me. She was *very* pleased when she left, which is a little alarming, obviously, considering the nature of the cards. I mean, for her to feel so strongly against you, clearly you must have something that she wants. Right?"

His nails scraped along the desk as his shoulders hunched. "She keeps mentioning how happy it makes her when I give her money to spend how she pleases."

No surprise there.

"Hmm." I bit down on my thumb, pretending to give the situation a lot of thought. "And she *has* mentioned marriage to me before in our sessions. So, that's troubling. Unless, you know, you aren't particularly concerned about her wanting to marry you for your money and then, well . . ." I tapped Death, just to make him squirm.

And squirm he did.

Back going ramrod straight, Hampton twisted from the

desk, hands on his hips. "If that's all you've got for me, Ms. *Lovelace*, I've got to get back to work."

"Oh, I don't want to hold you."

I slipped the cards back into their velvet pouch, tucked my folder into my jacket again, and moved toward the door. Only when my hand was on the doorknob did I pause and glance back to say, "Free will is such a powerful thing, Mr. Hampton. Just remember that nothing is ever set in stone."

He didn't offer a response, but I wasn't looking for one.

I'd planted the seed of distrust. For an already suspicious man like Joshua Hampton, I had a gut feeling that the seed was all he needed to attack anyone who threatened his kingdom.

But kingdoms rose and kingdoms fell, and one by one, I wouldn't stop until they all came tumbling down.

18

AVERY

"You need a date, and I don't care what Captain America says, I was your one and only first," Katie hollered from the doorway. "Which means that I deserve the chance to sweep you off your feet."

The eggs on the stove sizzled and popped as I flipped them over in the pan. "By that sort of logic," I repeated to Katie as she entered the kitchen, still in her work uniform of a skimpy tank top and even skimpier short-shorts, "you should be cooking *us* lunch today instead of the other way around."

Grabbing two plates from the cupboard next to the fridge, I tacked on, "And what are you going on about, anyway?"

"A fancy party, that's what I'm talking about."

Out of my periphery, I watched her toss an unsealed envelope on the counter. It slid to a slow stop inches from the pan. Curiosity weighing heavy, I moved the skillet off the hot burner to the back of the stove and then picked up the envelope.

"Party's set for tomorrow evening."

I lifted my gaze to my roommate's face. "Since you already opened it, why not just tell me what it is?"

"I'd hate to take away the fun from you."

I bit back a laugh. "You've already opened the damn thing up. I mean, the party bus has already left the scene."

"Good point." Tugging the envelope from my grasp, Katie promptly pulled a cream-colored card from it, and then cleared her throat. "Tomorrow evening at seven on the dot"—she wiggled her brows playfully—"you've been invited to a party being held in support of the announcing of a new mayoral candidate for the upcoming election." Pausing, Katie sucked in her bottom lip. Then, "Not going to lie, it's a little weird that they'd send you an invitation like this on such short notice. Who do they think you are? And what the hell sort of clients have you been seeing in the square that you nabbed an invitation like this in the first place?"

The kind who wanted me to play puppet to their puppeteer.

Stomach dropping, I gripped the edge of the kitchen counter for stability's sake. There was only one reason I'd be sent an invitation like that—and there was no doubt in my mind who'd sent it.

"Give me the card," I muttered, extending one arm.

"You look like you just bit into a lemon." The card was slapped into my waiting palm. "Newsflash, Ave, people *die* to get invited to stuff like this."

Yeah, that was my fear.

That, and the fact that the event was less than twenty-four hours away.

Twenty-four hours until I came face-to-face with Jay, my stepfather.

Twenty-four hours until I finally laid to rest the retribution I'd been determined to dole out for years now.

Forcing my gaze to the card, I skimmed the flowery prose of "winning back New Orleans" and the mention of "representing the people for the greater good."

Bullshit, bullshit, and more words.

Politicians in the city were all one and the same in this city—dirty and corrupt to their core.

Only, the name at the bottom of the card wasn't Natalie Lauren, as expected. Nor was it Big Hampton.

No, Jason Ambideaux was the man behind the invite.

Nat's ex-husband.

Lincoln's former boss.

My bare toes curled into the linoleum flooring, and I swallowed, hard. Had . . . had Lincoln mentioned me to him in passing recently? Or maybe Nat had dropped some sort of info about me, even though I thought they no longer spoke to one another anymore?

Maybe I was on Big Hampton's radar; maybe I was on Nat's.

But Ambideaux, the man who'd ordered someone to carve Lincoln's face? There was absolutely no reason for him to know me. Not to mention . . . how had he even known where to deliver the card? I wasn't listed in any registry, and no one knew I lived here at the Sultan's Palace aside from Pete, Lincoln, and Katie.

But the apartment and rent were in Katie's name, not mine—which meant that *someone* had to have told him where to send it. And that someone . . .

My cheeks hollowed with a harsh exhale. Or maybe it was a broken laugh.

I was so, so stupid. Still that naïve little idiot on the streets wanting to believe the good in everyone I met. And

I'd trusted Katie—maybe not with who I was, but in every way that mattered, she was my family.

My *only* family.

Heart thundering, I dropped the card on the counter like it'd caught fire. Took a step back, and then yet another, until the cool expanse of the refrigerator was at my back. I wanted to run—to dart out the front door and down the stairwell, until the breath I drew into my lungs tasted like freedom. Freedom, and a new identity—the way I'd always done.

Be brave.

Be bold.

Hands shaking at my sides, I curled my fingers in, clamping down on my thumbs. Kicking up my chin, I reined in the shock to grind out the words that needed to be said. "It's weird that I received an invitation at all, considering the fact that I don't know a Jason Ambideaux."

Katie's blue eyes went from my face to the glossy invitation. "Really? That's definitely . . . unexpected, then."

"Unexpected" didn't even cover it.

As much as I wanted to manipulate her into a confession, I wanted answers more. And I didn't believe, not even for a second, that Ambideaux's invitation was just a casual, *let's get to know each other* type of deal.

Not from the way Lincoln had described him.

One wrong move on my part and I'd have a damn *J* carved into my face, just like him.

"Did he pay you off?" Bitterness dripped from every word, and my trembling hands were suddenly trembling for an entirely different reason. Betrayal. Anger. And the underlying layer of hypocrisy—because hadn't I kept her in the dark, too? Hadn't I staged our first meeting because of *who* she was?

Jay Foley's niece.

My cousin by marriage.

Family, for whatever worth that word even held.

In silence, Katie grabbed the pan off the stove and made a show of dumping the eggs in the trashcan like the action was some sort of metaphor for our relationship. Straight down the trash it went.

Patience wearing thin, I snapped, "Aren't you going to say anything?"

After roughly dropping the pan in the sink, Katie's hands went up to tighten the elastic band of her ponytail. "What is there to say? Here's your invitation." Her gaze cut to mine. "You're throwing a bitch fit for absolutely no reason. Most people would be excited to party it up with the city's elite."

Most people didn't have to worry about staying in the shadows for reasons they *still* didn't understand. And since it wasn't like I could stroll up to my stepfather and pop the question—*hey, why did you want to kill me so badly?*—I was stuck in a permanent position of ignorance that kept me forever vulnerable.

Suspicion crawled like spiders over my flesh, raising the tiny hairs on my arm. "Just answer the question, Katie. *Where* did you get the invitation? Because we both know that it wasn't sitting in the mailbox for me downstairs."

Mouth tightening, she twisted away, presenting me with her back. "He saw you, you know."

My mouth went dry. Did she mean Ambideaux or Jay? *Who would be the lesser threat?*

I wasn't given the opportunity to voice the question. With a hand on the wall, her shoulders hunched, Katie's voice practically seethed with tension. "Outside of the police precinct with Captain-fucking-America. You had him all over you, so the way I look at it, you brought this on yourself."

Because I'd finally wanted a man? Because I'd finally grown the nerve to let down my guard and let someone touch me? How in the world was that *my* fault? Hell, it seemed like something Katie would usually applaud me for.

Only . . . "You're not making any bit of sense. *Who* saw me and what the hell does *that* have to do with this?" I pointed at the card. "You're speaking in riddles."

It was the wrong thing to say.

Arms flying up in the air, Katie whirled around, her expression so hard, so unlike her, that if I could have backed up without climbing into the fridge itself, I would have.

"Speak in *riddles*?" she hissed, storming toward me. "Are you fucking kidding me right now? You want to throw stones, then how about this? Ambideaux saw you that night, and then he saw you at the club with your precious sergeant." Her gaze glittered with fury, and my shock must have registered on my face because she let out a caustic laugh. "Oh, yes, *Laurel*, he saw you with the good sergeant's hand down your pants. Then Ambideaux visited me at work. He wanted to know who you were, how long I'd known you. Maybe if you'd been forthcoming with me from the start I would have told him to fuck off. But, no, I wanted answers, and I found them."

Laurel.

The fear was back, clogging my throat, turning my limbs to concrete, submersing me beneath the water.

"Katie, I would have—"

Her hand came up, cutting me off. "I gave you the opportunity to come clean after I went through your precious file cabinet and the rest you hid above the fridge. Was it wrong of me? I don't even care. And though the blond hair might let you believe otherwise, I'm not an idiot. I sat on that damn couch and called you out and waited for you to say *something.*" She breathed out a laugh that sounded like tangible disappointment, and I couldn't deny that I wanted to shrivel up where I stood. "But you only fed me another lie, which I should have expected. I mean, who *don't* you lie to?"

Her pointed question landed like a sucker punch to my chest.

Lying was my key to survival, but hearing it out loud was . . . oh, God, I couldn't breathe.

At my silence, my roommate snorted derisively. "That's what I thought."

I needed to apologize. Hell, there was a *lot* that I needed to do to make amends with my only friend, but as I stood there, my brain working in overtime, I only whispered, "Jay Foley killed my mother. *He's* the one who murdered her, the reason I've lived on the streets. You've got to understand that there are some facts I couldn't tell you in fear that you'd tell *him.*"

Fear ran my life.

Ruled my emotions.

And as Katie stared at me, her expression tight, I realized that my fear had also caused the death of my only friendship.

"Call me unreasonable or a bitch," she said in a thin voice, "but I'm gonna need space. And, ironically, I tried to warn you that running forever would land you in trouble."

She couldn't be . . .

Head pounding with panic, I muttered, "Twenty minutes ago you were demanding to go to this party with me, and now you're, what? Kicking me out?"

Katie snapped up the card from the counter and crumpled it up in one hand. "It's called finally coming to my senses and knowing when to call it quits. Maybe if you haven't totally fucked over your sergeant, he'll take you in."

Like a stray seemed to be her unsaid implication, and the thought alone was like having steel injected in my bone marrow.

I was completely aware of the fact that I'd lit the matchsticks for our imploding friendship. I'd approached her first. Warmed her up to me and broken down the walls until we hung out regularly and then we were picking out apartments together.

She'd trusted me, and I'd betrayed that over and over again for years.

You're not so much of a saint after all, are you?

My chest tightened at the truth. I could pretend all I wanted that every single one of my actions was justified, but at some point along the way I'd become unrecognizable even to myself.

A woman so determined to right a wrong that I didn't even blink at using others to put myself in a better place to manifest my own goals.

"I'm so sorry," I whispered. It was an apology to Katie, yes, but also to myself. For letting my rage overrule everything else, including my common decency. "I just—" I broke off, unable to put into words how I'd waged war within myself for years. "I'm sorry."

Katie nodded, then turned her head, as though she didn't want me to read her expression. "Don't go to that party alone, Avery. That's all I'm going to say. If you're smart, just don't go alone." Stepping back, she spun on her heel and headed for the bedroom. Over her shoulder, she said, "You can let yourself out. And if it makes you sleep any better, no, I won't tell my uncle about you. Your precious secret is safe with me—for whatever that's worth to you."

She closed the bedroom door, and I heard the lock click shut.

My palm closed over my mouth, and I bit down on my knuckle to keep from letting a sob break loose. I was strong, had always been strong, but never before had I wanted to admit defeat as much as I did now.

Jay Foley had stripped me of my identity.

But he wasn't responsible for the way I'd stripped myself of who I was at heart.

And, if I wanted to dig deep, I didn't even know the answer to that question.

Laurel.

Samantha.

Ruby.

Avery.

A figment of mashed identities, whose only purpose in life, for over a decade, had been to murder the man who'd had my momma killed.

Beyond that, I was no one.

And that, it seemed like, was the greatest loss of all.

19

LINCOLN

It wasn't Avery's face that greeted me after I'd spent five minutes banging my fist on her apartment door.

No, it was her roommate's.

The blonde.

I couldn't remember her name—but there was no mistaking her bloodshot eyes or the way her coloring was all off. She looked like shit, and I had a feeling that I looked no better.

Guilt could do that to a person.

"If you're looking for her, she's not here."

I went rigid. "You mean, she's at the square for work already?"

It was way too early in the evening for her to be reading cards. Hell, it wasn't even 6 p.m., which meant the gates of Jackson Square weren't even locked for the night yet.

The blonde lifted her chin. "No." She shook her head, then quickly averted her gaze to stare at my right shoulder. "I mean, I don't know."

There was something in her tone . . . something that didn't sit well with me, and even though I knew it was inherently wrong to scare her, I set my palm on the doorframe anyway. Used the size of my body to intimidate her.

I'd never said that I was anything less than a callous asshole.

My voice was low, hard, when I said, "I read liars for a living, and I know when someone's trying to bullshit me. So, let's try this again—where is she? And we both know Avery's not the sort to go somewhere without saying something first."

If she had been, she would have left this damn city years ago.

Like me, she had unfinished business.

And she has me.

Christ, I couldn't go there right now. Not until I'd unloaded everything I had to tell her about the case—and not until I confessed about the night I'd been sent to kill her. I had to come clean, even if it meant she'd never want anything to do with me again.

Avery's roommate folded her arms around her middle. Then, softly, she whispered, "I asked her to leave."

Ice slid down my spine, and my nails scraped the door-frame as my hand balled into a fist. "Why?"

"She . . ." Lifting one hand, she ran it over the bridge of her nose and drew in a deep, shaky breath. "That's between me and her. I shouldn't have—" Shoulders squaring off, she met my gaze and I could read the worry in her blue eyes. The blatant regret.

Join the party—there's more than enough room.

Clearing her throat, she muttered, "She turned off her phone. I've tried calling. I've been waiting here in case she . . . That doesn't matter. I'm rambling, and I doubt you give a shit."

If it had to do with Avery, I cared. More than I wanted to

admit, and honestly more than I liked. She'd wormed her way into my life, staking her claim and making me believe in shit I'd always assumed was a bunch of bull.

"Where would she go?" I couldn't quite hide the urgency in my voice, and the blonde noticed.

Her shoulders twitched and the smallest smile tipped up her lips. "Shit, you like her."

I wasn't having this conversation. Pushing off the doorframe, I made a solid effort to wipe any trace of kindness from my expression. "No bullshit," I bit out, "where would she go? If she's not here, what's the most likely place?"

Shifting her weight, Avery's roommate dropped her hands to her sides. "She left yesterday. I don't . . . I don't know where she slept, but she's resourceful. Probably the most resourceful person I've ever met."

A visual of Avery sleeping on the street hit me like a fist to the face, and it was a testament to my self-control that I didn't let loose the rage sweeping over me. My periphery blurred. Heart rate went into overtime.

I stepped back, half fearful that I'd react physically.

Do something I'd always regret.

As a teenager, I'd obsessed over studies—was human nature learned or genetic? Were the things that I did, the way I acted, a reflection of learned actions over time or something I'd inherited from my parents and their parents before them?

The way I looked at it, I was fucked either way.

I'd been taught to kill, taught to react with violence and anger. No one had ever shown me a kind hand, a loving touch.

But as I stared at the miserable-looking woman before me, I rejected both cases, learned and genetic.

Only opened my mouth and rasped, "I need one place you can think of—just one."

I'd go from there.

I'd tear this entire city apart until she either turned her damn phone back on or I found her—whichever came first.

The blonde wet her lips, like she was nervous to be standing near me. Then, "Flambeaux. The corner store over by St. Phillip. She's . . . she's friends with the owners."

It would have to be enough.

One curt nod later and I was taking the steps two at a time—but the roommate's voice stopped me just before I opened the door.

"Captain America," she called out, and I glanced up the stairwell. "When you find her, tell her that . . . tell her that I'm sorry. I overreacted and I just—it's not home without her here."

I had my own groveling to do, without adding someone else's into the mix.

"Sorry, Blondie, you're gonna have to tell her that yourself."

20

AVERY

I was too old to be sleeping on city streets.

Also too old to have, in the midst of fleeing the scene yesterday with Katie, made the critical error in forgetting my cell phone somewhere in the apartment.

Neither were particular highlights of the last twenty-four hours for me, but hey, what doesn't kill you makes you stronger. Right? Right.

I shoved my hand into the bag of cheddar popcorn and popped two kernels into my mouth, watching as two patrons meandered down the tiny aisles of Flambeaux. After almost a decade of having Pete pester me into working for him, I'd taken him up on the gig—temporarily—in return for letting me crash on his and Sal's couch.

Couches I could handle—streets weren't my thing anymore, and I'd never loved Pete more than when I'd come crashing into the corner store yesterday, holding back tears, and he'd told me to pull up my britches, dry my eyes, and get in his car before he threw me in, head first.

I was twenty-five and more than capable of finding new living accommodations, but there was something to be said about sticking with the familiar when you were bleeding from the heart.

"Y'all got any jambalaya mix in here?" called out one of the guys who'd wandered in a few minutes ago. "Told my wife I'd come back home with it."

I'd visited Flambeaux enough times to know where everything was located. "Aisle two! Next to the microwavable rice."

The bells jangled above the door with a newcomer. Hand shoved into my popcorn bag, I turned to welcome the person—and promptly dropped the snack on the floor as a muscular body leaned over the counter, hands wrapping around my biceps, and hauled me close.

Lincoln's lips crashed down on mine, domineering and possessive.

The other problem about being phone-less meant that I'd had no way to reach him, especially as I didn't even know where he lived. But, holy hell, he was here and there was *no* denying the tension that reverberated off his body.

His hands were tight on my arms, his kiss choppy but so damn hot, and I could almost taste his desperation as he devoured me. It was heady, addicting, and like a junkie of the first order, I swept my tongue along his lower lip, wanting more. Needing more.

With a rough groan, he broke away and stared at me, his familiar Haint-blue eyes flashing fire. "We're getting out of here. Now."

Beyond his right shoulder, I caught sight of Mr. Jambalaya eyeballing us, mouth gaping open. At my stare, he blushed and waved a hand. "Sorry," he muttered, "in a dry spell with the wife. I'll just, uh . . . find that jambalaya she wants so damn bad."

Before I could say another word, he'd hightailed it down

the aisle, and then Lincoln was lowering me back onto my feet, his muscles bunching under the fabric of his shirt as his arms unfurled.

I blinked up at him. "What are you doing here?"

His thumb came up to swipe over his bottom lip, like he was still absorbing the taste of me, and it was . . . I wanted him to do it again—preferably after he settled himself between my thighs.

"Your roommate told me I'd probably find you here."

My heart twisted at the thought of Katie, and I dropped my gaze to the register. "We had a . . ." A falling out? A breakup? It sure felt like a breakup. I squeezed my eyes shut. "She told me that Ambideaux saw us together, me and you. Outside the precinct. And then again outside the club when we'd—"

Lincoln let loose a rough curse, one hand coming up. "I'm going to need you to back up. He did what? And how the fuck does your roommate know Jason?"

"She didn't. She *doesn't*, not really, but he—"

"Five boxes of jambalaya, please."

I cut a sharp glance to the right, where Mr. Jambalaya himself was standing. He emptied his basket, tossing box after box of the pre-cooked New Orleans cultural dish onto the counter. My brows lifted, and he offered a casual shrug in return. "I'm praying that each box ends up with another round of sex with the wife."

"I . . ." Clearing my throat, I picked up the first box and ran it under the scanner. "You know, I really hope that works out for you."

"God, me too. You'd think she would want jewelry or some shit from here, but no, jambalaya was her only request. Honestly, it's weird, but if she sucks my—"

Lincoln growled, pulling himself up to his full height,

and Mr. Jambalaya immediately sucked in a sharp breath. "Damn, man," he whispered in awe, "you can do that on command? I'm not even into dudes but I'd bang you. Wait, hold on. You think you can do that again while I record it this time? Gonna send it to my wife and see if I can convince her it was me—"

It only took one step from Lincoln in the guy's direction to have Mr. Jambalaya shoving a twenty in my direction before nabbing his plastic bag off the counter.

He backed up, feet tripping over each other, and he headed for the door. "You two have a great day. Like, have awesome sex for me." His gaze flicked to Lincoln. "I want to be you when I grow up. Seriously, man-crush status over here."

Before Lincoln could make another move, the man was out the door and the flimsy door was clanging shut behind him.

"Fucking tourists," Lincoln grunted, and I held back a snort.

Bending down to grab my discarded popcorn bag off the floor, I tossed it in the trash can. "You've got a secret admirer."

"The only admiring I want to do is with you riding my cock and my gaze on your tits."

Heat erupted over my cheeks. "They're small."

Lincoln leaned in, hands on the counter. "They're perfect. Especially when they're in my mouth and you're moaning my name."

I hissed out a breath, and then sent a quick glance to the rest of the store. Empty, aside from one grandfather-looking fellow checking out the fridges housing the dairy options. He appeared completely in his own world as I returned my attention to the powerful man before me.

As much as I wanted to keep flirting, I couldn't quite disguise the worry in my voice when I said, "Not trying to get all Negative Nancy here, but why . . . why would Jason Ambideaux even care to follow me? Us? I mean, you—okay, I can see you, considering everything with Tabby and the others, but me?"

Expression sobering, the heat in his blue eyes cooled to a low simmer. "You're a way to get to me."

He said it so simply, so easily, and yet my mouth opened and fell shut in an embarrassing rhythm that was only broken up when I finally muttered, "He invited me to a party tonight. It's to announce a new mayoral candidate, and to be honest with you, I'm getting the feeling everyone in this city is trying to play the *whose-dick-is-bigger* contest and throw their hat into the ring." I paused, then belatedly tacked on, "They should probably be thankful that you're not entering."

Lincoln choked out a startled laugh. "My hammer would like to stay out of this narrative, thanks."

I grinned—it was big, and it was all teeth, and best of all, it was *real*. He did that to me, for me, and it was pure instinct alone that had me abruptly hooking a finger into the neck of his shirt and pulling him down for another kiss.

He let me, moving freely under my command, and that led to a rush I didn't expect. My hand left his shirt, skirting up to cup his cheek, and then *I* was the one who angled his face for a better fit. Lips brushing, tongues tangling.

I wanted to alternatively climb his body and force him to submit to me, just as much as I wanted to beg him to bend me over and take me from behind.

And, as much as I was loath to admit it, I almost wished that I wasn't on the outs with Nat, just so we could revisit the Basement again and experience more of the rooms.

Dropping back onto my heels, I broke off the kiss and pulled one of his moves—thumb brushing my lip, eyes lifting to meet his gaze.

He looked ready to jump the counter and fuck me right here, right now.

"We need to get out of here," he rasped.

"Because we need to talk about Ambideaux?"

Haint-blue eyes glittered. "Because I need to sink into your body, sweetheart. Because I'm fucking dying, and if I thought I could get away with taking you right now, I'd do it. No questions asked."

I eyed the elderly man again speculatively. "Not going to lie, I'm tempted."

"You're supposed to be the voice of reason."

I swung my gaze back to Lincoln. "When have I ever been the voice of reason?" Lowering my voice, I taunted, "When I let you put your hand down my pants on a not-so-private street? Or maybe it was when you went down on me in front of just about everyone and their mother in a sex club?"

His chest heaved with an inhale. "We're leaving."

I gestured to the store. "Can't go until Pete comes back."

There was a very good chance this was the first time I was seeing him close to coming undone. Stoic Lincoln, hard-ass Lincoln, dangerous Lincoln, reached down to subtly adjust himself. "How long?" he demanded roughly.

"How long until what?"

"Until Pete comes back."

I rocked onto my heels, thrusting my chest out, and peered at the digital clock on the wall. "Another hour."

"Another—" He broke off with a curse, hands going to the counter like he needed physical support.

I didn't know what possessed me to do it, but I patted his

chest—like he wasn't the most feared man in the city—and drawled, "Must be karma."

Blue eyes narrowed on me. "Karma for *what*?"

I shrugged. "Tossing my taser into the Mississippi? Stealing my underwear? Or how about—"

"Who's your friend, Avery?"

Pete.

I turned to the man who'd been a friend to me since I was a teenager, and although it wasn't at *all* like introducing a man to my father, nervous butterflies erupted in my stomach anyway.

Swallowing nervously, I made the introductions as quickly as possible. Awkward, so awkward, especially since my core was still throbbing for Lincoln.

Lincoln, who ditched his badass persona long enough to exchange a word or two with Pete about the Saints and the NFL draft.

Lincoln, who grinned just slightly when he asked if he could steal me away early.

Lincoln, who ushered me out of Flambeaux five minutes later, gently nudged me into the driver's seat, and then climbed in behind the wheel.

We weren't even two minutes into our drive to Destination Unknown before he turned down the volume of the car radio and husked out, "Drop your panties, Avery. Karma is making me so hard that I can't even see straight, and I'm in the mood to return the favor."

21

AVERY

Startled, I twisted my head to stare at Lincoln.

Mouth feeling parched, I croaked, "What?"

Fingers white-knuckling the steering wheel, he slid a quick glance over to me. "Underwear, sweetheart. Lose 'em."

Lose them? I laughed shortly. "Excuse me a moment while I have a flashback to me dropping ten feet from a fire escape stairwell while being *completely* bare below the waist."

"You enjoyed every moment that came before that."

"Yeah, *before* it." I watched the buildings pass us by as we left the French Quarter. "I can't say that I enjoyed everything that came after, especially the whole being-held-at-gunpoint bit."

"That shit isn't happening again." He flashed me a dark, serious look. "I promise. None of them are going to touch you. Not again, not while I'm here."

I thought of what Katie had said about Jason Ambideaux . . . about him watching us. A shiver of trepidation slid down my spine. It was one thing for Lincoln and me to hook up at Stage One, when we'd willingly participated in everything that was happening.

It was something else entirely to know that Ambideaux had followed us, watched us, and had gone so far as to even approach Katie about me after no doubt seeing us talk while she'd tended the bar.

That sick feeling returned, pushing aside the lust, the need, to settle like lead in my stomach. And that—that made me angry. That I could so easily let someone else taint my experiences with Lincoln that I hoarded like shards of treasure.

Sex with Lincoln was like piecing together fragments of my broken soul.

Without giving myself the chance to rethink my decision, my fingers went to the button of my jeans. I flicked it open.

The zipper coming unhinged was what caught his attention—his nostrils flared at once, his cheeks hollowing out.

It was the right side of his face that was presented to me, and it seemed almost fitting that he gave me his worst, unflinching under my perusal, and I barely noticed his scars. They were there but they weren't my sole focus. No, I just wanted him. Any way that I could have him.

I shimmied my jeans down to my knees, butt lifted off the seat, underwear going with the denim.

Lincoln hit the brakes a little too hard, and the car behind us let loose three consecutive beeps.

"Distracted?" I teased in a low murmur, drawing my finger up the length of my inner thigh just to play the seductress and make him sweat. Watching him lose control was hands-down my favorite part of sex with him. Besides the orgasms, of course. "I wonder . . . can you drive when you're focused on me?"

"Hands on the back of your seat."

I blinked. Then blinked again. "What?"

"Karma." Slowing to a stop at a traffic light, he took the extra second to look my way. "I get to tell you a little story—and you get to wait until I let you touch yourself."

"That seems like a bullshit deal."

"You'll like it."

Doubtful. But even as the thought crossed my mind, I couldn't help but think I was lying once again—this time to myself. There hadn't been a single thing Lincoln had done so far that I hadn't enjoyed.

And it was for that reason alone that my hands slowly lifted to the seat, as he'd said, and wrapped around the back of the headrest. Nails digging in, I glanced down—my legs were as wide as they could be with my jeans still hiked around my knees. It was a heady sensation, knowing that each time he dragged in another breath, it was on account of the fact that I was half-naked and driving him crazy.

"How long are you going to make me wait?" My arms flexed in the position, fingers re-clasping the seat. "Until we get wherever we're going?"

"If it came down to me circling the block ten times just so I could get you off first, I'd do it."

"I knew you were a gentleman under all that . . . bad-assery."

He shifted in his seat, his gaze momentarily landing on my legs with enough heat that I was surprised my skin didn't singe. "I'm no gentleman, sweetheart. Never have been, never—"

"Will be," I finished for him with a wink he didn't catch. "Let's stop ahead of the clichés, what do you think? I'm pretty much naked, the AC is cranked a little too high and I can tell *down there*, and I'm waiting to be wowed by whatever you have up your sleeve."

That brought out a startled laugh from him. "I think I liked you more when you were a virgin."

"I can't say that I feel the same."

"Fuck," he worked out after another bark of laughter, "you were made for me. I didn't laugh until you. Didn't see a glimmer of light within all the darkness." One big hand lifted from the steering wheel to run over the scruff along the bottom half of his jaw like he was embarrassed. "And now you've got me spilling my soul like I'm some sort of poet."

I couldn't deny it—*cliché* or not, my heart fluttered at the awkward way he continued to glance over at me before quickly fixing his attention on the road again. Smiling, I offered up, "I don't mind poetry. Are you any good with haikus?"

Adam's apple bobbing as he swallowed, Lincoln directed the car off the main throughway and onto a side street with a row of townhouses that were all identical. Painted brightly hued colors like they were straight from the Caribbean, each one was complete with a small area of grass out front and a narrow driveway.

Neat.

Orderly.

Cute.

For whatever reason, I'd pictured Lincoln living on the cusp of the bayou where wilderness thrived and the only thing more untamed than the man who owned the land were the feral animals that prowled the swamp.

"Change of plans," he said as he pulled up into one of the driveways in front of a teal house, "we're taking this inside."

My hands unclenched from the headrest, biceps sore from holding the position. "The disappointment is real, Sergeant. Here I am willing and waiting, bare to the world, and—"

The rest of my sentence ended in a gasp.

His big body invaded my space, seat creaking under his weight as he leaned over the center console, his warm hand between my legs. His thumb flirted with where I wanted him most, hovering just above ground zero. Palm squeezing my inner thigh, his lips grazed my ear. "Playtime's over, Ave. You like to be pushed to the edge. You like it when I'm rough. So, let's put it this way—pull up your jeans and go inside. I can promise you that the only disappointment you're about to feel is when you've come too many times and your body is too tired to go for another round."

Lips parted, I met his gaze as he pulled away.

Then I confessed: "I liked what we did at the Basement."

Thumb cresting over my clit, making me twitch with want, he lifted his hand and cupped my jaw, that same thumb brushing over my bottom lip. "I know you did."

"Is it wrong that I'm annoyed that we can't go back?" Even the pad of his thumb was calloused, and it was such a contradiction between the gentle way he touched me and the innate roughness that was so very much *him.* Giving in to pure lust, I licked the tip of his thumb just because I could. "Not unless we're keen to find ourselves jumping from a fire escape again, obviously."

His blue eyes darkened. "We don't need the Basement for you to feel like you're pushed to the edge. All you need is me."

He said it so casually, so easily, and as he twisted his body to climb out of the SUV, I scrambled to pull up my pants. Didn't even bother to slip the brass button through its hole.

I was out of the car in seconds, slamming the door shut behind me, lengthening my stride to the front door to cut the distance. Logically, I understood that I needed to be talking to him about Ambideaux's invitation—about the ultimatum Nat herself had given me—but Lincoln never failed to make me lose sight of everything but him.

And as he'd put it, if I wanted something, then I needed to take it.

I chose to take him, putting everything else on the back-burner, even if only for a few hours.

He keyed open the door. Pushed it wide. Ushered me inside with a hand to the small of my back. Quickly, I skimmed the space: a living room that opened to what had to be the kitchen through a doorway.

Lincoln's hand slid from the base of my spine up to the space between my shoulder blades. "Go sit on the couch."

He didn't have to tell me twice.

I swept forward, stepping around a small side table, and took a seat in the center of the sectional. Immediately I reached down to kick off my shoes, tossing them off to the right as Lincoln lowered himself to the single chair opposite the wraparound.

"I feel like you're a little far away." I motioned to the space between us, then tacked on, "You're big, Sergeant, but not *that* big."

His mouth twitched at my innuendo, but he otherwise didn't outwardly react.

Instead, he settled in to his seat, legs spread wide in that masculine way that seemed to be part of a guy's genetic makeup. His forearms landed on the armrests, like he was seated on a throne.

"The Basement caters to everyone," he murmured. "No matter what kink you've got, they'll take real good care of you. It's the reason they've got a waitlist a mile long."

I swallowed, hard. "You got a kink I should know about, Sergeant?"

He smiled, just a little. "I like to be in control."

"Right." I bobbed my head in a nod. "I was thinking more along the lines of . . . like whips or chains or something."

"Is that what you want? To be whipped?"

I rolled the image over in my head. Discarded it on second thought. "No. I'm sure it's . . . fun. But I just—"

"It's not for you."

"No."

"I spent a good amount of time at the Basement, back when I was too young to do anything more than sit and watch." He reached down, grasped the hem of his shirt, and pulled it up and over his head. It was the first time I'd had the opportunity to see his upper body in broad daylight, and it was . . .

Brutally savage.

Both the power that existed in his heavily corded muscles and the tattoos that were inked in his skin.

No, I thought as I stared at him, *he was beautiful.*

With his scars and his tattoos, he looked like a man who'd been through hell and come out the other side. And when he spoke, his voice a rough timbre, everything in me strung tight with desire.

"Kinks often reflect what a person has suffered in their past life. A man who has never had the opportunity to speak his truth, for example, might find that he likes to wear something during sex that limits his vocals."

Like Zak Benson.

I opened my mouth, prepared to mention that exactly, but Lincoln rolled on, his gaze impossibly astute. "I'd say that goes for you, too."

"What?"

"My hand around your neck, sweetheart. Years of keeping your secrets and never telling a soul." He rose, then. Came around the backside of the sectional until he was there, behind me, his arms wrapping like bands around my middle as he bent over the back of the couch. "You have no fucking idea how wet you get the second my fingers touch you here."

The pads of his fingertips brushed the underside of my jaw.

My core tightened, and I hated that I was so damn transparent.

"Not everything is about whips or chains," he husked, those fingers of his coursing down, over my chest, down past my belly, until they were resting on the waistband of my jeans. My breath caught when he silently encouraged me to strip off the denim.

They were gone in a heartbeat. Kicked off to the side.

And his hand was pushing me gently forward, until I was seated on the very edge of the seat cushion.

I twisted my head to look back at him. "Lincoln?"

My eyes went wide as I realized he'd shucked his pants, too. He was fully erect, fully naked, and I was fully in lust. Limber like an athlete, he jumped the back of the couch and dropped into the space behind me.

Reached forward to clasp me at the hips and pull me back into him.

Oh, God.

Despite the thin fabric of my shirt, I could feel his cock like a brand against my back. Could feel the heat radiating from his skin as his arms wound around me, keeping me in close.

I was surrounded by him.

His heat.

His power.

He grazed my earlobe with his tongue, sending shivers firing down my limbs.

"Should we see how wet you are?" he teased.

"*Yes.*"

Chuckling, he pressed a kiss to my shoulder. "Go ahead."

I swallowed, hard. "What?"

"Take what you want, Avery." Clasping my hand in his, he set it on my inner thigh. "I'll give you what you want . . . but I want to watch you first."

Oh, God.

My heart thudded in my chest, so hard that I was surprised we didn't hear it. It was one thing to touch myself at the Basement, when I wasn't alone in doing so. Another thing entirely to do it on my own.

Butterflies fluttered to life in my belly. I flexed my hand under his, then brought it to the apex of my thighs.

"Brave girl." His hot breath rustled my hair and I felt him harden even more against my back.

I wanted to be that brave girl, the way I was in everything else in life, but never here. Never with a man. Letting my head fall back onto the hard planes of his chest, I stared down at my hand as if it was someone else's but not my own.

Those fingers curled, the middle seeking my clit. It was swollen to the touch—and I was on edge. The slight brush of my finger sent my toes digging into the carpet and my free hand went to Lincoln's thigh, where my nails carved half-moons into his flesh.

"Fuck, yes," he growled behind me.

The clear-cut lust in his voice powered me on. I dipped my finger, sliding it along my slit, tracing my entrance. My core tightened, and I brought my thumb up to circle my clit as I teased my pussy.

There was something heady about playing for him this way, like I owned his pleasure, dictated its ebbs and flows. Lincoln Asher was a man who enjoyed being in control—but what happened when he lost it?

A grin flickered along my lips, and I tossed my head back in retaliation. I'd give him what he wanted, but it'd be on my terms. Not his.

"Oh, my God," I moaned, slipping a finger inside, curling it just right so that when I cried out, it was all too real. Putting on a show for Lincoln just might be the best sort of performance I'd ever attended—literally.

Releasing his leg, I skimmed my palm up my belly to my left breast. Tweaked the nipple over my shirt. Fingers thrusting down below, I hiked up my left leg and laid it over his, spreading myself wide.

"Christ," he grunted, his hands landing on my hips. "Don't stop."

I didn't.

Pulling my fingers from my pussy, I spread that wetness over my swollen clit. Rubbed in incessant little circles until my vision blurred and I was gasping for relief. Relief that Lincoln was determined to hold off, as though punishing himself just as much as he was punishing me.

He shifted me forward, his hard-on slipping between my ass cheeks.

It was a shock, the girth of him, the heat of his cock there.

All words fled my brain. My hand left my pussy to land on his knee. Using him as leverage, I lifted and fell, needing the pressure of his cock even though he wasn't inside me.

I wanted him to lose control, and I wouldn't stop until he did.

Turning around, I straddled his hips and sank my weight down on his body. Wrapped a hand behind me as I circled my fingers around his erection and rubbed the crown along my slit. Up I went, grazing his cock with nothing but the tantalizing hint of what was to come. Down I came, the crown teasing *me*, rubbing up against my clit and making my legs twitch.

It was seduction in its finest form, and Lincoln's blue eyes were wild.

His chest rose and fell with short breaths, and his fingers curled into the cheeks of my ass. "Holy fuck," he grunted harshly, "I need a condom. Avery, I need—"

I leaned in with a short kiss to his mouth. And then I said, "I think you can suffer a little longer, Sergeant."

If his gaze had been wild before, it was not even close to now.

He launched off the couch, me in his arms, bridal-style.

"I'm calling the shots on this one." His nostrils flared as he kicked open what had to be his bedroom door before dropping me on the bed. "I'm in charge."

My fingers dipped back between my legs again after I stripped off my shirt, and sure enough, his blue eyes tracked the path of my hand like a starved man. "No," I said, "I think it's safe to say that *I* am."

His big body stilled like he was cataloguing what I'd said.

And then he moved into action, and I didn't stand a chance.

My ass was in the air, my hands pinned to my sides, my face planted into the sheets. I heard the crinkle of foil and then a drawer slamming shut so hard that I was pretty sure he'd knocked over the bedside table.

The blunt head of his cock aligned with my entrance.

"You'll come when I let you come." His palm smoothed out over my lower back, keeping me in position. "Do you understand? If I want to hold off your orgasm until you're crying you're so desperate for relief, I will."

I turned my head, nose rustling with the cotton, and taunted, "Sounds like you might have to prove you're not a five-minute man."

His hand came down on my right cheek. It was pleasure and pain, all mixed into one, and my skin felt aflame as he pulled back and did it again. I bit back a cry, clamping down on my bottom teeth, as I fisted the sheets and held myself back from begging for more.

I wanted Lincoln as everything that he was: rough, wild, dominating.

I shoved my butt back against him, silently daring him to do his worst.

He thrust inside me a moment later, and I knew then that he hadn't given me his worst, but only his best. And he backed my theory up when he pulled out and buried himself to the hilt.

Oh.

My.

God.

I muffled my cry in the sheets, unable to stop myself from thrusting backward to meet him. I craved him like no other. Wanted him like no other. And then he was dragging his hand down my back, making me arch my spine like a cat lazing in the sun. His palm slid over one cheek and I prepared myself for the sting, for the want, for the way my core squeezed in excitement and anticipation and desire.

His hand never connected with my ass, not the way I'd expected it to. Instead, he spread my cheeks wide, and—

I swallowed. Fisted the sheets.

His thumb circled the puckered rim of my ass, and I didn't know whether to beg for more or run in the opposite direction.

But his cock kept hitting me at just the right spot and the pressure—oh, God, the pressure—of his thumb felt insanely good. He circled there, just like he'd do to my clit, and I moaned so loud I was sure they'd hear it in the townhouse one over.

"Your pussy is mine," Lincoln growled, "your ass is mine."

I cried out at the alternating pressures of his surging cock and the soft brush of his thumb. Struggled to gather my breath when I edged out, "You're at three minutes, Sergeant. A-almost there."

I was almost there.

I was spiraling in an abyss I'd never known existed, addicted to the feel of him dominating my body like he truly owned my pleasure. Dictated it, just like he ordered about all the cops in his unit.

Pleasure swept over me, my hair falling across my face, my sensitive breasts rubbing up against the sheets.

The pressure grew, his strokes more insistent, his thumb dipping down so that I felt him along my slit as his cock continued to power into me. And then the pressure at my ass was there again, heavier.

I couldn't breathe. Couldn't think.

Lincoln reached around, his free hand going to my clit, circling with two of his fingers. Stringing me so tight that I felt him everywhere, heard his deep groans and the way he said my name like I'd been made for him.

Like he'd been made for me.

Another circle of his fingers at my clit, another thrust of his hips, and I came, shaking so hard that there was nothing I could do but enjoy the ride. My lids slammed shut, and I felt Lincoln tumble along after me, his pace quickening, his hands on my hips as he fucked me.

He came, groaning my name, tucking me under him as we accidentally rolled off the bed and onto the floor. I tossed my head back with a laugh, the base of my skull connecting with the side of the mattress.

Lincoln chuckled, his blue eyes on me. "Wasn't quite the grand finale I was hoping for."

Shamelessly, I looked down at his cock. "All I need to know is . . . if my pussy belongs to you and my ass belongs to you, do I get to own *that*?"

As though aware that he was up for discussion, Lincoln's dick twitched. "All yours, sweetheart. He's all yours."

Stealing a big breath into my lungs, I watched him climb onto his knees and then move toward the small waste bin in the corner of the room.

"We made a mess." I lazily kicked the drawers that had tipped out of the bedside table. "A total mess." There was a deck of playing cards on the floor, a strip of condom packets, a bottle of Advil, and . . .

My heart stopped.

Shifting onto my knees, I leaned forward, my fingers grasping the bracelet that was jumbled in with the rest of everything else. I knew this bracelet. It'd belonged to me—

once. Back before Momma died and I ran from the house. Back when I'd been happy.

"Lincoln." My voice was raspy, and I cleared it. Ignored the ringing in my ears and tried again. "Lincoln, where did you get this?"

22

LINCOLN

"Lincoln, where did you get this?"

I was fucked, didn't matter which way I looked at it.

Lies tangled in my throat, each demanding their own chance to smooth over the situation and put everything back to rights.

Rights would be Avery and I in bed together, her tucked up against my side while I skimmed my hand up and down her frame and memorized every dip and curve.

Christ, I needed pants for this conversation.

With my dick still half hard, I scoured my bedroom floor for a stray pair—then moved swiftly toward my dressers and yanked the second drawer open. I threw a T-shirt back for Avery, then drew on a pair of sweatpants up my legs.

It'd have to do.

"Lincoln," Avery said, her naturally throaty pitch elevating enough for me to know that she was trying to hold it together. That space in my chest—which I'd always assumed was empty and dead—gave a pitiful jump at the sound. "Where did you get that bracelet? Don't lie. Please don't lie."

I wouldn't lie.

But she wouldn't like the truth either.

Hands on my hips, I faced her. Felt the strained look in her expression like a punch to the gut. If I were anyone but me, that look on her face would have brought me to my knees. They wavered now anyway when I stared into her hazel eyes and gave myself away: "From your family's tomb."

The words were like a sledgehammer to her knees.

They gave out without warning, and her ass hit the mattress a moment later. She didn't pull the shirt on over her head—didn't do anything but sit there, her chest rising and falling rhythmically, her bare toes curling into the carpet flooring like she was seconds away from bolting out of this room.

She was naked, exposed.

And, this time, I was the one responsible for the devastation that lined her features.

"I-I don't understand," she whispered hoarsely, the T-shirt tangling between her fingers as she fisted her hands in her lap. "Did you go there recently? After you found out who I was? Who I am?"

In ten seconds, maybe less, she would hate me.

I experienced my own slice of devastation, then. My fist came up to rub at my chest, directly over my heart where her number was tattooed. I wished . . . fuck, but I wished we'd been other people than who we were. That I'd met her at a restaurant or on a blind date or *anywhere* else but our true reality.

At the end of the day, though, *this* was our reality.

"I went there a week after they put your body to rest."

Her pretty hazel eyes went wide, the color draining from her face. "No."

It was all she said, and that dug the knife of guilt more deeply into my chest than if she'd asked me to repeat myself.

I was so sorry, so damn sorry, and seeing her gutted expression stripped my emotions raw. I was dangling, hanging from a precipice where I went from a man she thought she could trust to the enemy.

Now she knows what the rest of this city does about me.

I'd never been a good man. Never been a hero. I lived in the darkness and relied on violence to get my point across.

And I'd never hated myself more.

Knowing it would only make the situation worse, I tried to explain. My tongue felt swollen, though, and when I spoke, it was a jumbled, chaotic mess of shit. "The kid—the *teenager*—that Ambideaux ordered me to kill . . . there's no good way for me to say this. I wish there was. I wish I was somebody else, and not the man who—"

"No."

She launched from the bed, slipping my shirt over her head as she moved around me.

I couldn't let her go. Call me an asshole, a bastard like my father, but I couldn't let her leave. Before I even realized that I'd done it, my hand was locked around her arm, dragging her back. Keeping her from fleeing, from leaving *me.*

Please don't leave me.

Desperate. Pathetic. But to a man like me—a man who'd lived without light so long—I wasn't willing to let this relationship go down in a ball of flames without trying to fix it.

"Avery, please—"

She stared down at my arm like it was the source of the next Bubonic plague. Her lips pulled back, nostrils flaring, and then she yanked away sharply. Stepped out of my reach. "You weren't the man who killed my momma. I know that you weren't . . . your voices aren't the same."

"No. I have no idea who that was, but I can guarantee it wasn't me." Not wanting to frighten her off, I took a single step in her direction. My hands came up like she was a terrified colt. "The guilt ate me alive for years," I muttered, "that I'd sunk so low in my own life that I considered, even for a second, taking—"

"For taking my life?" Avery shook her head with a bitter laugh. "Is this where I thank you for not putting a bullet through my head?" Her hands landed on my chest and pushed to no avail.

I'd take whatever punishment she doled out.

It was my penance. My atonement.

My hands wrapped around her wrists, my thumbs pausing over her pulse. "You were a mark, a way for Jason to strike back at Foley. The same mark that, not just a few days ago, you comforted me over." I jerked her in, getting my face close to hers. "I know it feels different switching out the unknown kid for being *you*, but I didn't know who you were. Or why Jason had a hard-on for your stepdad. *I didn't know.*"

Her lip curled. "Then what *did* you know?"

This was not the way I'd planned to tell her about Foley and the case, but if I didn't come clean from start to finish, there'd never be another opportunity. Squeezing my eyes shut, I exhaled through my nose and sought the calm that was quickly eluding me.

"Foley likes teenage girls." The words sounded so clinical, too hard, and I tried again. "Jason . . . he was pissed off at Foley. He's hated him for *years*, and I suspect he knew that if you were killed, that would send Jay in a tailspin he'd never recover from. I could be wrong—it's speculation on my part, pieced together from information I've gathered over the last few years. Rumors I've heard." *Stories I've been told.*

Avery stared at me, her eyes glassy and unfocused. "He was obsessed with my mom."

"Maybe it was a front—"

"No!" Her throat worked with a rough swallow. "You don't understand—he was *obsessed* with her. Cooking her breakfast daily. Always coming home with these little chocolates that she could eat by the box. There wasn't anything he wouldn't do for her. Until he had her murdered."

Fuck, I hated seeing the pain in her eyes. I wanted to wrap her up in my arms, but it wasn't the right time. *If it will ever be the right time again.*

"Avery, I'm telling you—I've been in the trenches, trying to bring this thing to light over the last few years. Trying to get him locked behind bars for the shit he's done to these girls. None of them will come forward to testify. None of them will say *shit*, but they all have admitted to sleeping with Foley. Every single one."

"How old?"

My heart slammed against the cage of my chest, like I'd been in a car going from eighty to ten in under thirty seconds. "What?"

"How old were they? These girls you've talked to?" She didn't mention the case or the testifying, and I had a feeling she was trying to prioritize all the information I was spewing out like a broken sieve.

She was the strongest person I knew, and it gutted me to think that life experiences had molded her this way. That she could compartmentalize her own emotions in order to focus on the conversation at hand.

I'd called her brave before, but it was pretty obvious that "brave" was a gross understatement.

Releasing her, I shoved my fingers through my hair. "All ages. The youngest was sixteen. Two, rather. Two of them were sixteen."

Avery seemed to be working through something in her head—mouth moving, though no words emerged, and she pushed past me to head for the living room. I trailed her, trying to work the fuck out where her brain was going.

I was a cop and even I was lost.

"Looks?" she asked as she shoved one foot in her jeans, then did the same with the other. "What did they all look like?"

"Young. Young—I don't know, Avery. Where the hell are you going with this?"

Hands on the button of her jeans, she turned to me again. "Did they look like me?"

Since none of the girls had been willing to go on record or even come forward at all, my database with their information was slim. Practically nonexistent. I'd been running on fumes for years now, trying to make something of a case that no one wanted to bring to court but me.

But I was a man obsessed with redemption. Vengeance. It drove me every day, was the force that woke me up at morning, and was the reason I hardly slept.

"They didn't have dark hair like you," I said, "hell, I don't know. Maybe a few did, but it was clearly dyed. Heights were all over the place, no sort of similarity there. Eyes . . . I don't fucking remember."

"He used to fuck Nat," she said in an almost off-hand kind of way, "and call her 'Catherine' as he did so. She's not blond, but a man like that . . . a man like Jay doesn't kill his wife for no reason or sleep with girls because he can." She shook her head, then moved to shove her feet into her shoes. “No, a man like that screws anyone he can, and pretends that they’re all his dear wife.”

“Whom he *killed*.”

“Sometimes good people do bad things.” With a raised brow, she bit off, “I mean, I technically agreed to kill *you*, but I don’t think I’m a bad person.”

23

AVERY

The minute the words were out, and I registered Lincoln's look of betrayal, I wished I could stuff them back into my mouth.

Yes, he'd once been sent to kill me, but that was ages ago. I'd accepted Nat's offer just last week.

It didn't quite matter that I never planned to follow through, that I'd only entertained the idea for so brief a period that it barely counted. Because somewhere along the way . . . Lincoln had stolen my heart.

I didn't know anything about love—had gone years without even a glimpse of it.

Momma, once, had lulled me to bed with talk of the language of love. I remembered little of what words she used or the stories she spun, but I'd never been able to forget the warmth that radiated from her voice as she murmured in my ear and tickled my sides to pull giggles from my six-year-old frame.

The minute I'd heard the gunshot that had stolen her from me, that warmth and joy was replaced with fear, isolation, vengeance.

Until Lincoln had strolled into my life, my version of the language of love had encompassed dark streets and even darker secrets. Then he'd touched me, and I'd come alive, gasping, wanting, my skin ablaze with heat and my chest rumbling with laughter.

And maybe it was just that the stupid organ in my chest was so desperate for affection that I was making more out of my emotions than I should.

"Lincoln," I whispered, hating the tumultuous way he watched me, like he was torn between reacting out of his basic instincts and killing me before I struck first or crumbling right there before me. "I'm telling you right now that I had no plans to—"

"Who," he ground out, blue eyes locked on my face with an intensity that was almost unholy. "And don't lie, Avery. Who the fuck put you up to it?"

From the first time we'd met, I'd never completely feared Lincoln.

I'd been wary. I'd been suspicious of his attention.

Fear had never entered the equation—until now.

Rage radiated from him, making the whites of his eyes brighter, his muscles stiffer, which in turn only made him look that much bigger. More imposing.

With my fingers tangling in his shirt, which hung down to my thighs, I stepped back in trepidation. "Does it matter?" I asked, not because I wanted to protect Nat, by any means, but because I hadn't gone through with it.

Just like he didn't go through with killing you.

We were two pieces to a puzzle built long before we'd ever entered the equation.

"Was it Nat?" he demanded. "Hampton?"

"Let them implode."

Haint-blue eyes turned in my direction, and I despised

the inner struggle that I saw there. My heart twisted at the sight of his pain, his hatred, which so mirrored my own.

"Let them both implode," I said again, voice gathering strength. "I pulled a card for you, that first day we met. The present you didn't want to know. It was Cruelty, Lincoln." Squaring my shoulders, I approached him with caution. "Cruelty is a mind game. It's driving yourself into the ground, never allowing yourself to move forward. You're stuck in the same cycle. *I'm* stuck in the same cycle."

Chest hitching, he cut eye contact. "The cards mean shit. This is real life, Avery. And, in real life, you don't sit around waiting to be picked off while your guard is down. That's not the way this works."

"So, what are you going to do? Just *waltz* into their homes and kill them all?" I'd be the first to admit that I'd spent years wanting just the same, but from the look on Lincoln's face . . . it wasn't nearly the same thing.

He was spiraling. Retreating back to the violence that had been ingrained in him since childhood. And it seemed like a strike of fate that I realized . . . I couldn't do the same. I wanted the love my momma had whispered to me about so fervently. I wanted to live, my conscience clear, knowing that I had taken the high road to my redemption. Through the courts, the way I should have done so long ago if I hadn't been so fearful of my own shadow.

Be brave.

Be bold.

My momma had guided me for years now, and I'd never listened over the furious pounding of hatred that seethed like poison in my veins.

I had to listen to that guidance now.

"I'll testify." Jaw clenching, I swallowed my fear and stepped in front of Lincoln, so that he had no choice but to look down at me. "Whatever you need to lock Jay up for what he did, I'll testify. He never touched me, but he killed my momma, and he can rot in hell for that."

Heart catching in my throat, I gently touched Lincoln's chest. Over his heart. Over the numbers and dates that reflected a life of horror and death. Somewhere in all that ink, I had a sneaking suspicion that he'd marked my death with a number, too.

"Tell me what you'll need me to do," came my whisper, "tell me, and I'll do it."

Hard blue eyes dropped to my fingertips on the even harder planes of his chest. And I knew it—I knew it before he even spoke—that this wasn't my Lincoln, the man who brought me to orgasm and protected me from anyone who dared to pose a threat to my safety.

"*Lincoln,* c'mon. Don't be impulsive. Think clearly. I lo—"

He spun away, leaving my hand to suspend in mid-air, forever grasping a ghost.

My momma.

My identity.

Him, a man who stood before me, though the ghosts of his pasts were drowning him still.

"I need you to stay here."

My jaw dropped. "Are you serious? You're not going to just *leave* me here while you go do all of—"

"You're a liability." Without waiting to see if I'd follow, he strode down the hallway. Ducked into his bedroom.

I followed like a lemming, ducking into the bedroom a heartbeat after him. "How the hell am *I* a liability?"

He stripped off his sweats. Naked as the day he was born, he yanked open his closet and began pulling out dark clothes. Pants. Long-sleeved shirt. Boots. One by one, he pulled them on—but not before arming himself. His trench knife, his two guns.

A walking armory, always and forever.

My gaze flicked to the rumpled sheets, and then fury displaced all else as I snapped, "I'm not a liability, Sergeant. I can take care of myself. I'm not—"

"You're a liability to *me*." The words shattered the otherwise silent bedroom like a crack of thunder. "I can't think straight when you're near me. If it came down to making a move against Jay or protecting you, I'd choose you. Every. Single. Time."

"Then why—"

His mouth came crashing down on mine, stealing my fury and giving me his own in return. The kiss was brutal, unromantic, a stake of claim and possession—but who was claiming who . . . I didn't know, not anymore.

Tearing away, his blue eyes flashed with heat. "I don't deserve you, Avery. You're . . . you're light where I'm dark." He shook his head, a wry laugh escaping his lips. "I picked the Dominion card for you, and I'm going to make that happen."

"And what about you?" I worked out, an edge to my voice.

"You picked Death for me, remember?" He gently nudged me to the side, stepping out of the room. "Stay here." One glance over his shoulder revealed a touch of sadistic humor in his gaze. "I once asked if you knew how to obey—here's your chance to prove that you can follow an order."

The slamming of the front door coincided with me picking my jaw off the floor from his high-handed arrogance.

And even though he was gone, and the house was

empty, my soul fractured anyway, belting out my anger in a way that I'd always kept locked inside before.

"I lied!" I shouted to no one. "I *lied*!"

Death was meant to be his new beginning, *not* a suicide mission that landed him in a tomb with me grieving yet another person I'd loved being taken from me too soon.

The man thought he was invincible.

He wasn't.

Would never be.

But I'd be damned if I let anything happen to him.

Be brave.

Be bold.

There wasn't any other choice.

24

LINCOLN

Anger had long been my biggest motivator.

It ruled my heart. It sabotaged my hopes for something more than the life I lived. It wrapped its claws around my ankles and dragged me back into the flames whenever something good entered my world.

Avery was that slice of good—and like all those who'd come before her, she'd been forced to make the decision between taking me out or letting me live.

Unlike the others, she'd given me life.

But that was the thing about anger. It was hard to shake. Harder to ignore. And as I flung open the door to Whiskey Bay, anger was the sole force driving me forward.

"Asher?" said a familiar voice to my left. "Man, I'm gonna be honest, you're persona non grata over here right now. Nat's not going to want to see your face, so I'd get the fuck out—"

Kevan's sentence died when my hand wrapped around his throat.

Our eyes met.

Fear swirled in his, and his hands came up to grasp at

my hand, desperation making each move sloppy. Blunt nails scratched my flesh. His mouth popped open, and I heard his ragged gasp. Noted the reddening in his cheeks as I kept him suspended an inch off the ground.

My grip never slackened.

"You're going to let me upstairs." Quiet, lethal, my voice barely reached a pitch high enough to draw attention to us. The Birkenstock crowd was too concerned about the women dancing to even glance in our direction. *Perfect.* Jerking Kevan close, our noses almost brushed. "You tell Nat that I'm here and I'll finish what I started." My gaze dropped to my hand encircling his throat in a clear threat. "Don't fuck me over, Kev. It never ends well."

Lips purpling, his tongue darted out to wet the bottom one. "P-please—"

"It's a yes or a no. You let me upstairs and tell her nothing. That's the way this shit is going to play out."

His head bobbed, fingers scrambling for purchase, and I dropped him a breath later.

Legs quivering, his hands went to his knees as he dragged in air. "W-what the fuck is *wrong* with you?"

In a rare moment when Nat hadn't explicitly showed her hatred for me, she'd once ruffled my hair and teased, "Lincoln, our resident killer."

That'd been before I'd murdered her brother on Ambideaux's command.

Before she and Jason had separated and then divorced.

Before she'd requested Avery handle the honors and end my life.

For twenty-seven years she'd been at my throat, waiting for any opportunity to throw me under the bus and watch me suffer. I was done playing by the rules. Done letting her have the upper hand because she didn't have a penis and should be left alone.

I wouldn't kill her—she wasn't worthy of being taken out quickly—but I'd make her life hell.

I turned my gaze on Kevan, who'd always been Nat's part-time fuckbuddy when she wasn't busy screwing dignitaries as a full-time gig. "Unlock the door to the Basement."

He laughed, the sound crude and hollow. "It's your head or mine if I do that, Ash, and I like mine just where it—"

He didn't see it coming.

My arm around his wiry chest, the other locked over his mouth to keep him from shouting and making a scene. I knew Whiskey Bay like the back of my hand, and I dragged his thrashing body back, back, back, until we were ensconced in a side closet brimming with cleaning supplies.

"I hope she fucking kills you for this shit. You're no better than Jason—"

His words died with my fist colliding with his cheek. Head swiveling to the left, a grunt broke free from his mouth—and I didn't miss the irony with this little setup. Ambideaux had done the same to me in my townhouse. Had shoved me into a chair and tried to break me.

I wasn't trying to break Kevan. Wasn't trying to kill him either.

But I'd be damned if he ruined my chance to catch Nat unaware.

Snagging a length of velvet cord off a shelf, I spun Kevan around and wrapped the rope around his wrists. Once I'd tied him off like he was Thanksgiving dinner, I sat him down on the floor—back to the wall.

His eyes were fluttering, breathing uneven. Groans were pitiful.

I'd dealt with worse, and I had no doubt that he'd live.

Dropping to my haunches, I quickly dug through his pockets for the building keys. They were hooked to his belt, and five second later, they were hooked to mine.

I shut the door behind me on my way out, locking it from the outside.

With a quick glance from right to left, I moved toward the back of the room, heading for the long hallway that'd lead me to the Basement. No one said a word as I brushed past them, my head down. They were too busy drinking, too drunk on the sight of almost-naked women twirling on the poles throughout the room.

Shoulder to the General Storage Closet door, I flipped through each key individually until I found the perfect match. Inserted it into the lock, twisted the metal door handle, and quietly entered the darkened room.

At this time of night, the Basement would just be rearing up to go. The gambling tables would be popping though the stages would still be quiet and unused. Which meant that Nat would be circulating each table as she observed her den, watching for weaknesses in the players, instructing the house to make certain moves.

I took the steps up to the second floor, two at a time.

By the time the night was over, Nat would rethink ever trying to eviscerate me—*or* using Avery to do so.

My heart thudded at the thought of how I'd left her. I'd sensed her disappointment in me. Hated the desperation she'd voiced in wanting me to step back, to rethink, to not act impulsively.

She didn't understand.

Jay Foley may have tried to kill her *once*, but my neck had been positioned under the guillotine by too many people over the years. I was done with the threats. I was done with stepping back and keeping my head down and trying to stay away.

If they wanted to dance, then I'd fucking dance them right into their graves.

My eyes adjusted to the dark slant to the room, its seductive shadows rippling like water along the walls and the floor. Only two of the almost ten stages were open so far: a female masturbating on one, and then a couple fucking on the other.

I turned away, clinically skimming my gaze as I searched for a glimpse of Nat. Hand on the butt of my gun at my hip, I hunched my shoulders and sank deeper into the shadows along the wall. She'd be here, I knew she'd be here.

And if I had any luck, Hampton would be here too.

I'd given him the benefit of the doubt the night at the shack in bumfuck nowhere. A benefit that had bitten me in the ass when I'd turned my back and given him room to play.

That was my fault.

My mistake, but one I wouldn't make again.

I tracked each figure that entered my periphery, and then—

"Bingo," I muttered beneath my breath.

There was only one woman who'd be dolled up in a gold dress that shimmered and glowed like that. Like a beacon of falsehood, she threw her head back with a tinkling laugh, her hand pressed to a man's shoulder as he sat at one of the tables.

Limbs loose, I waited. It was part of the hunt, the waiting. Couldn't move too soon for fear of giving myself away.

Two minutes later, a man appeared at her side and bent to whisper in her ear.

Her laughter died. Giving a brief nod at the man, she

made her exaggerated goodbyes at the table, and then followed the newcomer away from the gambling. They bypassed the rooms where I'd owned Avery's pleasure, and then breezed past a doorway just left of the bar.

Her offices.

Time to go.

I trailed them at a safe distance, and either the guy bartending was new and didn't recognize my face or he didn't give a damn because, just like Nat and the stranger, I breezed past the bar, too.

Flexing my fingers, I angled my body to hug the walls.

It'd be too easy to pull out my firearm now and unload a round the moment I saw either her or Hampton—but I was a civilized bastard, as much as was possible, anyway, and I only listened for the distinct sound of their voices.

Stepped down the hallway.

Paused. Listened.

Kept going.

"I'm glad you were able to meet me. It's been so very *long,* and I have such an interesting bit of information to tell you."

Here we go. Back to the wall, just beside the door, I strained to hear the response—tried to gather how many people might be beyond the closed door.

"It has been, Natalie. Quite long." There was a small pause, and then the masculine voice added, "Wasn't expecting to find Quinn here with you."

Feminine laughter drifted out into the hall. "Quinn's loyalty has been on my side for a *very* long time, sir. Since the end of my marriage, at least."

"How fascinating."

My eyes slammed shut as I recognized that voice—Jay Foley. My deadbeat, socialite of a father.

Fuck.

He never traveled without security which meant that there were at least four people inside: Nat, Foley, the stranger Quinn, and at least one detail assigned to my asshole father. Give or take another one or two, just depending on how paranoid Foley felt this evening.

The situation wasn't ideal.

Actually, it was *far* from ideal.

But I'd been in worse positions. Hell, the first and only time I'd ever met my father had been during one of the annual first-responder galas. I'd had no interest in going, but Delery wouldn't have it—and it'd been with a shock of disbelief when the mayor walked up to me, out of nowhere, and said, "Heard through the grapevine that you're my son."

The introduction had been impersonal.

And the fleeting happiness that had entered my heart at being recognized—maybe even wanted—was extinguished in the very next second when the mayor cut a glance at me and muttered, "I've heard of you, of course, and what I've heard is disturbing. Man to man, I thought you should know who I am to you but"—he'd looked away—"I've got no interest in having a son, Mr. Asher, and particularly not one like you."

Particularly not one like you.

If I'd been quick enough on my feet, and not reeling from shock, I would have gotten in his face. Told him that the only reason I was *like me* was due to the fact that I'd been dumped as a child. Maybe if I'd been shown love, hugged on occasion, told that I was more than "our little killer," the mere mention of my name wouldn't have disturbed *him* or anyone else.

I never learned who told him about me.

It could have been Ambideaux, my mother's close childhood friend.

Could have been Nat, on a bender after the poker game gone wrong with her brother, and wanting me to hurt. Years had separated her brother's death and when Foley had approached me, but she held grudges longer than even I did.

Back to the wall, I drew in air, filling my lungs, and debated my next steps.

There was no other way about it: I'd have to stroll in there like a casual son of a gun. Act like it was all part of my plan to be the odd number out.

Now or never.

25

LINCOLN

Pursing my lips, I whistled like a damn lunatic and popped the door wide open with the toe of my combat boot.

Then slammed to a dramatic stop as I went faux wide-eyed at the lot of them in the room. “Hot damn,” I drawled with pure sarcasm, “I must have strolled into the wrong room.”

For a solid two seconds, there was pure silence.

And then everyone launched into motion: Nat leapt up from her seat and Foley dragged her back, while Nat’s lackey—Quinn—hurled himself toward me, the mayor’s detail in tow.

I ducked the swing of Quinn’s arm on instinct alone. Came up on the other side, one hand clamping on his extended arm to swing him around by the elbow until I’d put him in Ambideaux’s favorite hold.

Wrists at his lower back. Knees buckling as I shoved my leg against the back of his thighs.

“Sorry to barge in,” I grunted as Foley’s detail came at me from the other side. I had a split second to feel guilty for doing what I was about to do but—*fuck it.* I swiveled Quinn to the left, positioning him before me like a shield at the last moment, and *crack!*

Quinn's head whipped to the side from the blow of the pistol connecting with his face.

As I'd been taught growing up, an opportunity gained was never an opportunity wasted—I helped myself to the gun at his hip, and then let his shocked body fall to the floor. Stepped over him and announced, "Not exactly the family reunion most people dream about, but pretty par for the course for me."

Foley's security detail didn't make it two steps before the mayor was barking out, "Everyone, stop!"

The detail froze.

I didn't abide by the mayor's orders and took the seat Quinn had vacated before trying to take me down. One ankle propped up on my opposite knee, I rested the butt of the gun on my thigh, pointing the mouth toward Nat.

"Why don't you take a seat?" I murmured with a motion of a free hand at her empty chair. "We've got some shit to discuss."

Her elegance had long since left the building and she came up spluttering. "I will *not*. Are you out of your mind? Why are you here?"

"Heard you wanted me dead. And I figured what better way to put the shit to bed than to nip it in the bud." Idly, I stroked the polymer frame of Quinn's Glock. At Nat's wide-eyed glance at the gun, I quirked a brow. "You've always thought the worst of me, Nat. I'm not going to *shoot* you."

When the stiff set to her shoulders loosened, I murmured, "Although, trust me, it's tempting as fuck. Between you and your husband, I can't catch a break." A bitter laugh rolled through me like a shard of ice. "To think, at one point I'd considered y'all family."

I'd meant it as a throwaway comment.

There was not a chance in hell I could have predicted the way her red-painted lips twisted in a sneer. The florescent lights caught on the shimmer and glimmer of her gold-sequined dress, making her look like the modern-day equivalent of a disco ball.

"I am *not* your mother," she hissed, chin jutting forward, eyes narrowed into slits. "You were a leech on my marriage, always there, always *existing*. But no matter how much Jason kept you around, you were *never* a son to me."

It wasn't anything I hadn't heard before—Nat had never been good at concealing her feelings for me, and I'd long ago built steel armor to protect myself from her vicious tongue. To be likened to a leech, though? Christ, something had crawled up her ass and died today.

Stroking the Glock, just to keep her off-balance and twitchy, I met her gaze. "I don't know who you're trying to shock right now, Nat. You hate me. That isn't anything I didn't already know—that I haven't known for years." I couldn't help glancing at Foley, just to catch his impression of this showdown, especially since he already found me *disturbing*.

Being this close to him, though . . . fuck, I wished that I had all those testimonies to lock him up for good.

You could have had Avery's.

Maybe. But I'd let my thirst for vengeance and violence override her offer. Even now, I couldn't deny the pulse of anger that sharpened my vision and vibrated just under my skin. It was the anger that pressed the words off my tongue: "And it's not as if I don't have experiences with mothers hating me. I get enough of that shit with my biological one, so I don't need you—"

Jay Foley's deep laugh interrupted me.

I stared at him the way I hadn't done when I'd first walked in—the salt and pepper hair, the dark eyes, the strong jawline. The New Orleans media had once likened him to George Clooney, and I could see it easily. Dressed in a crisp, gray suit, there was an air about him that was deceptively friendly. Easygoing.

It was all too easy to see why all those females had fallen victim to his charms.

As for me, I was too much of a jaded bastard to do anything but stare impassively at him, my thumb coming to rest on the trigger guard. He may have knocked up my mother, but he was as much of a father to me as any other stranger I'd met along the way in my life.

"Care to share what's so funny with the class, Mr. Mayor?"

With his thumb, he swiped at his right eye. "It's heartless of me to laugh, of course."

My grip tightened on the Glock. "There's no press here for you to put on the gentlemanly act. Whatever you've got on your mind, just fucking say it."

His dark eyes swung to Nat, whose brow was once again unpuckered. She smiled, just a little, and there was something in her expression . . . something about the way she turned to me with clear eyes and that smirk . . .

Blood chilling, I growled, "Someone want to get on with the program?"

The mayor shook his head like he was utterly flabbergasted. "How does he not know?" he asked the room, not making eye contact with any one of us. "Jesus, this is rich. How does he *not know*?"

Energy spiked down my spine, and I rose from the chair. I kept Quinn's gun in front of my hips, clasped between my two hands in caution. "What the fuck don't I know?"

"Your mother is *dead*."

Four words from my father's mouth, and I staggered back. Victoria Meriden hadn't loved me, hadn't ever shown me even a smidgeon of affection, but she was still my mother. Still the woman who'd brought me into this world.

Pain slipped over me, needling my skin like the sharp tips of a blade, over and over until I'd been torn open. Gaping wounds. Bleeding profusely.

"How?" I worked out hoarsely, my gaze volleying between Nat and Foley. "When did you find out? Did Jason"—I swallowed, hating the vulnerability in my voice—"tell you?" I looked to Nat. "Is that what happened? He told you?"

Not even a hint of pity lined her features when she stared at me, not saying a word. If I'd wanted to throttle her before, it was nothing compared to the rage that seeped into my marrow now.

"Someone answer me—when did she *die*?" My voice boomed through the room. I spun around to face Quinn, who was now hauled up against the wall, touching a palm to his cheek. Foley's detail was next to him, standing guard.

She couldn't be dead. Yeah, she'd had medical complications over the years. The car accident had robbed so much from her—the use of her legs, her mind, it seemed, which included her memories of me. But Ambideaux had more money than God, and he kept her lifelines steady. That was our deal. Had always been our deal.

I worked for him, and he ensured that my mother—

My legs wavered under my weight. *No*. No, he wouldn't have . . . I was going to be sick. Right here, right now, I was going to lose the contents of my stomach in a way that I'd only ever done three times in my life.

The night I'd committed my first murder and brought the body to the Atchafalaya Basin.

When I'd learned that Avery—Laurel—was dead.

And when I'd driven Tom Townsend out there, just a few weeks ago.

Foley, my father, cleared his throat. "Put the gun down, Sergeant."

I shook my head. The gun wasn't going anywhere.

Firearms weren't capable of betrayal. No, that feat only belonged to humanity.

To people like Nat and Ambideaux and Foley and Hampton.

"When did she die?" I asked again, eyes on my father's face. "*When did she die?*"

He looked at me, and it was the first time that sorrow lined his handsome features. "She's been dead since you were two years old, Lincoln. She died in the car accident."

26

AVERY

When push came to shove, I'd hailed a cab from Lincoln's townhouse in Bayou St. John and high-tailed it straight back to the Sultan's Palace. Katie had kicked me out. She'd vowed that she needed space.

She was my family—my only family—and as I barged up the steps and tried the lock on our apartment door, I prayed that we could get past this.

I needed her.

No matter how I'd entered her life, she'd always been my support system. With Lincoln on a suicide mission, I didn't know where else to go.

The door was locked, and I smashed my fist on the wood in a desperate knock. "Katie! Katie, open the door. Please!"

A second passed.

And then yet another.

And then the door was pulling open wide and my best friend, my roommate, my step-cousin, was standing there looking like a hot mess with rumpled PJ's and hair that looked like it hadn't been brushed in days, even though it'd only been twenty-four hours since I'd walked out.

Her blue eyes blinked back at me.

A half-second later, her arms were around my back and hauling me close. She was taller than me, and my nose ended up in her armpit.

"Katie—"

"Oh, my God, you're back," she whispered, her hand petting the crown of my head like I was her most prized possession. "He said he wouldn't tell you but I'm so glad that he did. I'm so sorry. I'm so fucking sorry, Ave."

I opened my mouth and managed to inhale straight B.O. Coughing, I pushed as much as I could out of her embrace. "I don't even know what you're talking about. *Who* wouldn't tell me what?"

She didn't let me go.

With a palm to my back, she yanked me into place, my nose getting reacquainted with her armpit all over again. "Captain America," she muttered, "he came here looking for you and I said that I was sorry about what happened. And I *am*. I'm so sorry. All the things I said—telling Ambideaux about you. I'm so sorry, Avery. I'm so fucking sorry."

"It's okay." It wasn't okay. Because Katie had only been reacting to my deceit. "I'm the one who needs to apologize," I rushed out, squeezing her back because this was family. *She* was my family, just like I wanted Lincoln to be. "I lied. I lied so many times and you were right to call me out and put me in my place. I left because you were *right*, and what I did . . . it's not excusable, Katie. There are *no* excuses."

Her shoulders sagged. "Friends?"

I nodded into her armpit. "Always."

She released me, and I spent a solid five seconds inhaling fresh air before I stepped into the apartment and fisted my hands on my hips. There was no easy way to phrase what I needed to say, and it didn't escape my notice that for the first time in my life . . . I was asking for help.

Katie sat on the armrest of the sofa, hands folding in her lap as she stared up at me. "What's the matter? You've got a look on your face that I *really* don't like."

I swallowed. Pushed the nerves so far down that I wouldn't choke on them as I spoke. "I need your help." I dove a hand through my hair, still somewhat tangled from sex with Lincoln. "I need . . . I need you to create a distraction."

Katie blinked. "A distraction? Where?"

Here goes nothing. Straightening my spine, I went for broke. "At Ambideaux's party that he invited me to. I need to go, and I need you to go with me."

I couldn't be in multiple places at once, but my gut told me that Lincoln would inevitably show up there. It would either begin with the Basement or with Ambideaux, and I was going for the latter for no other reason than it was a scene I could prepare for. While Katie created a distraction for the guests, I could . . .

Eyes squeezing shut, I tried not to think about what I'd do if needed.

Take a life in order to save Lincoln's.

Sacrifice my own freedom to see that he kept his.

It wasn't what I wanted, and if I had the opportunity to talk some sense into his stubborn head, I would. But if I we showed up too late . . . if he'd gone to Ambideaux's first, instead of to the Basement, where I imagined he would go to begin his reign of death, then we were all fucked.

Think positive.

It was hard to do so when the man you were in love with was determined to ruin his life just to prove he was not someone who should be crossed.

Spinning on my heel, I went into the kitchen and climbed up onto the countertop. Resting one hand on the roof of the fridge, I pulled open the cabinet and took out the gun I'd never used.

"Ave? You're freaking me out."

I glanced down at Katie, who'd trailed me into the kitchen. Turning the gun around, I handed her the butt. "Hold this so I can climb down." When her brows arched high, I added, "Please don't shoot me."

"Trust me, of the two of us, I'm pretty sure we're better off with me holding this thing."

I hopped back down to the kitchen tile. "You know how to shoot?" I asked, bewildered at the familiar way she handled the firearm.

The grin she gave me could have lit up a room. "Bonding with my dad meant going to the range. He's an enthusiast."

An . . . enthusiast?

And then I was grinning, too. "You think you can teach me how to use it by the time we make it to the cocktail party?"

Katie didn't even blink. "Hell no. We're going to need more than fifteen minutes."

Refusing to let my confidence waver, I dropped my eyes to the firearm. "You think you can at least help me *look* like I know what the hell I'm doing?"

"Slightly more realistic but if you keep looking at it as though it's a snake, we're going to have some problems."

I didn't know whether to laugh or to feel grateful for having Katie at my side, as we'd always been since meeting a few years back.

In the end, I offered her a shaky smile and muttered, "I *really* need to get a new taser."

27

LINCOLN

My finger hovered over the trigger, the palm of my hand slick with sweat against the polymer frame.

"You're lying." Feet rooted to the tile floor, I jerked my gaze from Foley to Nat. "You've seen her," I said, "for years you've *seen her.*"

For fuck's sake, my mother lived with Ambideaux. Sure, she had her own wing in the home, but she wasn't a ghost. She wasn't just a figment of my imagination. Nat had seen her countless times over the years, though my mother hadn't moved out of the hospital and into the house with Jason until some time after he and Nat had divorced.

My throat closed up, and I swear to God my heart iced over as I stood there, waiting for someone to fucking say something that wasn't cryptic. Waited, even longer, for the sensation of being run over by a truck to ease off my worn body and steamroll someone else for a change.

With a nod to his detail, Foley took one of the empty seats and sat down. Like he was preparing himself for a conversation over tea and baked goods.

Fingers tightening around the gun, I tracked his every

movement. "Stop with the bullshit." One step to the left set my back against the wall, giving me the chance to note everyone in the room—as well as the empty doorway. "I know my mother's alive, so if you're hoping to fuck with my head, you're going to need a new intimidation tactic—"

"Jason always was obsessed with your mother." Foley flicked a stray piece of lint off his suit pants. "They were childhood friends. All of us were next-door neighbors. But they were each other's firsts in every capacity of the word."

Nat's expression tightened, and I bit my tongue to keep from saying anything that might encourage Quinn or the security detail to put a bullet through my temple.

He hiked on his pants, pinching the fabric at the knees, and resettled himself in. Foley continued, then, arms loose on the chair as he pinned me in place with an unwavering stare. "And then she had you, her precious boy. You lit up her world. Stole her heart, and there was nothing she wouldn't have done for you."

I couldn't hear my heart pounding—it was buried beneath the blood roaring in my head.

And yet I stood there, back to the wall, hands locked around the gun's grip, my goddamn soul bellowing out for it all to stop.

"She'd died whereas you lived," my father went on, his face completely impassive as he watched me. "But, of course, no one dwelled too long on a death of a girl like Victoria Meriden. Her family were nobodies, but unlike myself or Jason, she never went on to make something of herself. Sweet, beautiful, but a stripper on Bourbon. She was a nobody. *No one cared.*"

I cared.

I cared that Foley was fucking with my head, just to get past my defenses. I cared that he was making shit up—shit that I knew was untrue. I cared so much that I shot forward and, with a hand to the back of his chair, I shoved the frame backward. Foley was big, but I was stronger, and the chair teetered on its hind legs for two interminably long seconds before I gave it another push, and my father and the chair went tumbling down with a crash.

"Is he fucking *insane*?" spat either Quinn or the detail, and I did nothing but glance up, aim my weapon, and shoot at their feet.

Not close enough to get them, but too close for comfort.

"Stay in your lane," I growled, "this shit has nothing to do with you, and the only place I'd ever send your fucking boss is to jail." I shoved my face into Jay's, and his dark eyes stared back, wide but cool. Not even a hint of panic.

Apparently, I'd inherited at least one thing from the bastard: remaining unattached, no matter the situation.

Like Big Hampton had done to me on that damn ride out to the middle of nowhere, I shoved the muzzle up against Jay's jawline. "We're going to try this again." I canted his head, angling the firearm at a sharper slant. Then moved my free hand to my pant leg, where I removed my weapon and positioned that one to face Quinn and the lackey. "You want me to believe that my mother died thirty years ago? Fine, let's play pretend." Breathing heavily, I leaned in. "Jason's version of Victoria, who I've always known . . . who is she?"

A dark chuckle greeted my ears. "Victoria's sister. Your *aunt*."

I would have gone stumbling if I wasn't so determined to maintain the upper hand.

Only, Jay's revelation rocked me. My ears popped and my vision turned red at the periphery, and my weight tipped forward. *No.* "I don't believe you. It's been over thirty years since the accident. She can't walk. The tests, the hospital visits. There's no way he would be able to keep all that going for—"

"You know Jason." My father's mouth twisted angrily, and even though he was flat on his back, his tone remained calm like the politician he was. "You know him better than almost anyone. Do you think he'd risk it all just to get caught? He's a monster. Always has been, even when we were kids."

It was a struggle to pull air into my lungs. If what he said was true . . . "She can't walk," I repeated again, voice fainter than the first go 'round. "The car accident—"

Dark eyes bounced from my hand holding the gun and then to my face, and for the first time, Foley's face turned wary. Nervous. He licked his lips, then grunted when I amped up the pressure of the gun to his jaw. "He gave you those scars on your face, didn't he?" he said at last. "Jason was the kid in the neighborhood popping the heads off of animals. The one our parents never let us spend any time with alone because he wasn't quite right in the head, they said. He did that with her—Samantha—crushed her legs so she couldn't walk. So she fit the part. I knew it. Nat knew it, too."

Behind me, Nat let out a keening sound that rang in my ears and pierced my soul. It was a cry of a wounded animal, and I wasn't sure if she were making fun of the story, adding to the dramatics, or if her own memories were so traumatizing that even the mention of her ex-husband was enough to send her into hysterics.

I thought of my mother—the woman Jason had always claimed to be my mother—and my heart sank, fracturing into a thousand little shards. Just like the antique vase I'd broken at Ambideaux's house. I felt shattered, balanced on the lip of no return, the pieces of my mind unable to fit together what Foley told me now.

It made no sense.

And still it made more sense than anything else ever had.

The way she refused to look at me.

How she'd always rejected me as her son.

He crushed her legs.

The words registered, horrific and horrible, and I fell back onto my ass. "Why?" I demanded, my throat raw. "Why would he do that?"

It wasn't Foley who spoke up, but Nat, and the words she said sent a chill down my spine.

"With her under his care, you couldn't strike back. He manipulated you, Asher, his son—the baby boy I could never give him."

28

LINCOLN

I heard nothing at all.

Not the voices around me.

Not the music echoing from down the hall in the main area of the Basement.

Not the beating of my heart erupting in my chest into a wild staccato that could not be tamed.

Nothing.

If I'd already visited each circle of Dante's hell, I must be in a new one now. Purgatory, maybe. More likely an undiscovered one that was meant only for me—designed and constructed to drown me until the fight left my body and there was nothing left but grief.

This wasn't how it was all supposed to go down.

Foley was meant to be in jail for everything he'd done over the years.

Nat was meant to be so frightened, she'd leave New Orleans for good.

Hampton . . . fuck, I couldn't even think that far right now.

Everything had been a lie. I should have seen it coming,

I should have been able to narrow down why Jason had a hard-on for everyone around him.

"Why?" I rasped to no one and everyone all at once. I blinked, focusing on Foley, the man who'd come to *me* and said he was my father. "Why would you assume that you were my dad?"

What kind of fucked-up, Jerry-Springer shit did I just land myself into?

The mayor of New Orleans rolled over onto his knees from where I'd practically tackled him to the floor. "Jason told me so a few years ago. Who the fuck ever knows why with him?"

The numbness faded, replaced by the familiar sting of fury. Rising onto my feet, I whirled around to face Nat. She'd known. All these years, she'd *known* and had said nothing. I neared her, closing in, both guns clasped in my hands.

She didn't cower. Like Avery, Natalie Lauren never shrank back in fear. Her chin tipped up and she met my gaze as she stared at me over the bridge of her nose. "Furious?" she hissed. "Imagine what it's been like for *me.* Married to a man who became so obsessed with another that when she died, even after cheating on me, he got himself the next best thing—her sister. I've hated you. I have hated you for *years*, and the fact that you will not die . . ."

I should have expected it.

The band of arms that wrapped around my chest and yanked me back. Rough hands that ripped the Glocks from my grip. My heels dragged along the tile as I tightened my core and tried to slow the momentum of being taken off to God-knows-where.

"Stop struggling, asshole," said a deep voice in my ear.

Screw that.

My hands went to his forearms, latching on, holding

tight, preparing to send him to Timbuktu when he tightened his grip and grunted, "You want to live? Shut the fuck up and let me do this."

Eyes drifting to the right, I caught sight of Foley yanking on the sleeves of his suit as he traded an inscrutable glance with Nat. Behind him, his detail watched me, eyes narrowed, jaw clenched, gun trained on my face.

The man behind me had to be Quinn. Nat's right-hand man.

And now he was promising to drag me to safety?

I grit my teeth. It was against my innate nature to let him take the wheel. I didn't know him worth a damn—had never seen him before tonight—but there were times when you had to rely on fate.

I let him drag my ass out of that room.

Away from the man who wasn't my father.

Away from the woman who'd wanted me dead for as long as I'd drawn air to breathe.

I struggled in Quinn's hold for the sake of appearances. Spat out vile words and elbowed him in the gut. Let out a quintessential, "Let me go, you fucker!" just before my feet crossed over the threshold of the room.

By the time the door shut, Quinn was heaving like a newbie sprinter. He released me. Then, hand to my back, he corralled me down the hall.

"You need to get out of here," he muttered, giving me no other option than to keep walking forward. "Nat might be playing nice, but she wants your head on a platter."

That stopped me.

Ducking under his arm, I twisted around to face him. He was even in height with me. Older, maybe mid-forties. Gray peppered his dark hair, and he walked with a distinct limp that made me wonder if he'd been shot before.

"I've been in this world too long to know that you aren't just going to let me go because you feel bad." I got in his face, careful to keep enough of a distance that if he held a knife, I was still out of direct reach. "If you're Nat's bitch, then—"

My back slammed against the wall. His fingers grasped my shirt, fisting the fabric as he jerked me in. "I'm nobody's bitch, Sergeant."

I danced my fingers to my back, skimming my waistband to circle the butt of my trench knife. "No?"

"No." His dark eyes narrowed. "No," he repeated, voice low, "I'm the man who kept your girlfriend alive when her stepfather wanted her dead. The one who opened the window downstairs for her to escape and locked her bedroom door so she had the chance to run. That was *me*."

The trench knife dropped to the floor, my grip going loose.

"Yeah, not expecting that, were you?" Quinn's mouth drew up in a dark, sadistic grin. "*I* let her go, and it cost me my right leg."

"You killed her mother."

His hold on my shirt tightened. "She knew it was coming and refused to leave. That was her choice, her decision, and I did what I could. I made sure her daughter got out alive."

Where I'd been sent to kill her.

Because of Ambideaux.

Because of my *father.*

Because Jay Foley had done something so awful that Jason sought nothing but retribution.

"Why did he want her dead?" My gaze cut over to the left. The hall was empty. Quiet aside from our hushed voices. "Why the hell did Jay want—"

"Because she'd inherited money—her father's living will

left everything he owned to her when he was diagnosed with cancer, and he owned most of the city." Quinn squeezed his eyes shut, color cresting on his cheeks. "I wanted her to leave. I *begged* her to leave. She refused, and Jay would have killed her no matter what. He'd so much as told her so."

I'd spent years reading expressions, diagnosing liars, and Quinn . . . Jesus Christ, but he was worse than them all. "You didn't kill her, did you."

Not a question.

He answered anyway, his voice raw, cracking, as the past swarmed over him—looking at his face, it was clear that he might be standing in this hallway, but he wasn't here with me now. Not really.

"She wouldn't leave—her house, her family, the life she knew." Adam's apple dipping, the man swallowed, hard. "I couldn't do it. I'd loved her for years, and I couldn't fucking do it. She pulled the trigger. Ended it all. Wasn't in her right mind and wouldn't listen no matter what I told her. When it came to Laurel . . . she didn't know me, but I knew her from Catherine. I let her go. I don't regret it."

I let her go. I don't regret it.

I'd thought the same thing when I'd left Avery on that front lawn. I couldn't kill her—couldn't do what it was that Ambideaux had asked of me.

Realization hit me square in the gut.

And the words fell from my lips as though they'd been pushed up from my heart: "He was pissed. Holy fuck, Jason was pissed that Foley was about to walk away with the entire city in his pocket."

Quinn's eyes, red with grief, narrowed on me. "What the hell are you talking about?"

"Nothing." I swallowed. "Everything. Shit." I shoved him

back with a hand to his chest. "I gotta go. You"—I met his gaze—"you want to make sure Laurel is safe for the rest of her life? Testify."

"*What*?"

Christ, I didn't have time to explain. Dropping to my heels, I grabbed my trench knife off the floor and, snapping it closed, shoved it at his chest. "It's monogramed," I said, kicking my chin toward the knife. "Go to the eighth district station and ask to speak with Lieutenant Stefan Delery. Tell him exactly what you just told me and tell him that Avery —*Laurel Peyton*—will testify too."

When he didn't make a move to grab the knife, I gave it another push at his chest, forcing him to take hold. "If Nat asks where you went, tell her . . . tell her that you brought me out to the Atchafalaya Basin. She'll know what that means, and here's to hoping it gives me enough time to go meet you at the station with Avery ASAP."

She'd been right.

There was a way to end this without total bloodshed—at least when it came to Mayor Jay Foley. Nat would go down, too, there was no denying that. She'd left crumbs throughout the years that made her as much a suspect as the city's beloved mayor.

Ambideaux . . . Skin tightening at the thought of everything I'd learned, I hurried down the steps of the Basement. I wanted to take him down. Wanted to string him up and feed him to the goddamn gators, the way he'd done to me—his own fucking son.

I thought of Quinn, the way he'd been in near tears thinking of Avery's mother. He'd loved her—however that had happened, he'd loved her, and he put her first over his own life. His choice had been to save her.

I chose Avery.

She'd entered my life when I'd least expected it, knocked me on my ass with her wit and her perseverance and the goddamn bravery she radiated like a second skin.

I was a man who'd never known love, but I'd fallen in love with her.

Her safety was priority. Her *life* was priority.

Between me and her, I chose her.

Always.

29

AVERY

"He's not here."

Katie glanced over at me, then locked her arm with mine. "You don't know that. He might be."

He wasn't. I would have sensed his presence or at least spotted his broad frame above all the people milling about.

Lifting my chin, I scoured the room, taking note of all the black cocktail dresses and black suits. It seemed that the whole of New Orleans was packed in the parlor and dining room of Ambideaux's house. No matter which way I turned, I was on the receiving end of an elbow to the side or a splash of a cocktail landing on the silk dress I'd borrowed from Katie.

Worry spliced through me.

He had to be at the Basement, then, going after Nat. *Dammit*. I'd taken a guess and had guessed wrong. By the time we even made it over there . . . I couldn't imagine the sort of damage he might cause.

Or the death.

I understood his anger, had thrived in that anger for years, but it wasn't worth risking his life. My life. The life we might have together if we managed to get out of this alive.

"We've been here for an hour," I muttered to Katie. "The likelihood that we missed him is slim to none."

She nudged me. "What about the second floor?"

I lifted my gaze to the circular stairwell just beyond the dining room. "I doubt he's up there. He'd be where Ambideaux is, and Ambideaux is . . ." I trailed off, hastily looking for the man of the hour. "He was just there. By the grand piano."

Katie craned her neck. "Bet he went to the bathroom. The man has been tossing back vodka like he's going for a liquor baptism session." Her hands went to her dress and, without even acknowledging that we were surrounded by some of the wealthiest people in the city, shoved her hand down her dress and adjusted her breasts.

My eyes went wide. "What are you doing?"

"Your distraction is here and willing to work." She tugged on the thin straps of her dress, letting them snap against her skin when she released the bands. "I'm going to stalk Mr. Future Mayor by the loo. You go upstairs. Make sure he's not there."

"You do realize you're not British, right?"

Katie winked. "You do realize that you brought me here for a reason, right?"

Dammit, she was right. Leaning back, I checked out the grand piano again, just in case. Nada. Looked like we were going for Plan B, with Katie leading the breast troops over by the loo.

When she stepped back, I circled her arm with my hand, pulling her to a quick stop. "Be safe," I told her, giving her a quick squeeze before letting go.

Her lips pulled up in one of her trademark smiles. "Be

brave, Ave. Go get your man before he does something idiotic and you're forced to visit him in jail for the next fifteen years. You'll be horny for life, and he'll be getting it up the ass from a prison friend. Don't let that be your future."

Well, when she put it that way, there wasn't a shot in hell that I was leaving this house without turning it over first.

We gave each other a little salute, then went off in opposite directions.

My purse slapped my leg as I hustled to the stairwell. It was heavy, my gun tucked inside for safekeeping, and at the sight of the velvet cord hovering above the third step, I climbed over it and hurried up the stairs. They creaked under my weight, no doubt as old as the house was, and I cursed every wooden whine.

Cursed, also, Lincoln's damn stubbornness for not setting aside his need for vengeance.

He wasn't a monster, just a man, and I knew that all men were fallible. But that didn't mean he should go risking his neck just to ensure that he wasn't caught unaware sometime down the line.

The second floor was carpeted, but I stripped off my high heels anyway and hooked the back straps over my finger. Cocked my hip as I walked and gave a little stumble—Katie wasn't the only one good at performing. If someone caught me up here, I'd rather they think I was a drunk wandering than, well, doing what I was *actually* doing.

Ensuring Sergeant Lincoln Asher didn't commit murder and end up somebody's personal friend in prison for the next twenty years.

Peeking into one room, I came up empty and went for the next.

Did the same with the next two rooms, one of which led to a bathroom.

Also empty.

Heart pounding, I neared the end of the hall. There was only one door left. Like the others, it was tugged shut. The ratio factor told me that Lincoln wasn't in there, but I couldn't leave without checking first.

On silent feet, I approached it, hand moving toward the doorknob. Pressed my cheek to the door. Hearing nothing at all, I twisted the handle and glanced inside.

"Who's there?" snapped a feminine voice. "Who is that?"

Don't go in there.

Leave.

Turn around!

I'd never been good at following orders, not even my own.

I stepped inside. Shut the door behind me.

And stared at the woman who couldn't be anyone but Lincoln's mother.

30

LINCOLN

My townhouse was empty, the front door unlocked but closed shut.

Desperation crawled through me, weighing down my limbs as I stalked down every room, hoping that I was wrong. That she hadn't left. That she hadn't gone looking for me.

"Fuck!"

Fury ricocheted through me, and I twirled around on impact and slammed my fist into the nearest wall. The plaster cracked. My knuckles cracked. My damn heart cracked as I tried to clear my thoughts and assess the situation.

In thirty-four years, I'd always managed to operate with a clear head because I had nothing to lose. *No one* to lose. That wasn't the case now—hadn't been since Avery entered the picture and tossed my life into a blender and flicked the switch to ON.

I couldn't think beyond the stampeding of my heart and the blood thundering in my head.

If she wasn't here, and she hadn't gone to the Basement,

then there were only two other options: Big Hampton's or Ambideaux's cocktail party that she'd received an invitation to attend.

Laying a hand on the now-fractured wall, I dropped my chin and inhaled sharply.

If I had more time, I'd go to the Sultan's Palace in the off chance she'd stopped by there to meet with Katie.

But I didn't have time. It wasn't on my side.

Swiping a hand over my face, I pushed away from the wall and beat it to the still-running SUV on the front drive.

I had to take a lucky guess, and my guess was that she'd gone to Jason's.

My father's.

Stomach churning at the thought, I climbed into the SUV and fumbled for my new cell phone. Flicked through the sparse number of contacts until Delery's name was blinking across the screen.

He picked up on the second ring. "What do you want, Ash?"

For the first time in my life, I would try to play by the rules. "I need units at Jason Ambideaux's house."

There was a minute pause. "What the fuck are you talking about?"

It wasn't the first time I'd heard that today.

Palming the steering wheel, I whipped the SUV down along the bayou. "Units, L-T. Police officers. Trust me on this."

Laughter echoed in my ear. "Ash, man, you feeling okay? I'm telling you that—"

"No," I bit out, "I'm telling *you* that unless you want shit about one of your officers being blasted all across the news tomorrow morning, you'll send me some backup so things don't get that far."

“Well, shit.”

Yeah, that about summed up my day.

“L-T?”

Delery breathed into the phone. “Please tell me you don’t have anything else to say.”

Swinging a right, the SUV went airborne when I hit a massive bump crossing the intersection. “Yeah,” I grunted, gunning the car once I’d hit the back road that would lead me to Jason’s, “I sent someone over to you. About the Foley case. Turn him away and I’ll shoot your dick off the next time we see each other.”

“That threat’s been old since we were in the East.”

“Yeah, well, I never said I’ve gotten more original with age.”

Canceling the call, I tossed my phone onto the passenger’s seat.

Hold on, sweetheart. I’m coming for you.

31

AVERY

She was blindfolded.

Shock skated down my spine as I took in what had to be Lincoln's mother.

Posted up in bed, her wiry arms were crossed over her chest, her legs hidden beneath swaths of comforters and sheets. A TV sat opposite her, on top of a waist-high table. Large murals graced the walls, turning what would have been an ordinary room into something resembling a rain-forest. And, to the left of the bed, a wheelchair waited, angled toward the mattress.

"Jason?" she called, her arms jolting into action. Shaky fingers reached up, up, up, searching for the scrap of fabric over her eyes. "Jason, is that you?"

If I said nothing at all, she'd know in three seconds when she whipped the blindfold off and spotted me by the doorway.

I cleared my throat. Swallowed, hard. "No, not Jason."

She stiffened in the bed. "Who are you?"

Seeing her like this, all trussed up in the bed, made pity beat a steady pace in my heart. Handicapped or not, no one deserved the pure isolation of being unable to see—because someone else wanted to remove that ability from you.

Dropping my heels to the plush carpet, I moved to her side and did the honors—sliding the black fabric up and off her face, until she was blinking up at me with eerily familiar-colored eyes.

Haint-blue, the same as Lincoln's.

God, I hurt for them both. Lincoln, who'd been forced, through no fault of his own, to put up with the moods of a woman who was clearly in pain. For his mother, who clearly had been held here like some sort of captive.

Everything was in perfect order. The wheelchair, the TV, the paintings on the wall. But who blindfolded a woman with a condition like hers? *Someone cruel, like Ambideaux.*

"I'm so sorry for intruding," I whispered, my tongue swollen with nerves. "I'm a . . . guest downstairs. Of Jason's."

Her mouth firmed into a thin line. "This is a private room."

There were so many things I wished to say, the most important being: did Lincoln know how she was kept here?

I balled the scrap of fabric in my hand. "Yes, I'm sorry."

What else was there to say? I needed to go. Lincoln's mother wasn't like the strays I picked up or the homeless that I brought food to whenever I could. She wasn't in need of a savior, and she certainly didn't need me—but I couldn't turn away.

"You need to go."

Yes, I thought, *you're completely right.*

My feet wouldn't budge.

"Does Jason treat you well?"

Her thin, dark brows lifted. "That's not your business."

No, it wasn't.

The blindfold tangled in my fingers as I held it up. "Do

you like this?" I asked softly. "If so, then there's no concern. None. But I can't help but feel as though you're kept blinded on purpose. You're not . . . are you?"

Her already fragile-like features winced, pinching at her brow and then again in her jawline. Her fingers fluttered in her lap. "He said it would help me to focus when I want to think about something. I have a hard time focusing. Always have, but especially after—"

"Lincoln was born?"

It was the wrong thing to say.

I saw it immediately, the way her gaze shuttered, and her chest heaved with a big, uneven breath. "Get out."

"Ma'am, I'm—"

"*Get out!*"

She shrieked the words at the top of her lungs. I knew it was only my imagination, but it seemed like even the walls shook with the force of her rage. There was no doubt that even the party downstairs had heard her bellow, and I backpedaled, feet tripping over the carpet in my haste to get the hell out of dodge.

"Get out!" Her coloring turned red, the color of the murals on the wall. The color of blood. "Get out! Get *out*!"

Her arm shot out to the left and she smacked something on her bedside table. When her hand came away, I saw that it was a button. A button that was clearly important to her because her palm came down again and again and again on it.

Oh, *shit*.

The straps of my purse swung left as I went right.

Lurching toward the door, I ripped it open to the chorus of Lincoln's mother losing her shit behind me. Slammed it shut to another verse of "Get out!"

The music downstairs was still playing. Thank God.

Maybe no one had heard her catastrophic shrieking.

Please, let no one have heard her.

Shoeless, my feet padded over the floor. It was time to go. Maybe Lincoln had gone to the Basement or maybe he'd developed a lick of sense and had gone straight to the police station. Maybe—

Footsteps that weren't mine drew my attention up off the floor and to the end of the hallway.

Jason Ambideaux stared back at me, his black hair slicked back, his suit pristine.

Then, his mouth curved in a smile that made me sick. "How wonderful of you to join us, Miss Peyton."

My gaze jerked to the left and to the right—there was nowhere to go.

Nowhere to escape.

Like when I'd heard Momma die, I was stuck. Frozen. Unable to move.

He took a step toward me.

I wouldn't be my mother, dead on the floor with the blood coating my hair.

I spun on my bare heels and ran.

"There's nowhere for you to go, Miss Peyton," Ambideaux said, his voice a pitch above a menacing murmur. "Or should I call you Miss Washington?"

The rooms were prison cells on this floor. There were no fire escapes that I'd seen from the outside when walking up. No big bushes to catch my fall if I leapt out.

Be brave.

Be bold.

My gaze caught on Lincoln's mother's room. She was still shrieking, still yelling at the top of her lungs. There was no other option, and I didn't dare take the time to risk looking back at Ambideaux.

With my shoulder, I burst the door open like a battering ram, which did nothing to calm the woman's shrieking from the bed.

"Get out! Get out! Get out!"

"Sorry, lady," I muttered, turning the lock and stumbling backward, "we're stuck together for the time being."

The doorknob jiggled a second later, and then there was Ambideaux's voice, no longer so smooth or cajoling. "Victoria!" The door visibly shook on its hinges, like he'd thrown his body against it from the other side. "*Victoria!*"

Behind me, Lincoln's mother didn't miss a beat: "Get *out! Get out!*"

The door creaked. And then, beyond it, again: "Victoria!"

My head swirled from the cacophony of noises. Heart thudded against my ribcage. Stomach churned as I clutched the strap of my purse and turned in a slow circle, assessing my surroundings. The closet was an obvious—and dumb—choice, and so I shot toward the window as the next best thing, hoping, praying . . .

Forehead kissing the glass, I glanced down and bit out a curse. No fire escape. No bushes to catch my fall. If I didn't break my neck, I'd be lucky to be the recipient of a bum leg, which would do me no favors when I couldn't flee.

Taking the time to move furniture to the door might work in the movies but wouldn't do me much good. I didn't have the time.

I was a sitting duck.

"Get out! Get out! Get out!"

Gaze snapping to the woman panicking in her bed, I swallowed.

Don't do it.

Don't you dare fucking do it.

The door squealed as a metal hinge whined in protest, then gave way.

Sometimes good people did bad things.

I didn't give myself time to rethink my decision. Popping my purse open, I ignored the flames of guilt and shame in my belly, and then pulled out the Glock Pete had given to me years ago. It was bulky in my hand, so foreign, and with a squaring of my shoulders, I set the mouth of the gun to Lincoln's mother's head.

And then I waited for Ambideaux to come bursting inside.

32

LINCOLN

The units weren't at Ambideaux's house when my SUV squealed to a stop in the middle of the street.

Which meant that either Delery hadn't dispatched them or they simply hadn't arrived yet. I was praying for the latter. Hoping for miracles I didn't actually believe in.

The front lawn was packed to the brim with guests all decked out in cocktail attire. Suits for the men; dresses for the women. I shoved past them all, fully cognizant of the fact that this was the first time I'd ever entered the house while a party was taking place.

I'd always been relegated to security. Peering in through the windows.

Today, I didn't stop to appreciate the beauty of the house or the guests.

Avery, where are you?

Bursting inside, I swiveled my head to scan the parlor. Clusters of people were tossing back cocktails and laughing.

"Can you believe it?" said one, her voice tinkling like chimes in the wind. "I mean, I know that *I'm* excited to see what the city will look like with Mr. Ambideaux in charge. He's just so charming."

"And hot," teased another. "I wish he'd let his hair go gray. Total silver-fox status."

Putting Ambideaux in office would be the equivalent of setting a city ablaze. Jack the Ripper would be a better alternative.

I powered through the groups, moving them aside, constantly scanning the rooms with the hope that I'd spot a familiar dark head. When I found her, I'd kiss her, owning her mouth with mine. And then I'd bend her over my knee and clap my hand down on her ass until she learned—for once—what it meant to fucking obey an order.

"Captain America?"

My heart leapt, and then resettled with disappointment when I realized it wasn't Avery's voice.

Fingers wrapped around my bicep, and I glanced down. It was her roommate.

"Katie," she supplied without missing a beat. She dropped her hand, only to set it to her collarbone. "I'm so, so glad you're here. We've been looking for you—"

"Avery's here?"

"She's been looking for *you*. So, yes, she's here. We're both here. Where have you been?"

All over this fucking city.

I shook my head, my palm glossing over my stubble. "Doesn't matter. We need to get her and head out." I peered over Katie's head, searching the crowd. "Where is she?"

The light in Katie's eyes dimmed. "I saw her thirty minutes ago. Maybe forty." Swallowing, she bit down on her bottom lip. "I figured that she'd found you. I've been watching Ambideaux this whole time—making sure he stayed where I could see him."

The way her brow puckered was not an encouraging sign.

"But?" I pushed, my patience already wearing thin.

"But he took a door I couldn't enter through about fifteen minutes ago. I've been waiting, figuring he'd come back out." Another swallow. "I was going to give it another five minutes before I went searching for her. I was hoping . . ."

There wasn't any time to listen to her hopes, not right now.

"Wait outside," I told her. "I had my lieutenant call units over here. They should be arriving."

Katie's head bobbed. "Sure, yeah. Okay, I can do that." She stepped back, hands going to the skirt of her dress as she went to spin around—but she slammed to a sudden halt, and then peered back at me. "Cap, I'm just going to say this once. She loves you. She might not know how to say it, but I know she does. Keep her safe or I will personally shoot you."

Despite the bad timing, my lips twitched. "10-4, Black Widow, 10-4."

She preened at that.

And, as pathetic as it was, I preened a little myself.

Avery loves me.

Christ, I was a sap.

Until I found her, there wasn't cause for celebration though. I eyed the stairwell. Palmed my one remaining Glock, and then ascended the stairs.

33

AVERY

My hands shook around the gun.

They shook even more when the woman's gaze jumped to my face. Those familiar blue eyes of hers were startling clear. No fear at the gun pressed to her temple. No quivering lips.

"Do it," the woman rasped.

My stomach dropped. "What?"

When the door squealed again, the woman's hands went in the air, trying to grasp my arm. "Do it," she said again, desperation tingeing her voice, "*do it.* Please, please, please—"

The hinges gave up their fight.

I twisted at the waist, forcing impassivity to my face when all I felt was frantic energy pulsing through my body. "Mr. Ambideaux," I drawled with false bravado, "how wonderful of you to join us."

He stumbled, the momentum of throwing his body at the door making it hard for him to stop. Dark eyes volleyed from me to Lincoln's mother.

"Victoria and I were just having a lovely conversation."

My index finger hovered over the trigger, and I immediately slipped it to the left. Just in case I got jumpy. Although, who was I kidding? I was beyond jumpy already.

My lungs seized the air, and I struggled to appear unaffected.

"Back away from her," Ambideaux barked. "I'm telling you right now, Miss Peyton, if you pull that trigger, I will end you for good. Better yet, I'll hand-deliver you to your stepfather." Mouth tugging in that same awful smile, he added, "Is that how you want this to end? *I would love nothing more.*"

Beside me, Lincoln's mother began a new, softly uttered chant: "Do it, do it do it do it."

I had no idea if she referred to me still or if she was egging Ambideaux on. I re-grasped the gun, hating the sweat pooling in my palms. "I've got no interest in going to see the mayor."

"Then put the gun down."

I forced steel into my tone. "Screw you."

Eyes narrowing into slits, he swept aside the fabric of his suit jacket to reveal a holstered gun at his hip. "Let me tell you what happens to people who cross me, Miss Peyton." He palmed the gun, bringing it up to eye level before turning it to point at me. "I shoot them, but of course, nowhere where they're particularly likely to die . . . not right away. I want them to suffer. I want them to bleed."

His leather shoes slipped over the carpet silently as he approached.

"Only when they're begging me for life do I move on to the next step." The mouth of his pistol went to his cheek, where he drew a line down the length of his profile. Slow. Menacing. I immediately thought of Lincoln, and the *J* he'd been forced to carve into, just to show that he would never be owned by this man. "They're all marked by me in some way. Tattoos on the living. Scars on the almost-dead. And then, of course, they're then brought out west for the gators to feast on."

The image made my stomach hurt.

My heart, too.

Voice releasing on a rasp, I said, "You're insane."

"No, Miss Peyton," he said with an odd little grin on his face, "that is not at all what I am."

"Do it," whispered Lincoln's mother again, "please, please, do it."

Ambideaux's gaze cut to her. "Victoria—"

"Samantha!" she shrieked, startling me. The gun jerked in my hand, accidentally shoving forward on her temple, and the damn woman didn't even flinch. She tilted her head, giving the gun more space to play along her hairline. "I'm not Victoria. I'm not Victoria. I'm not—"

Confusion gripped me, and then a moment later, a gunshot erupted.

The window to my right shattered just as Ambideaux went down, his big body crumpling as something hit him from behind.

A familiar frame bulldozed Ambideaux over, rolling the older man onto his back while he straddled his midsection.

Lincoln.

Oh, God.

I didn't dare make a sound, fear clogging my throat that I'd distract him and he'd end up with a bullet in his head instead of it sailing through a window.

Hands wrapped around my wrist. "Please," the woman —Samantha?—whispered urgently, her eyes fixed on the gun. "Please kill me. I can't"—a sob wracked her body—"I can't do this anymore. He'll never let me go. Please. Do it, do it, do it."

My mouth went dry.

Lincoln had said his mother had never cared about him, but I couldn't kill her. *I can't end someone's life.* The gun had just been a threat. A way to bend Ambideaux to my demands, letting me escape unscathed.

"*Please.*" She yanked on my hand.

Masculine grunting tore my attention from her to land on the men wrestling on the ground. Lincoln nailed Ambideaux in the face, a fist so powerful that it whipped the man's head to the side and no doubt loosened his teeth on impact.

"I should have killed you," Ambideaux growled loud enough for me to hear, his hands scrabbling for purchase around Lincoln's throat, still wielding his gun as his arm slashed through the air. "I had so many damn opportunities over the years and I was too soft."

Lincoln didn't say a word. His face was a mask of concentration as he weaved out of the way of Ambideaux's grasping hands. Leaning forward, Lincoln hooked his legs around the other man's, and then rolled them over until Ambideaux was eating carpet and Lincoln was on his back.

His gun trained on the back of the man's head.

34

LINCOLN

I was aware of Avery's beautiful hazel eyes on me.

Aware of the woman I'd always thought of as my mother making incoherent pleas that didn't register beyond the thundering of my heart in my chest.

Adrenaline pulsing like I'd been injected with Epinephrine, I kept the muzzle steady on the back of my father's head. *My father.* Bitterness joined the adrenaline, and I leveraged my pistol forward, digging the mouth into Jason's skull.

I leaned down, the Glock brushing my unscarred cheek when I hissed, "Not exactly going down as you'd planned it, wouldn't you say? *Dad.*"

His body twitched under mine, and I laughed.

Fuck, I laughed. Long and hard and so damn bitter. "I always wondered why you'd taken a liking to me in foster care. Me over anyone else. And here I'd been thinking that I was special."

I heard Avery's gasp, but I couldn't let myself be distracted.

The sight of Ambideaux pointing a gun at her would forever be imprinted in my head. It'd twisted my vision, driven me to the brink of insanity, and now here I was, holding my old man up at gunpoint and not regretting a damn thing.

No one touched her. No one threatened her.

I would fucking send them to hell first.

"What?" My palm landed on the man's head, and I roughly forced him to turn his face to the right, so that his left cheek was planted against the carpet. The gun, I dragged over the side of his profile exposed to me. His right side. "Too bad I'm all out of knives," I drawled, voice low, "or else I'd carve your face the same way you did to mine. To *your son*."

His Adam's apple bobbed. "I love your mother. Don't do this in front of her, Lincoln. Don't make her see—"

"She's not my mother!" I bellowed, which prompted more incoherent mumbles from my mom—*Samantha.* Ambideaux's mouth popped open, cheeks hollowing, as I pushed the gun deeper. "I learned a lot today, Jason, but mostly I learned that you are out of your mind."

He wheezed, and I felt his legs thrash as he struggled to flip me over. "I made you," he bit out harshly, "I made you who you are. A killer. A monster. Just like *me*."

The words arrowed into my heart like pinpricks.

"It's not true."

I glanced up, past the brutal scene before me, to stare at Avery. Her arms were down by her sides. Her gaze transfixed on me.

She wet her lips. "It's not true," she said again, louder this time. "You know that it's not true, Lincoln."

"Do it," chanted Samantha in the bed, her arms around her middle, "do it, do it."

Beneath me, Ambideaux thrashed some more. "You will always be what I made of you. A killer, Lincoln."

The endless noise was an assault on my ears, but I couldn't tear my gaze away from Avery. I watched her move, the way her lips formed the words that I couldn't hear over the roaring in my head.

Don't, she mouthed, *you are better than this. So much better.*

It didn't feel that way. It felt like I wanted to sink into my reality and pull the trigger, ending my father's life. One less threat hanging over my head for years to come when I didn't bend over backward to do his bidding.

I'm better than this.

I wasn't, not really.

But I damn sure wanted to be—because of her, Avery.

Unwilling to loosen my grip and have the roles reversed, with Ambideaux riding cowboy on my back, I sent a quick glance over the room, trying to find something I could use as rope. "Ave," I grunted, "get me—"

"Get out!"

I started at the shriek, my hands jerking from the unexpectedness of it.

"Get out! Get out! Get out!"

I looked to my right, dread lifting my chin slowly, and made eye contact with the mayor of New Orleans. His gaze was on Avery, transfixed in much the same way that guests do while watching a fascinating performance on stage.

The gun he held clasped between two hands was trained on her.

Fuck.

"Get out! *Get out!*"

Weeks ago, Avery had pulled the Death card for my

future. It'd matched my fears for so long, but I refused to go down. I had a life to live. A woman to love.

My gun left Ambideaux's temple and I rolled out of the way. Rose up onto one knee at the same moment Foley grimaced and turned to engage with me.

One . . .

Two . . .

Pft! Pft!

"Jesus Christ."

Foley dropped to his knees, hand going to his stomach where I'd hit him. The stomach, with all of its organs and intestines, would lead to a slow, excruciating death—unless he received medical help soon.

Relief sank into my system.

It was short-lived.

Arms locked around my chest, driving me backward onto the floor. *Jason.* My back landed with a thud, my molars cracking together as Ambideaux straddled me. And, just as he had in my townhouse weeks ago, he shoved the mouth of the gun into my forehead so that all I saw was the barrel and all I heard was his harsh breathing and Samantha's chants and Avery's scream.

"I love her," Jason whispered, his hair disheveled, his suit even more so. "I love her more than anything."

Air expelled sharply from my nose as I fought to remain calm. "More so than Nat? Your wife?"

Mouth flatlining, he shook his head. "Nat had it good. I gave her the world. It's because she's a greedy bitch that she couldn't handle you, that she couldn't look at Victoria." A grim mask settled over his face, and he leaned into my chest, giving me his full weight and making it hard to breathe. "No one crosses me, son. No one. It's a point to prove, to keep the fear moving in my favor in this city." His finger slid over the trigger, taking my long-dead heart right along with it. "I'm sorry that this has to happen. But you deserve it, just like they all did before you. You deserve—"

There was a low *thud* that echoed in my ears and robbed me of air, and then Ambideaux stared down at me, dazed, swaying, before collapsing on top of me.

Avery stood behind him, a gun gripped in her two hands, a look of resigned horror on her face.

I'd once said that my heart was dead. I'd fully believed it. A person couldn't do the things that I had done and still remain human inside—I'd been a monster, just like Ambideaux had raised me to be. But with my father's slumped weight on top of me and Avery standing just a foot away, her eyes as round as saucers, I knew that wasn't true.

If I'd been a monster, there wouldn't be regret and grief seeping into my marrow.

Regret that Avery had had to take this step when she'd made the decision to abstain from taking another's life.

Grief that Jason, the one man I'd leaned on while growing up, had, at some point, lost his mind so that his delusions became his reality . . . and threatened everyone else in his wake.

Avery's tongue swiped along the cushion of her bottom lip. "He's not dead, I don't think. You were right—I don't know how to shoot a gun. I didn't want to risk killing you instead if I aimed wrong. I-I slammed the barrel on his head."

Rolling Jason's body off mine, I pressed a finger to his throat, just beneath the jut of his jaw. His pulse was light but it was there. A strange mixture of relief and disappointment slid through me, and I didn't bother to sort it all out. Not right now.

My gaze went to Samantha, the woman Ambideaux

had kept here in captivity. Her smashed legs. She hadn't been intentionally cruel, I saw that now. Like me, she'd been in her own prison of Ambideaux's making, unable to escape.

"I'm sorry," I rasped when her blue eyes, so much like mine, swung my way. "I'm so sorry, Samantha."

Her eyes went wide and her shoulders shook and a distraught cry pulled from her mouth. "Samantha," she whispered, "I've always been Samantha."

A hand landed on my back, comforting in its softness, in its slight pressure. For years, I'd been strong. Unshakable. The man who got things done and didn't ask questions. My chest was littered with dates and numbers of those who I'd put in their graves way too soon.

In this moment, though, I turned to Avery—the woman who saw beneath my hard veneer—and I swallowed her in a hug that lifted her feet off the floor and had her hands jumping around my back to keep her balance.

"I'm okay, Lincoln." She kissed my chest, right over my heart, right over her number. "I'm okay."

My nose nudged her neck as I inhaled her scent. "I didn't ask for a savior." My lips found the pulse at her neck, and I lingered there, gratification filtering through me that she was safe, she was okay. "I didn't ask for a savior, but you found me anyway."

And then my Avery, the bravest girl I knew, kissed my chest again and propped her chin on my pec, lifting her gaze to mine. Her lashes were wet with tears. Her beautiful face open and transparent as she murmured, "You found me in the shadows, Sergeant, when I was afraid, and you brought me back to the world of the living."

We were two untethered souls who'd found each other, and, Christ, holding her felt so good. So right. "You're mi—"

Commotion at the doorway had me lowering Avery to her feet.

Katie was there. Quinn. Delery. And, to my biggest shock of all, Big Hampton stood before them all. He looked from me to Avery. And then, to her, he said, "I've heard that sometimes good people do bad things, Miss Peyton. I'm making an effort to be good all the way around, so I hope you won't mind that I took the liberty to go to the NOPD in your stead and"—he looked down at the mayor of New Orleans, who was clutching his stomach and moaning—"see to it that things were put into place to make things right."

Avery released a strangled cough. "Well, damn."

And if that wasn't a proper slogan for the last month's events, I didn't know what was.

35

AVERY

SIX HOURS LATER...

"Can I sit here with you?"

Since the showdown at Ambideaux's house, and the bloodshed that had followed, Lincoln and I had been shuffled to NOPD Headquarters. The building was a 1960's monolith with stark, uncompromising lines, and a general air of sterility that made my skin run cold.

Or maybe it was just that, after learning everything that I had today about Foley and Momma, and then Lincoln and Jason Ambideaux and his poor Aunt Samantha, I felt chilled to the bone.

"Miss Laurel?"

Throughout the day, I'd had to answer to Laurel and Avery, and my brain had lost track the number of times I'd failed to turn around when spoken to. For a woman who'd adopted too many identities, I'd grown to know one—Avery—and nothing else seemed to fit any longer.

I glanced up at the familiar husky voice—Quinn—he'd introduced himself to me, earlier, when we'd all first found ourselves at headquarters and camped out in uncomfortable seats to wait our turn to speak with the police.

The man who let me live.

The man who didn't kill Momma.

I knew, somehow, that he'd seemed familiar when I'd first stumbled across him at Whiskey Bay.

I nodded jerkily. "Of course. Sure."

His ass hit the seat next to mine, and he immediately hunched over, elbows on his knees. For a moment, he was quiet. And then, "I thought I was seeing ghosts when you walked into Whiskey Bay a few weeks back. My past coming back to haunt me and all that."

I swallowed, then dropped my gaze to my clasped hands. "Not a ghost," I said softly, "just a girl who learned to hide for a very long time."

A dark noise reverberated in his chest, and he shoved one hand through his salt-and-pepper crewcut. "You didn't deserve any of what happened. You were a child and Foley was a greedy son of a gun. She knew what he'd do to her—what he'd done to others—and that he'd never let her get out alive. I've wracked my brain so many times, so many conversations we never got to have. I wouldn't do it, she knew that, and I think she worried about Foley moving to the next person who'd kill her, no questions asked." He shoved a hand through his hair again, tugging on the short strands. "I want to believe she knew what she was doing and that she'd thought everything through, including what might happen to you."

I stared down at my hands. Watched them curl and unfurl in my lap. "She drank a lot. I remember her falling asleep with the bottle tucked to her chest. I remember her crying at all hours of the day, a glass of wine in her hand." She'd been lightness and shadows, when I really looked back on it—laughter and thunderstorms, a troubled combination that probably had crumpled upon learning what Foley intended.

It pained me to think that Momma had been in such a dark place . . . that she probably hadn't been thinking clearly when she'd pulled the trigger. That maybe she'd felt like she had nowhere to go, nowhere to turn.

Just like I had for all these years.

It hurt to swallow, but no more than my heart already hurt, knowing all that I knew now. And what I'd never know.

"I know you feel guilty, but I promise that it's okay. From what I understand, you were stuck. She stole the decision from you and you did what you could—you kept me safe."

I didn't want to understand—I wanted to cling to the rage that had fueled me for so long. But at what purpose? You couldn't reverse the actions of the dead, and you couldn't question them after they were gone. If any of that were possible, the world would be a different place. Momma had made her decision that night, and I had to live with that.

Quinn's Adam's apple bobbed as he continued to stare down at his scarred hands, and it hit me then that he and Lincoln were one and the same. Their loyalties had laid with different people, but at the end of the day . . . two killers, two so-called monsters, two allegedly heartless men who lived for the violence and nothing more.

Quinn swiped a thumb under his eye. Cleared his throat. "I met her first, you know. In Jackson Square. She was twenty-four to my nineteen, but goddamn, she was beautiful. All long, blond hair and brilliant hazel eyes, the kind I wanted to lose myself in."

My heart rocketed to a stop. "In Jackson Square?"

His jaw clenched. "She was one of the artists along the gates. Painted the most beautiful scenes of the city that you'd ever see. I didn't have the courage to do more than talk to her that day, and the next time I saw her, she was on Foley's arm. My boss, the girl I couldn't stop thinking about." He laughed, the sound hollow and sad. "She remembered me because I'd made a fool of myself. I remembered her because I'd never seen another soul with so much light. You were six then, I think."

The heartache in his voice broke my own heart, cleaving it in two. Without giving it a second thought, I touched his forearm in sympathy. He looked like he needed it. Like maybe this was the first time since Momma had passed that he'd had the chance to say what he wanted to say.

"I wasn't allowed to be around you," he added a moment later. "You weren't even his child, but there were rules in play. Like Cat, you belonged to him. He was—*is*—a controlling man, but the night he came to me and told me that I needed to be the one to kill her, I refused. Said no."

It was hard to breathe, harder to digest it all. "Lincoln mentioned something about an inheritance? I just don't understand."

Quinn's shoulders lifted. "From what little I know, your mom was cut off from her family when she had you. She made her living down in the square, sometimes bartending here or there, but then Foley swept her off her feet." His feet began to tap the floor, nervous energy radiating from him. "Your grandfather was dying, and I guess there was no one else to leave the money to—so he gave it to your mom with a single stipulation: if something were to happen to her, the money, the countless properties throughout the city, would go to her husband."

"And not to me."

"Not to you," he repeated, his voice cut with an edge. "I'm sorry that he wasn't progressive or that he didn't see you as—"

"I'm not."

And I wasn't. I'd never met my grandfather. The sparse memories that I had of life before Jay were of me and my mother living in a small apartment over a corner store in the Marigny. There were no cousins to play with or family to smother me with affection, just me and Momma. I'd done fine without the money all these years, and though it balled my fists to think that she was dead on account of a greedy bastard like Jay wanting to own it all, I knew he felt his own form of regret.

He'd called Nat by my mother's name whenever he screwed her.

He'd found women—sometimes teenagers—throughout the city who looked like her, to do the same.

He'd get what was coming to him, but I . . . I just wanted to go home for tonight. Wherever that was.

"Sweetheart."

That voice.

I blinked up at Lincoln, at the hand he offered me, at the harshness of his features, and the beauty of his Haint-blue eyes.

"Harlonne let me know we can take off for the night." He paused, fingers curling when I didn't take his hand fast enough. Doubt flashed like a bolt of lightning across his face. And then, "Come home with me."

We were two broken souls, our lives somehow aligning parallel throughout the years without either of us knowing. My eyes watered, and just before his hand would have dropped back to his side, I caught him by the fingertips. "Yes," I whispered, "please."

At my side, Quinn cleared his throat again. "I'll let you go, then." He stood, clapping Lincoln on the shoulder.

"Thanks for using me as a human body shield today. Much appreciated."

Lincoln barked out a laugh. "Desperate times."

"Don't I know it." He glanced back at me, brow furrowed. "Before I go . . . Nat's already getting out of the city. We all got the alert, so I—well, I thought you should know. You're not going to have to worry." He turned away without another word, head down. His limp was more pronounced than the first time I'd seen him at Whiskey Bay.

"Quinn!" I shouted, and he immediately checked over his shoulder. "Give me your number. Maybe . . . maybe we could get lunch one day? Talk about my momma or the Saints or whatever it is that you want?"

The man's face lit up like a beacon, and I felt the warmth inside my chest, too. "Fuck yeah. I mean, yeah. Yeah, that would be good. If your boyfriend promises not to clobber me over the head, maybe we can invite him too."

Lincoln's smile was all badass charm. "No promises, man. Bad habits are the hardest to break."

And then my own Captain America, my own Thor, was swooping me up in his arms, just like he had outside that shack when I'd wanted to clobber *him* over the head. He pressed a kiss to my cheek, to my forehead, to the crooked slant of my nose, broken from a skateboard accident gone wrong as a kid.

"I'm taking you home," he said in my ear, "and that's an order you're gonna have to obey."

I grinned. "Funny enough, *no* isn't a word in my vocabulary right now. Better take advantage while you can."

"Oh, I plan to, sweetheart. I plan to."

36

LINCOLN

I took advantage, as I promised—and Avery didn't have a single complaint as she sank into the steaming bathwater two hours later.

"God," she groaned, her head tipping back as the water lapped at her small breasts, "that feels so damn good."

I snapped open a shampoo bottle. Squeezed a healthy dose into my palm. "Lean forward," I said, my voice pure grit as my cock hardened in my sweats. "Let me take care of you."

She did as I ordered, leaning forward without question, droplets of water clinging to her smooth skin as she pulled away from the side of the tub. Like a lot of old homes in New Orleans, I was the proud owner of a claw-foot tub. Normally, I hated the damn thing. Now, I counted my lucky blessings as I inched my chair closer to the porcelain and set my hands in Avery's dark hair to massage the shampoo into her scalp.

"Will you keep it black?" I asked. I didn't give a shit one way or the other, but with Jay Foley in the hospital—and then on a one-way ticket to Louisiana's infamous Angola prison—she was free.

Free to be who she wanted.

Free to look however she pleased.

Free to leave me.

If I had it my way, she'd be suctioned to my side for the rest of our lives. My wife, my anchor, the future mother of our children. Fuck, I wanted it so bad. When death had always been my fated future, however I looked at it, it felt surreal to think that I had a chance for something else now.

"Yeah." A moan escaped her lips as I rocked my thumbs into the base of her skull, kneading the muscles at the nape of her neck. "God, yes."

Laughter rumbled in my chest. "Is that a yes to the dark hair or a yes to me making you feel like heaven right now?"

Her head fell forward. "All of it. Particularly the heaven bit."

My hands glided down the expanse of her back, thumbs digging in along either side of her spine. She was perfect under my touch. Beautiful. Expressive. Her arms went to the sides of the tub, and then she arched her back. The mirror on the wall opposite us showed me what my vantage point didn't: her breasts thrusting forward, her eyes open and homed in on me, the slope of her belly rising above the water as she stretched upward gracefully.

Fingers teasing the sides of her ribcage, I blatantly flirted with the outer swells of her breasts. "What do you want, sweetheart? Tell me what you want."

If she heard the urgency in my voice, it only seemed to spur hers on. In the mirror, her hazel eyes rounded. She reached back over her shoulder, seeking my hand. I dunked my hand in the water, rinsing off the shampoo and then tangled our fingers together.

"I want to be wanted," she said, and I didn't miss the slight quiver in her hands. "But more than that, I want to be loved." She swallowed. Squeezed my hand. "By you, though. Only you."

I'd never been particularly sentimental, but as I brought her hand up to my mouth to press a kiss to her knuckles, I realized that I'd never let my guard down long enough to fall either. "Make room for me, Ave." I let her go. Shucked my sweats and my shirt and put all the horrors of my life on display for her to see. "I'm coming in."

The water swirled around her diaphragm as she moved to the opposite end of the tub. Craned her back and rinsed some of the soap from her head. Steam enveloped me as I set one foot into the water, then did the same with the other. And when I lowered myself to sit, the water rose from her diaphragm to her collarbone. It flirted with the lip of the tub, splashing over the side.

I didn't give a fuck.

"C'mere," I growled. "Let me love you."

A small smile played at her lips as she crawled on her hands and knees toward me, the water caressing her bottom lip. She looked like a sea goddess, sent to ruin my piece of mind.

Gorgeous. So fucking gorgeous, and she was all mine.

My hand gripped her waist, spinning her around so that her back was to my chest. She floated up, and I clamped my legs over hers to keep her in place. Bent my legs, so that hers would do the same, driving her open for me down below.

The back of her head fell to my collarbone. "I feel like there's so much to say." Her fingers teased the short hairs on my thighs, dragging her nails down, down, down until they came mighty damn close to grazing my cock. "I want to say everything—how shocked I feel that Momma took her own life, knowing that he would kill her anyway. That I'm trying not to feel disappointed that Jay will probably live or that Ambideaux . . ."

The blow she'd delivered him had shaken his brains, that's for sure. He'd fallen into a coma—maybe I was still that heartless bastard I'd always been because I felt no remorse about hoping he never woke up from it. A tiger couldn't always change his stripes, and I'd done enough changing in the last few weeks. For the better. I may not be a monster, but I'd never be citizen of the year.

I kissed Avery's damp shoulder. "We'll watch and see how it goes with the medics. He might come out of it."

"I wish I felt guiltier, for your sake more than mine. He was your father, but what he did to Samantha all these years . . ."

The way I looked at it, Samantha was the true victim in this situation. The doctors had found both heroin and Methamphetamine in her system—no doubt injected by Jason himself to keep her hooked and sedated. She'd told me over and over again that I wasn't her son, and instead of feeling dejected over it, I should have wondered why. Should have done something more instead of giving Jason more time to buy off the doctors so they told me what he wanted me to hear: her head was scrambled from the accident.

No, her head was scrambled from decades of drug usage that had been forced upon her.

My grip tightened on Avery's waist, and I wrapped an arm around her front like a band. "They'll wean her off," I said into the curve of her shoulder, "and if he survives, he'll rot in jail the way he should have for all these years."

Avery's soft hand, wrinkled from the water, closed over mine. "Look at me, Lincoln."

I met her gaze in the mirror, my chin on her shoulder. Struggled to not let her see the pain that I couldn't shake. "It'll all be fine. All of it."

Her nail bit into my knuckles. "Stop being so strong."

I smiled—and the one that reflected back in the mirror was just as weak as I suspected it was. "Thought I was Captain America. Thor, whatever. I have to be strong."

She shook her head, the strands of her hair brushing my face. "What did you once tell me? I'm a brave girl." Gently, she removed my arm from her middle and turned around. "Sit on the edge of the tub and let me be the one who takes care of you."

I wanted to tell her no. I wanted to be the one who cared for her, who made her feel safe.

Fuck it.

The bathwater surged as I ripped my body from its fold and sat on the edge of the tub, my hands going to the curved lip. Avery licked her lips. Glided closer. Rose onto her knees and circled my cock at the root.

My stomach tightened at the feel of her. I'd had her only hours ago, but, Christ, it felt like ages. Months. Years, even. With her eyes on my face, she brought her mouth to my hard-on. Swiped her tongue along the crown, and I'd be lying if I said that the one touch didn't light me up like an inferno.

"Ave," I grunted, hands still on the lip of the tub. *Don't push her to go faster. Let her set the pace.* It went against my nature to do that, to take the backseat . . . but with her, I'd done a lot of things that weren't very *me*.

Picnics under the moonlight.

Conversations that didn't stick on sex and only sex.

Falling in love.

Her mouth enveloped me. Her wet heat. The water

splashing around my knees as she worked my cock until my eyes were crossed and my breathing came in hard pants that sounded choked even to my own ears. Her tongue glided along the base as she sucked me in deep. Her fingers tugged on my balls.

She was pushing me, testing my limits with a playful glint in her hazel eyes whenever she looked up at me, her pink lips opened wide. It was the exact visual I'd had when I met her in Jackson Square.

Avery was the girl who could handle my darkness, who dusted off the glowing embers with a flick of her hand and pulled me from the roots of hell to make love to her under the moon.

She licked the tip of my dick, then challenged me with a saucily delivered, "Give me everything, Sergeant. I can take it."

With a deep-seated groan, I submitted.

My hands went to her head, tangling in her hair. My hips rose off the porcelain as I drove my cock into her mouth, deep enough that I glanced off the back of her throat. My heart thundered with the words I only knew with her: *I love you, Iloveyou, Iloveyou.*

And then I was tearing myself away, watching my cock pop free from her mouth, as I dragged her up from the water and spun her around to stand. With me seated on the edge of the tub and her standing, she was at the perfect height. I nudged her legs together, so that her thighs touched, and then positioned her in front of me.

Her pussy hovering just above the tip of my cock.

"I want you like this," I said, voice low, my hand following the curve of her ass. "You taking your pleasure from me, no barriers between us."

There was a minute pause where I worried that I'd come

too strong, that I'd demanded more than she was willing to give just yet.

Then, her sweet, throaty voice greeted my ears and I almost came right then and there: "Challenge accepted, Cap. Challenge accepted."

The first glide in was a tight fit, and we both groaned.

"Oh, God, you feel big." She sank back, testing the waters by inching down the length of my cock. "You feel so big . . . like this."

I squeezed her ass cheeks and tried not to blow my load. "The hammer doesn't mess around."

A half-laugh fell from her mouth. "You always make jokes at the very worst times." Her fingers dug into my thighs as she slipped down another inch. "First when we're jumping out of windows and now this?"

Glancing down, I watched my cock sink fully into her. Gritting my teeth, I bit out, "Trust me, sweetheart, this isn't a joke."

Arching her back, she rose up, straightening her knees, before coming back down on me again. And then did it again. And again. Her ass moving up, her pussy sucking me in, she controlled the rhythm, the pace, the goddamn way that I breathed.

My skin felt like it was on fire, burning like I'd sat amidst the flames as opposed to the gradually cooling water lapping at our legs. I barely noticed, not when I sat there, letting Avery take me exactly how she wanted me.

Fast. Then slow. Then fast again.

My palm glanced off her ass cheek, punishing her the way that she was punishing me by never keeping the same rhythm for long. The pleasure was addicting. The way she rode me, like I was here to quench her desire alone, was addicting.

Circling her hip, my hand cupped between her legs and her pace jerked to a halt.

"Keep going," I muttered, the pad of my middle finger finding her swollen clit.

On shaky legs, she continued. Her back arched. Her ass bouncing. Her head dropped forward as she let out a moan that rattled my soul. I couldn't see her face in this angle, the mirror too far to the right.

"Are you watching me?" I demanded.

Her only response was a jerk of her hips and a loud, "Oh, my God, *Lincoln*."

My balls tightened, my orgasm creeping in. Fuck, not yet. *Not yet.* I applied more pressure on her clit. Gripped her hip with my other hand, forcing her to take the entire length of my cock with every downward thrust she gave me. "Are you watching me play with you?" I said again, pushing us both to our limits. "One finger or two?"

"Two," she gasped, her pussy squeezing me like a vice when I rubbed her clit with two fingers, just as she wanted. "*Please,* Lincoln."

She felt so damn good.

Air pumped out of my lungs, so uneven with each exhale that it almost hurt. Hurt even more when I managed a guttural, "Please what, sweetheart? *Please what*?"

"Love me. Just love me."

She burst apart in that moment and I jerked her off me just in time for my own orgasm to hit. I came all over her back, wishing that I'd come inside her instead. *Soon. Just not yet.* I wasn't a patient sort of guy—I took, knowing that no one would be waiting on the sidelines to give me what I wanted.

But Avery . . . I wanted her for forever. We'd get there.

Cupping the water in my hands, I washed her back.

Grabbed a loofah and drizzled soap into it, and then soaped her up. I turned her to face me. Swept the loofah up her flat belly to tease at her nipples.

And then I gave her my heart, for whatever it was worth: "I love you, Ave." I swallowed past my nerves—ones I'd never experienced before. "I walked into your world and then dragged you into mine. I've never been a gentleman—one look at my face and you know exactly what I mean. I'm rough around the edges. Dark all the way to my soul. My past is Ruin, as you told me with the cards. But the way you look at me . . . like you know I can be someone better . . . Christ, I want to be that man for you. The good one. The one who you know would do anything for you, no matter what it is." I dropped the loofah. Brought my hands down on her hips. Soaked up her warmth like it was a balm to the ice that had always coated my skin. "You're not looking for a savior, but I fucking hope you might be looking for a guy like me . . . the kind of guy who loves you, even if he knows he'll spend the rest of his life trying to be worthy of a brave girl like you."

My confession wasn't pretty.

It was barely articulate.

And yet, Avery dropped to her knees before me. Water splashed her chest, the underside of her chin. Her hazel eyes were red with unshed tears, and her nails dug into the back of my calves. She could draw blood and I wouldn't give two shits, so long as she—

"I bow to no man," she whispered, her gaze locked on my face. "I tattooed the words on my skin on my momma's ten-year anniversary." She inhaled sharply, and a lone tear fell from her bottom lash to land on her cheek. "I made that vow, knowing what had happened to her. I made that vow, determined to keep my heart safe and my body untouched from those who abuse me. I bowed to no one . . . until you. Until you walked up to me like the king of darkness and forced me to shed the shadows. You pushed me. You baited me. You made me *come alive* when I'd been dead for so damn long."

She kissed my knee, pressing her lips to the skin as her lids fell shut. "I wanted you, even when Big Hampton dropped the bomb that we may or may not be related. I wanted you, even when you showed me your darkness and I matched it with mine. And I love you, knowing that your rough edges will always be outweighed by the size of your hammer and the goodness in your heart."

I blinked. Rewound her words in my head to replay.

Stared down at her when she grinned brilliantly back at me, another tear joining the first on her cheek. "I'm trying to be romantic here and you're cracking jokes."

She nipped my knee. "Like you said before, your hammer is *not* a joke, Sergeant. Although neither was me jumping from a fire escape with no underwear on either. Could this be . . . karma, maybe?"

Reading the intent in my eyes, Avery launched from the bathtub and nearly slipped when her feet hit the tile.

I swiveled around, keeping my ass on the tub and my feet now on the floor. Water dripped from every inch of our skin and I didn't even care.

"You still feel good about following orders?" I asked her when she righted herself and skipped out of the bathroom, her perky ass making me hard all over again.

She glanced at me over her shoulder, her hazel eyes bright. "Catch me and see for yourself."

I caught her. Down the hall, where I then pressed her up against the wall and hiked her leg up, spreading her wide as I thrust into her.

"I love you," she whispered into my chest, kissing my heart.

All my life, I'd been a man resigned to death. But maybe the tarot cards had it wrong. Maybe it wasn't death in the literal sense, but maybe something like a new beginning. A fresh start. I could get down with that, so long as I had Avery at my side.

I slid my arm behind her, then pressed my mouth to her neck, just the way she liked. "I love you, sweetheart. Christ, how I love you."

EPILOGUE

AVERY

A year and two months later . . .

Jay Foley survived his gunshot wound.

Most days, I tried not to be bitter about it.

But because he didn't die, I sought out to ensure he'd never make it outside of a prison. When I wasn't taking my GED classes or working in the women's shelter I'd helped to found with the help of Lincoln's Aunt Samantha —who'd finally weaned herself off the drugs with the help of her nephew and the good doctors at University Hospital —I tracked down every female Lincoln had ever spoken to about the case against Foley.

I had lived in the shadows of New Orleans for over a decade, and because of that, I knew where to look. Like me in my teenage years, they'd feared men. They'd feared Lincoln, even when he'd assured them he only wanted to help.

In the end, I was the one who convinced them to testify against a man who had ripped families apart because of his greed. I was the one who stood next to them in each court date, my encouraging words the persuasion they needed to come forward.

"Corruption and New Orleans go hand-in-hand, and have since 1718," I told the judge when I began my testimony, using the words Jay once had repeated to me. Mayors in this city weren't immune and they weren't gods. They murdered, they sinned, they embezzled money like every other criminal to sit behind prison walls.

The judge dismissed court with a hammer of his gavel, but we already knew what his judgment would be. The city wanted Foley's head on a platter, and unless the judge wanted to face serious criticism from the public, the former mayor would be sentenced to Angola by the time the day was over.

I glanced back at the row of people who'd come to support me. Lincoln with Aunt Samantha. Pete and Sal were seated beside Katie, who was next to the city's new mayor, Joshua "Big" Hampton. He was an unlikely ally, no doubt driven by guilt for the way he'd manhandled Lincoln and me. Over the last year, though, he'd stood by his word to right his wrongs.

Sometimes good people did bad things—I was willing to overlook his faults for the way he'd turned the city around and led by example.

Quinn was here, somewhere, watching my back as he'd grown to do over the last year. I was a tarot reader in Jackson Square, a twenty-six-year-old woman studying for her GED, and part-owner to a shelter—but to Quinn, I would always be the daughter of the woman he'd loved. I didn't need a bodyguard just like I didn't need a savior, but the men in my life didn't give a damn when it came to seeing me safe.

Foley met my gaze when I stopped before his row. His handsome features were sallow, drawn, with deep, dark circles beneath his eyes. He looked like hell personified . . . and I'd never been more satisfied.

"Laurel." The metal cuffs around his ankles clanged their presence as he climbed to his feet. "I . . . I wanted to say that—"

I didn't shrink into myself, not the way I had outside our dining room all those years ago. Kicking up my chin, I forced out the words I'd rehearsed all morning on the drive in with Katie and Lincoln. "It's Avery."

Those weren't the words I'd rehearsed. Digging into my purse, I pulled out the one tarot card I'd brought with me today. The illustration was dark, composed of greens and blues and grays and drowning fountains. I set the card on the balustrade that separated us.

"What is that?"

"Gluttony." When his eyes narrowed, I added, "I hope that your stay in Angola is a frequent reminder that every step that led you there was on account of your own greed." I nodded toward the card. "I used to think that I wanted death for you, but I think . . . no, I think the sort of lifelong suffering you're in for is so much more appropriate."

Nodding, more to myself than to him, I turned on my heels and started to head over to my people. My family.

"Avery."

That voice, that sickening voice which had been the source of comfort to me as a child. I didn't look back—wouldn't give him that sort of satisfaction.

The silence stretched uncomfortably, and then: "She would be proud of you. Your momma, she would be so proud."

I knew that.

Be brave.

Be bold.

Sometimes being brave meant holding your tongue and letting someone else drown in their own guilt. I said nothing in return.

After all these years, I'd come face to face with Jay Foley —and I'd ensured, after saying my piece during today's session, that I would never have to do so again.

Vengeance, sometimes, was best served by legal professionals.

"LAGNIAPPE" - BECAUSE NEW ORLEANS ALWAYS GIVES MORE THAN YOU ASKED FOR

LINCOLN

Later that night . . .

My wife was exhausted.

The signs were there in the dark thumbprints beneath her hazel eyes and the quiet way she watched a recap of today's court proceedings on the TV opposite our bed. Over the last few months, she'd run herself ragged trying to get everything in line to send Foley to lockup for good.

Hell, she'd done a lot more than I had when Ambideaux's court date had rolled around. I'd shown up, dressed in my Class-B's from work, my new lieutenant patch all shiny on my arm, and did what needed to be done. Jason and I hadn't exchanged a word, but I hadn't expected anything less.

And when news had broken three months ago that he'd been killed in a prison fight, a knife straight to his gut, I'd simply driven to my Aunt Samantha's new place and poured her a glass of her favorite lemonade, and said, "You don't have to worry anymore. The fucker's dead."

She rarely smiled in my direction—too many years, I guessed, from having to put up with a life that wasn't hers—but she'd opened her arms wide and a tremulous smile had graced her thin lips as she said, "Give me a hug, nephew."

Nephew, never son.

But goddamn, had it felt good.

She loved Avery, though, and I'd sensed her seething hatred for Foley as she sat beside me in court today, her fingers digging into the cushioned armrests of her wheelchair.

I'd seethed hatred all day, too. Even now, as Avery lay beside me, her eyes glued to the TV, I seethed. Pushed it down, squashing it into a million little places so I could be the man my wife deserved.

"You did good today," I murmured, coasting my palm up along her arm. "Phenomenal."

She fiddled with the engagement ring I'd purchased for her from a shop in the Quarter. Gold filigree and topped off with a ruby, it'd reminded me of her. Delicate but with a badass outlook on life that turned me on in a way that no one else ever could. The simple gold band nestled along it had been slid onto her finger a month ago in Jackson Square, at the base of the steps of St. Louis Cathedral where we'd met.

"Love you," she said, craning her neck to plant a soft kiss on my neck. "Sorry, today has me all messed up."

I covered her hand with mine, then dragged it up to hold to my scarred cheek. "Don't apologize for doing what you needed to do."

Her fingers curled against my skin, and she swept her thumb over the corner of my mouth. "Don't tell me you weren't thinking about unloading a round in the back of his head the entire time."

With a kiss to her palm, I flashed her a quick grin. "Guilty as charged." I waggled my brows. "Too soon with the legal talk?" I slid on top of her, and her legs immediately separated to make room for my body. "Or maybe just right?"

The pucker between her brows cleared when she gave a light laugh. "Always making jokes when you shouldn't."

Leaning down, I nipped her exposed shoulder. "Haven't made a joke at a funeral yet."

"That's because the opportunity hasn't presented itself to you."

I winked. "Good point."

Dropping my mouth to hers, I sipped at her lips, pulling her out of her shell and back into the light. We'd shared a million different kisses. Soft, hard, challenging. This one, though, was all comfort.

She clasped the back of my head, and I chuckled against her mouth. "There's my brave girl."

Her hips rose off the bed to press against mine. "More than you know."

I rolled away. Ignored the tent in my sweats as I motioned for her to stand. "I'm gonna need you to be brave for me tonight."

Avery sat up, her hair mussed from the pillow. "Lincoln," she drawled, "I'm pretty sure I've slept with you enough times by now that you don't need to give me the *be brave speech* just before you drop your pants."

Laughter climbed my throat as I threw her a skirt from where she'd left the folded laundry earlier this morning. One fault we had? Neither of us enjoyed putting laundry away. We'd get to it, at some point.

Tugging a shirt over my head, I said, "We're going on a little drive. Something to perk you up."

"Oh, really?" She jumped out of the bed, then yanked

her skirt up her legs and settled it around her hips. A second later, she had a top on and was ready to go.

Christ, she could be fast when she wanted to be.

On the drive, she propped her chin on her hand and stared out the front window. "Are we going to our picnic spot?" she mused, reaching forward to turn down the volume of the radio. "Or maybe we're going to satisfy one of your late-night frozen yogurt cravings?"

She knew me way too well. When I wanted to play Mr. Romantic, I brought her to the same spot on the side of the levee with the view of downtown New Orleans. And when I wanted to make her laugh at me for having the same food cravings as a kid, I took her to the frozen-yogurt joint over on Magazine Street, where we could watch the traffic pass us by from the floor to ceiling windows.

Avery Washington Asher wasn't just my wife, she was my favorite person in this world.

I squeezed her thigh, then left my hand there. "Wrong," I said as I took us on the I-10 and headed east. "Try again, ma'am."

She settled her hand over mine, overlapping our fingers. "All right . . . not a picnic, not frozen yogurt. Are we heading to the Quarter? You know how I feel about going down there on my nights off from the square."

"Are you saying that you *don't* like convincing tourists to give you more money now that you fully believe in the cards?"

"I always believed in the cards."

"That's because I taught you the best way to do it—pick the card you want and then tell everyone around that you're about to make the magic happen."

She snorted, fingers squeezing mine. "Guess it's going to be a surprise then."

Hell yeah it was.

Sliding my hand out from hers, I reached into my pocket and pulled out one of her scarves that she bought every other week from her friends in the French Market. "Put this on."

"Are we going to do something scandalous?" Her tone was playful, but she slipped the scarf around her head anyway, blindfolding herself, trusting me explicitly.

Maybe. Yes. One-hundred-percent.

With her sight blocked, I gunned the gas pedal and brought us into the Bywater. A few minutes later, we were parked, and I was walking around to Avery's side of the SUV. "Don't peek." I wrapped my hands around hers and pulled her from the car, careful to make sure she didn't tumble out. "It'll ruin the fun."

I led her up to the large brick building, ignoring the front entrance and choosing instead the new side door that led club members to the recently renovated second floor. Whiskey Bay wasn't Whiskey Bay anymore, and the Basement was a thing of the past—Nat had fled the state, taking with her my old coworker Josiah Templeton, and a few other folks like Kevan.

Quinn took bets that his old boss was living it up in Vegas.

Avery tossed in her vote for California-dreaming.

And I knew exactly where she was, thanks to Zak Benson trailing her out there and leaving crumbs wherever he went—but some shit was better to just keep to myself. So long as she stayed out of Louisiana, I didn't give a damn where she went.

"Watch your step," I told Ave, my hand on her lower back.

We climbed the steep staircase. Only when we were

fully upstairs, the door locked behind us, the club-member key in my pocket, did I pull the scarf off Avery's head. Her delighted gasp was like fireworks in July, and I stepped behind her. Lowered my mouth to her ear, and murmured, "Like what you see?"

The new owner of the building had changed things up.

The old stage lights had been exchanged with fairy lights, strung up to create a romantic glow over the myriad couples that were positioned throughout the room. A four-string quartet—yes, a *quartet*—was seated in the far-left corner, playing a song that made the space less about the kink and more about the romance.

The sex was still the sex.

That would never change, no matter who owned the building.

"I feel like I should say no," Avery said, falling into me.

"Because we're married?" I nuzzled her ear, nipped the lobe. "You like what you like, but if you ever think someone else will touch you . . . that shit's not happening. You're mine, and I don't share."

"You don't even share your frozen yogurt."

"Damn right I don't." Squeezing her hips, I gave her a little push. "Find the stage you want, and I'll meet you there after I buy us cocktails."

She twisted to stare up at me. "How will you find me?"

Another nudge, this one to her ass. "I'll always find you, sweetheart. Always."

And I did.

Stage One wasn't the same—the couple up there weren't fitted with ball-gags—but I'd known she'd come back here out of memory's sake. She'd selected the same position on the sofa, though the furniture was all new. I sat next to her, handing her one of those frozen margaritas she liked so much.

Our cheeks grazed as we both leaned in.

"What's on the lineup?" I asked at the same time she said, "I don't think he knows what he's doing. I mean, he's slapped her ass so many times I think I'm . . . I can't believe I'm about to say this, but I might be bored."

I glanced up at the couple on the stage with the fairy lights hanging so low that they were almost swimming in the cords. Sure enough, the dude was slap-happy. My brows arched when I counted ten in as many seconds.

"She's not going to be able to sit down for a week," I muttered out of the corner of my mouth.

"I know!" Avery shifted in her seat as if she were experiencing sympathy slaps to her ass. A second later: "My butt hurts just looking at them."

I set my beer on the small table to my left. "Don't worry, Captain America is here to save the day."

Avery snorted with laughter. "Please don't tell me you're about to pull out the hammer and show the poor guy on the stage exactly how it's done. You'll embarrass him while he's on the clock."

My fingers went to her skirt, and I pulled the fabric up, up, up until it was around her waist and she was thrusting her hips forward, no matter the protests that fell from her lips. And, no matter who owned the Basement now, and no matter what name it was called, Stage One would always be just about the same.

I got down on my knees before my wife, the soles of my shoes rubbing up against the stage, the sound of incessant slapping behind me. And for memory's sake, I ripped her underwear straight from her hips and jerked her close, so that my tongue could run along her slit.

"Don't worry," I said, just before I put every other man to shame in this room, "I won't make you jump out of any fire escapes tonight."

And then my mouth was on her clit, my hand clutching her quivering leg, and all I heard was her gasp and the throaty way she whispered, "God, I love you."

I swallowed my laugh and set about making my wife come so loud she'd have an encore after. I probably would never know what I did to deserve her, but I would never give her up.

I love you, too, sweetheart. So damn much.

The End.

⚜

Do you need to talk all things *Defied?* Be sure to join the private Blood Duet Spoiler Room group on Facebook!

DEAR FABULOUS READER

Hi there! Thank you so much for reading *DEFIED*, and I so hope that you enjoyed the wild ride that Lincoln & Avery found themselves on.

If you are new to my books, I always love to include a behind-the-scenes glance at the back—where did some of my inspiration come from? And are there any locations mentioned in the book that can be found in real life? All of that and more is below! (I like to think of it as the Extras section on DVDs, LOL).

As always, we're hitting it up bullet-point style! Enjoy!

- I hardly know where to begin! But I suppose I can begin with one of the names from the book... Pershing University, anyone? Some who know New Orleans may have noticed that it is seated on St. Charles Avenue (think: gorgeous, gorgeous mansions) alongside Loyola University. Loyola is my alma mater, and Pershing (in my head) is Tulane University next door. There's always been a longstanding competition between the two schools, so it was fun to play on that! "Pershing," however, comes from General Pershing, the street I lived on once upon a time in the city.

- Flambeaux, the corner store that Pete and Sal own: did you know that "flambeaux" in New Orleans actually refers to the people who hold the lanterns during Mardi Gras parades? In much earlier years/centuries, these "flambeauxs" (as they were called) tended to be inmates who were allowed to come out and help and also earn a coin or two for providing light (and heat) along the route. Nowadays, parades still have "flambeauxs" but they aren't inmates - although tips are still appreciated! Pete's store is my little nod to this little part of New Orleans culture that is so firmly rooted in history.
- Captain America & Thor: Yes, I have an obsession. Yes, Mr. Luis knows. Yes, he also has man-crushes! Therefore, it had to be involved ;)
- The story Nat tells Avery: Do you remember the small anecdote that Nat tells Avery at the Basement? When she mentions the policemen who tried to cover up a murder? Yes, that is a *true* story, dating to the early 2000's. For many years, it was very hush-hush because of the gravity of the crime they committed, but the police involved were eventually caught and sentenced to jail. When I asked Mr. Luis for a story that would rattle our souls and show us just why Avery would have a hard time trusting anyone, that is the one he gave me. It's heartbreaking, terrible, but goes to show the nature of humanity, both the good and the bad.

- Algiers Point: Fun Fact (and get ready to learn how naive I was to Louisiana geography when I moved here a decade ago), Algiers is actually located just across the river from the French Quarter! Yes, I once fully believed that New Orleans was the farthest south you could go. Yes, I was promptly corrected *multiple* times by friends. No, you can't swim across the river, LOL. Since moving to this area of the city, I've found that it's actually one of the most romantic - especially at night when the city glitters across the river - and I couldn't resist staging a moonlight picnic with lots of steam and heat because...why not? LOL.

As always, there are many more but here is just a sampling! If you're thinking...that seems rather fascinating and I want to know more, you are always so welcome to reach out! Pretty much, nothing makes me happier :)

Much love,

Maria

PREVIEW OF SAY YOU'LL BE MINE: A NOLA HEART NOVEL

The NOLA Heart series is now complete! Keep reading for a sneak peek of Say You'll Be Mine, the first book in the series—featuring a hot cop and his high school sweetheart. This is a second chance romance that will heat up your kindles and keep you up at night reading.

"Need help with those?"

Shaelyn jerked at the familiar masculine voice and nearly pantsed herself. Picking a wedgie in public, while sometimes necessary, was embarrassing, but losing her shorts in front of Brady Taylor, strangers, and the all-seeing eyes of her parish church might actually spell the end of her.

Then again, problem solved. Meme Elaine would have to find someone else to inherit their ancestral home, of course, but Shaelyn could work some serious magic from Upstairs.

"Nope, I've got it," she bit out. She didn't look at him.

One glance and there was a decent chance of her good sense going MIA.

"You sure?" Black Nike tennis shoes entered her peripheral vision. "Looks like you might need a hand."

His toned calves were dusted with short, black hairs. It was a sign of weakness, she knew, but Shaelyn couldn't stop the upward progression of her gaze. Settled low on his hips were maroon basketball shorts with cracked-gold lettering running up the side. The first and second O's were missing, so that instead of Loyola, it read "L Y LA." She wondered why he wasn't wearing his alma mater, Tulane University, and then reminded herself that she didn't care. Her gaze traveled up to a faded-blue NOPD T-shirt that—

Shaelyn inhaled sharply as she realized just how awful *she* must look. Boob sweat was the least of her worries when her underwear had officially integrated itself between her butt cheeks. She reached up to smooth her short, curly hair, which she'd tamed with a headband straight out of the '90s. Her bedroom was proving to be a treasure trove of forgotten goodies.

"You've got something . . . " Brady reached out a hand toward her butt.

"Hey!" She swatted at his long-tapered fingers. He wasn't wearing his hat today, and she finally had her first glimpse of his blue-on-blue eyes. She'd once compared them to the crystal blue waters of Destin (where their families once vacationed together in Florida every summer), and she was annoyed to find that time had not dampened their appeal. Straightening her spine, she snapped, "Hands off."

Holding both hands up, he dipped his chin. "You might wanna check out your behind then." Those blue eyes crinkled as he grinned, with small laugh lines fanning out from the corners.

Shaelyn twisted at the waist. Three leaves were stuck to her butt, suctioned to the fabric of her shorts as though hanging on for dear life. Sweat, apparently, was the proper glue foliage needed for attachment.

She was never working out again.

"You got it?" Brady asked, humor lacing his husky drawl. "I'm good with my hands, if you need help."

An image of Brady's large hands cupping her butt snapped her into action. She swiped at the offending leaves, sending them fluttering to the ground. "I'm good. Thanks."

His sweeping glance, one that traveled from her tennis shoes all the way up to her face, left her wondering if he liked what he saw or if he was glad he'd dumped her years ago. Finally, he murmured, "I can see that."

The key ring came loose from her belt loop with an extra hard tug of desperation, and she started for her car. "Right. Well, nice to see you."

Brady effectively ruined her escape by leaning against her car door with his arms crossed over his hard chest. Hadn't she suffered enough today without having to deal with him, too? Boob sweat, wedgies, and leaves suctioned to her ass were all a woman could take, thank you very much.

She gestured at him. "Do you mind?"

His answering smile was slow and easy. "Not at all."

Her fingers curled tightly around the car keys. "I've got somewhere to be."

"Yeah?" His tone suggested that he didn't believe her. "Where are you going?"

She toyed with the idea of blowing off his question, but if there was one thing she knew about Brady Taylor, it was that he was annoyingly persistent. "I've got a bachelorette party tonight."

"Oh, yeah?" He said it differently this time, as if

intrigued, perhaps even despite himself. "Didn't realize you had many friends left in N'Orleans?"

She scowled, placed a hand on her hip, and then realized that she must look about five seconds away from throwing a good ol' Southern princess tantrum. Hastily she folded her arms over her chest to mimic his stance. With determination she ignored the way her sweat-coated skin fused together.

"For the record, I do have friends." She didn't, not really, but he didn't know that. "And secondly, my job is hosting a bachelorette party."

He seemed to digest that, his full mouth momentarily flattening before quirking up in a nonchalant smile. "Where do you work nowadays, Shae?"

The bells of Holy Name chimed again. She really had to be going, but something stopped her from walking around the hood of her car, climbing in, and speeding away. She didn't want to think about what that *something* might be.

"I work at La Parisienne in the French Quarter. On Chartres."

One of his black brows arched up in surprise. "The lingerie joint?"

Only a man would call a business that sold women's underwear a "joint." Rolling her eyes, Shaelyn let her weight rest on her right leg. She bit back another moan of pain. "It has a name, but yes, I work at the 'lingerie joint.'"

"And they host bachelorette parties?"

She shrugged. "Sometimes. Tonight we're cohosting it with The Dirty Crescent."

"The sex toy shop?"

"Yes."

His blue eyes glittered, and when he asked, "Can I come?" his voice slid through her like that first shot of whiskey she'd downed in his grandfather's office years earlier. Shocking at first, and then hot and tingly as it heated her core.

Then he ruined everything by laughing.

Nothing ever changed with him.

"You're such a jerk," she snapped. She stepped forward and pushed at his chest to urge him away from her car. He didn't budge, which only infuriated her. How dare he tease her like he hadn't broken her heart? So what if she'd been young, naïve, and fifty shades of stupid? Being a gentleman was not overrated.

He was still laughing when he caught her by the shoulders. "I could arrest you for harassment." His hands were warm on her exposed skin, hotter, maybe, than the late afternoon sun toasting the back of her neck.

Shaelyn glared up at him, not the least bit pacified by the mischievous glint in his blue eyes. His thumbs stroked her collarbone. Once, twice. If she'd been a weaker woman, she would have curled into his embrace. "You should arrest yourself."

"For what?"

"For being an ass."

His head dipped, his breath a whisper against her ear. Goosebumps teased her flesh. "You gonna do it yourself? Maybe buy a pair of new 'cuffs from that party tonight and put them to good use on me?"

ACKNOWLEDGMENTS

It's crazy to think that the Blood Duet is now complete! (I'm not ready to let it go - I love Lincoln & Avery way too much!) In all truth, though, I can't even begin to express all of my thank-you's for *DEFIED*. When this book threatened to do me in, my friends and family brought me right back up and keep me afloat.

As always, this book wouldn't have been possible without my amazing team:

-Najla, girl, these covers are everything! Thank you for being you, and for always rocking it out. You are the best.

- Kathy, I'm so thankful to have met you. Thank you for being the best editor a girl could ever want, and for always supporting me. I'm so, so lucky to have you.

- Tandy, thank you for making this book sparkle!

- Tina, I couldn't do this without you. Thank you for keeping my butt in line, and for making sure I'm alive/eating/sleeping/stepping away from the computer. You are amazing.

- To my beta readers, Brenda and Viper - your endless support means everything to me! Especially when you see my book in its unedited form, and still don't judge, LOL. I love you!!

- To my VIPers, y'all are the foundation of my career. This author business wouldn't be possible without you, and I'm so lucky to have you all on this journey with me.

- BBA: This book is for you. Thank you for encouraging me to write it, for showing Lincoln & Avery all the love. Without you, this duet wouldn't even exist.

- To every blogger, reviewer, or reader who passed on word about *DEFIED* and told your friends about this book or took the time to write a review, I can never say thank you enough. It means the world to me, and I send so many virtual hugs!

- And to *you*, Dear Reader, thank you for making my author dream a reality. There are no other words, but thank you.

Much love,
Maria Luis

ALSO BY MARIA LUIS

NOLA Heart Series

Say You'll Be Mine

Take A Chance On Me

Dare You To Love Me

Tempt Me With Forever

⚜

Blades Hockey Series

Power Play

Sin Bin

Hat Trick

⚜

A Love Serial

Breathless (.99c)

⚜

Blood Duet

Sworn

Defied

ABOUT THE AUTHOR

Maria Luis is the author of the sexy NOLA Heart and Blades Hockey series.

Historian by day and romance novelist by night, Maria lives in New Orleans, and loves bringing the city's cultural flair into her books. When Maria isn't frantically typing with coffee in hand, she can be found binging on reality TV, going on adventures with her other half and two pups, or plotting her next flirty romance.

Printed in Great Britain
by Amazon